BENEATH
THE
SHADOWS

BENEATH
THE
SHADOWS

SARA FOSTER

MINOTAUR BOOKS

A THOMAS DUNNE BOOK

NEW YORK

This is a work of fiction. All of the characters, organizations, and events portrayed in this novel are either products of the author's imagination or are used fictitiously.

A THOMAS DUNNE BOOK FOR MINOTAUR BOOKS.
An imprint of St. Martin's Publishing Group.

ISBN 978-0-312-64336-2

First published in Australia in 2011 by Bantam, Random House Australia

For the Curlew Cottage family

The past is still too close to us.

The things we have tried to forget and put behind us

would stir again . . .

—DAPHNE DU MAURIER, *Rebecca*

BENEATH

THE

SHADOWS

1

They should be home.

The thought scratched at Grace's mind as she peered out of a narrow upstairs window. The sun had long since been banished behind a blanket of thick grey cloud. In front of her, the wild moorland rolled away to be absorbed by the gloom of twilight.

Grace turned and trailed through the cottage, flicking at wall switches, shaking the shadows from their slumbers and driving them out. She moved as though in a trance, the surroundings still surreal to her, although it had been over a week since they had moved in. The upstairs corridor was poky, and the ceiling so low that she had spent the last few days watching Adam stooping under the beams. The staircase was steep, the wood beneath the carpet uneven, so it was better to tread on the outer edges of each step rather than stumble into the indentations of myriad footsteps gone before.

She made her careful way downstairs, through the small living room that was littered with packing boxes, and headed into the kitchen, moving again to a window, unable to stop herself from looking out across the sloping moors towards the distant road that wound in and out of sight. A few trees were silhouetted on the horizon, their brittle skeletons bent from regular lashings by the coastal winds. The view before her was utterly still.

She took a deep breath, trying to quell the worry that was winding her nerves into knots. Adam's note had unsettled her. *"Won't be long. I have to talk to you when I get back, don't go anywhere. A x"*

Back in the lounge, Grace threw herself into an armchair, one hand brushing over the raked leather where a long-dead cat had once regularly sharpened its claws. She looked around the cottage—*their* cottage, though it was nearly impossible to think of it that way.

"It's an incredible gift," she could still hear Adam enthusing, over and over, when they had first found out his grandparents had bequeathed Hawthorn Cottage to him. "It's like fate is giving us a bloody great shove in the back. Our own place, no mortgage, away from the rat race, a chance for Millie to start life among nature rather than believing that trees grow through cracks in the pavement. Come on, Gracie, let's give it a go."

At that point Grace had been overwhelmed by pads and pumps and nappies, and had somehow found herself agreeing with every point he made. Adam was right. Who wanted red-top buses flying past their London flat at all hours; noise, lights, people everywhere? This way they could escape their financial pressures for a while. She didn't want to leave Millie while she was tiny, and go back to her marketing job, with its meager wage and demanding retail clients. It wasn't her vocation, and to satisfy her demanding boss she often had to stay long after office hours were over.

They couldn't avoid the fact that their priorities were changing. Adam and Grace had begun their relationship to a backdrop of fine restaurants and raucous weekends away with friends. Now, in their thirties, most people they knew had children, their social life had dwindled, and they wouldn't be the first ones to make the move out of the city. Grace began to imagine the possibilities that the cottage in North Yorkshire would present: the chance to cook proper meals for a change, taking Millie for long country walks in the fresh air, and snuggling up to Adam in the evenings. She wouldn't have to give up anything either—she could take the maximum maternity leave she was allowed while they gave it a try. To top it off, they'd be free of the extortionate repayments on their tiny two-bedroom flat; so instead of struggling, they might even save. And, as Adam said, if it didn't work out, they would simply come back.

"Six months," she'd agreed. "We'll try it for six months, see how it goes."

But as they packed their belongings, and the moving date drew nearer, something had begun to niggle at her. She couldn't put her finger on what it was that woke her in the early hours, well before the baby stirred. Eventually she had dismissed it as understandable nerves at such a big change. And yet, the nagging voice refused to quiet.

Now, she picked at the torn leather on the armchair as she thought about their first few days in the cottage. The unsettling silence as she had unpacked boxes. The stillness each time she looked out the window. The black descent of night; and the relentless ticking and chiming of the grandfather clock in the hall. As she sat there, it was hard to imagine the throngs of people and traffic swirling around central London, an endlessly shifting kaleidoscope of color and movement. The last week at the cottage had felt like the longest of Grace's life. The six months she had promised Adam now lay interminably before them.

She looked at her watch. *Where the hell were they?* Adam's car was out the front, so they couldn't have gone far. Just the thought of the two of them made her heart quicken. Since Millie had been born her emotions seemed to bubble fierce and strange beneath her skin, threatening to spill over at any moment.

Her mobile rang and she fumbled around for it among the packing debris, snatching at it before it stopped.

"Gracie?"

"Annabel," she sighed, sitting back down.

"You could at least pretend to be pleased to hear from me," her sister grumbled. "Or have you forgotten about me already now you've moved to Timbuktu?"

"Sorry, Bel, I'm getting a bit worried about Adam and Millie—they've been out since I got back from town. They should be back by now."

Annabel laughed. "Grace, you're such a worry wart. Adam's probably chatting over a fence post somewhere. You know he has to show Millie off to everyone. Stop panicking. Now, tell me when you're coming back—you can't stay a country bumpkin forever. I miss you too much."

Grace smiled at that. "You still can't believe that I've moved away, can you? Come and see us, Bel. You never know, you might like it here."

"So you're planning on staying then?"

"Yes," Grace said, as emphatically as she could manage. She had never felt the need to pretend to Annabel before, but she was determined to give this move a chance. In truth, she missed her sister terribly, knew the feeling was mutual, and was afraid that Annabel would exploit any opportunity she saw to encourage them to come back to London.

"Grace? Are you listening to me?"

"Sorry, what were you saying?" Grace replied, tuning back in to the voice on the other end of the line.

"I was asking you to tell me just what Yorkshire has that London doesn't?"

"Well, fresh air, for a start. And you can move without someone knocking you over and then swearing at you."

"Okay, okay," Annabel acquiesced. "Well, at least I don't have to see you and Adam wandering around with soppy grins on your faces quite so often. It can get pretty sickening after a while, you know."

Grace ignored the jibe. "Come for a visit, Bel—we've got a pub!"

"Hmmm. I guess I might have to if you won't come back. London misses you, though. I miss you."

"You shouldn't have helped me pack everything up then."

"I know, I'm my own worst enemy."

Grace smiled again distractedly as Annabel chattered away, getting up to gaze once more through the kitchen window. All was quiet. She walked slowly to the front of the cottage and glanced out into the dusky garden.

There was a dark shape on her doorstep. She couldn't quite see it at this angle, or make out much in the shadows. She frowned, listening to Annabel reporting on her week as she headed to the front door. Once there, she twisted the key in the lock, pulled it open, and stopped in shock.

In front of her was Millie's pram. She peered inside, to find her ten-week-old daughter fast asleep, her cheeks rosy and cold, her tiny chest rising and falling steadily underneath the tightly tucked woolen coverlet.

Grace ran her fingers gently over her daughter's forehead, then glanced around and said, "Adam?"

No one answered. She waited, watching her short breaths bursting into the frosty night air. She called a little louder, "Adam, where are you?"

Silence. Then she heard a small voice saying. "Grace? *Grace?*"

She looked down absently at the phone in her hand. She lifted it up to hear Annabel's voice, alarmed. "Grace, what's going on?"

"I just found Millie asleep in her pram on the front doorstep," Grace said, her confusion growing with every word.

"So they're back then. See, I told you it would be fine."

Grace stared out into the deepening darkness. "I'm not sure, Annabel. It's only Millie here. There's no sign of Adam."

"He must be caught up with something—he'll be there in a second, I'm sure," Annabel reassured her.

But he wasn't.

2

TWELVE MONTHS LATER

It waited in the shadows, golden orbs for eyes that burned with hellfire. A continuous low growl hummed in her ears. And then came the snarl and a frenzied flash of fangs.

When she heard the scream, Grace came to with a start. The noise weakened to a wail—a high-pitched cry that sent a shudder through her. She checked the clock—three a.m.—then flung back the covers, jumped up, and rushed into the small room next door, swatting the landing light switch as she went, rubbing sleep from her eyes.

Millie stood holding the crib bars with one hand, the other clutching Mr. Pink, the small teddy bear Adam had brought to the hospital after she was born. Her eyes were squeezed tight, lashes glistening with unshed tears, while her fine brown hair had risen up in a defiance of curls. She had already worked herself into an exhaustion of gulping sobs and whimpers, and Grace went swiftly towards her and gathered her up into the safety of her arms. Millie huddled against her mother's breasts, her wet nose and mouth dampening Grace's nightgown.

"You're safe now, Mummy's here," Grace whispered as she rocked her daughter gently, chanting the words over and over, whether to Millie or to herself she wasn't sure. "It was just a nightmare."

Soon, Millie began to quiet, and as her breathing slowed, so did Grace's racing heart. While she cradled her child tightly, she tried to push away her thoughts—but it was no use. She feared it had been a mistake to come back.

They had driven to the village that morning through the sodden November countryside, their car sloshing along the winding roads, while Grace's reasons for returning became more and more muddied. But through the endless days and restless nights of the last twelve months she had been sure of one thing: she would come back. The shock of Adam's disappearance had finally begun to fade, but Grace's yearning for answers had not. She had come to realize that if she had any hope of discovering what had happened, she needed to begin retracing her husband's steps in the place where it had all gone so horribly wrong.

It had taken much longer to reach the village than she remembered. Eventually they had crossed a cattle grid at the bottom of a steep hill, then listened to the car's protesting whine as it climbed up the bank in second gear. As they reached the bare, brown moor top, Grace's memories began to unfold. The back of her neck prickled as the hill plateaued out and took them gently downwards, and the sensation moved to her throat as she saw the village sign—Roseby—set into a jagged piece of stone. Then the road dipped abruptly, revealing first of all a brick house, then a neat sloping row of terraced cottages. She drove until she reached the last one, halfway down the hill, then pulled onto the grass in front of a low stone wall, and switched off the engine. One year ago, Adam had been here with them, parking a large removals van ahead of their car. Grace remembered catching his eye through the windshield, his grin as he came across to unbuckle

Millie from her seat, and the way he had cradled his tiny daughter close, pointing at the cottage and telling her, "We're home."

Now, Grace's hand shook as she pulled the keys from the ignition. She peered over into the back seat, murmuring to her sleeping child, "We're here."

Millie had been reluctant to wake, her head drooping against her mother's chest as Grace struggled with the stiff front door lock, eager to escape the icy wind. Once inside, warmth hit them, taking Grace by surprise. She moved through the small entranceway into the lounge. There was a note on the coffee table: *Have left a few things in the fridge for you. Meredith.*

Looking around, Grace was touched. Even in this scant neighborhood of half a dozen buildings, she'd had little opportunity to get to know the neighbors. Meredith lived in the grandiose house only a short walk from Hawthorn Cottage, but the first time they had met, Grace had been dazed. Police had been bustling in and out, while she stared in bewilderment at Adam's dirty mug on the benchtop, his jacket slung over the kitchen chair, his toolbox left open on the worktable.

Meredith had volunteered to help and made cups of tea for everyone, but Grace would have barely remembered her if she hadn't turned up again a week or so later. This time it was Grace's mother who made Meredith tea, explained that they were taking Grace home with them, and accepted her kind offer of looking after the cottage until Grace decided what to do next.

However, Meredith had gone above and beyond what Grace was expecting. There was no air of neglect to the place: the surfaces were freshly dusted, the radiators were warm, while the air smelled faintly of lavender. It took the edge off Grace's apprehension, and she was overcome with gratitude.

She had put Millie down on the floor with a drink. Then she had walked into the kitchen, to find it waiting neat and expectant, before heading back through the living room and into the hall, climbing the stairs, tiptoeing like a trespasser.

Her emotions had finally caught up with her as she took her first tentative look into the main bedroom. There was the bed—their bed—made up neatly. She had gone across, turned back the covers, and pressed her face into the pillow on Adam's side, but all she could smell was clean linen.

She stood and gently shushed Millie in her arms, using the soft glow of the landing light to watch as Millie slowly succumbed to sleep. After a while, she carefully laid her little girl back down and returned to her own room. A loud, insistent ticking kept pace with her footsteps. She had forgotten about the damn grandfather clock. The last time she had been here the ticking and chiming had begun to drive her crazy, though Adam had reassured her that she would get used to it. "It's been with the family for generations, it's got to be valuable," he'd said, opening the oak casing at the front and beginning to wind it. "My grandfather used to call it the heartbeat of the cottage."

Now, Grace attempted to ignore it, as she lay under the covers and tried to drift off. But suddenly her eyelids were aglow, and the deep crackle of tires outside made her jump. She padded out of bed again and eased one curtain back a little, resting her hand on the cool windowpane.

A black Land Rover was parked a short distance up the sloping lane, just visible by the faint moonlight that cut through the clouds. It had stopped outside the redbrick house that crested the hill. The Land Rover's headlights were now off and the interior light was on, but Grace was too far away to see anything more than a moving shadow inside. The light disappeared, the driver climbed out into a darkness her vision could not penetrate, she heard the slight creaking of a gate, and then all was silent.

She could feel her heart thudding beneath her nightgown, but tried to calm herself, realizing how silly she was being. It was perfectly reasonable for people to arrive home in the middle of the night. She had to stop letting her imagination play games with her.

Grace settled back into bed again, but sleep wanted nothing to do with her now. She remembered the first night she'd ever spent here, when Adam had pulled her to him and wrapped her tight within his arms. He had been wearing a thick sweater—in fact they'd both been only semidressed, having underanticipated the biting cold of the northern winter. She could still feel the fleece soft against her skin, warming the cheek that had lain against it while the rest of her face stung with cold. "I'm scared, too," he'd said, holding her close. "But I know we've done the right thing, Grace. I promise it will be all right."

Grace remembered how she had relaxed at his words, so much so that she had slept soon after. But a week later he had gone out and never come home.

Now, she did her best to ignore the empty space next to her, and wrapped her arms around a pillow, trying to pretend she could bring Adam back for a moment, make believe that he'd kept his promise after all. But sleep kept its distance.

She tossed and turned for a while in an effort to get comfortable, then her eyes flew open as the silence was shredded by a jarring screech. It's a bird, she told herself, pushing away the image of some tormented ghost out there in the black maw of night. Shuddering, she switched on the bedside lamp and cast a glance around the room, at the old furniture, the sepia photo of Adam's grandparents on their wedding day that hung above her half-unpacked case. Then she remembered the small bookshelf on the landing. She threw back the covers and tiptoed across the carpet, hoping she wouldn't wake Millie. The bookshelf was right outside her door, barely visible in the light cast by the bedside lamp, but she could just make out the spines on the top shelf. They were all classics. *Wuthering Heights. The Turn of the Screw. Jane Eyre. Great Expectations.* She'd read a few of them at school. Then her eye fell on a book she had always wanted to read, but never got to. *Rebecca.* She plucked the tattered copy from among the others and took it back to bed with her. She pulled the covers over her, opened it, and read the first few lines of a long-ago dream. And soon, her grip loosened on the book, her eyes closed, and she found herself lost amid thick overgrowth, gazing towards the mullioned windows of a dark, abandoned house.

3

When Grace woke again it was to silence. Light had begun to seep through the curtains and saturate the darkness as the day broke. She was grateful, in fact strangely exhilarated, to have gotten through the first night alone in the cottage, and felt full of energy for the day ahead. She intended to begin going through the contents of the cottage, quickly and meticulously, packing up while searching for anything that might explain the mystery of Adam's disappearance. She was anxious to get started.

She had a chance to have a bath before she even heard Millie stir, then went to get her little girl. Millie was sitting up, playing in her cot, and Grace observed her for a moment without being noticed. Millie was nearly fifteen months old, on the verge of walking, almost unrecognizable from the tiny bundle that Grace and Adam had first brought to the cottage. Adam had missed all the changes, big and small, that had happened over the past year.

Grace closed her eyes briefly, and when she opened them again, Millie was holding out her arms, saving Grace from her daydream. Grace was relieved to see that whatever had terrorized Millie in the night seemed to have been absorbed by the morning's light. "We have a visitor coming today," she told her daughter, smiling at her reassuringly, hoping Millie would smile back. Instead, Millie reached out to touch her mother's mouth, watching her intently all the while, as though checking she was real.

After breakfast, Grace unpacked the rest of their luggage, while Millie played by her feet. She put away all her clothes except her jeans and thickest sweaters, looking longingly at a pair of high-heeled brown suede boots that she'd worn all the time in London. They were consigned to the bottom of the wardrobe behind the trainers and Wellingtons, which were all she needed right now.

When they returned to the living room, Grace scanned the area and, satisfied there was nothing too dangerous within reach of little hands, set Millie on the floor to play. Then she picked up the phone and called her parents in France. Her father answered and sounded pleased to hear from her, even if there was a note of concern in his voice. She recalled their last conversation a few days earlier, before she had left for England.

"What the hell do you want to go and live there again for?" he'd roared when she'd announced her plans.

"It's only for a short time," Grace had replied. "There are things to sort out, and I think it's time I went and did it. I can't stay here forever."

"You can stay here for as long as you like," her dad had replied, his voice gruff and indignant. "You can't fool me, Grace, I know why you're going."

Grace bridled at her father's intimation of the truth. She didn't want to discuss Adam, or her overwhelming need for answers. "I need to pack up the cottage properly, Dad. There's nobody else to do that job except me. And it's Millie's inheritance, remember? Everything there is part of her family history."

Her father made a noise that sounded like *hmph*, and walked over to the living room window, from where, if you looked between the huddled villas opposite, you could glimpse a patch of sparkling blue sea. Then he turned and glared at her. "I'm sure we could find someone there to do that for you."

Grace had folded her arms, stood her ground and waited, until her father added, shaking a finger at her, "Just don't you go chasing shadows, you hear me? Get in, do what you need to, and then go somewhere else—somewhere far away. Your mother and I have no idea why Adam took you there in the first place."

She'd gone across to him and put her hand on his arm. "I'll be fine," she said softly.

He hadn't met her eyes, simply patted her hand and said, "I know you will."

She and Millie had left the next day.

Now, she was glad to hear their voices, though this time it was her mother who couldn't hide her worry completely.

"Remember to take any legal documents you find to a lawyer. You need to know where you stand. Your father and I will pay for it."

"I have enough money," Grace replied, although she was secretly alarmed at how rapidly her ample savings, the proceeds from the sale of their London flat, were vanishing. "Besides, we know where I stand," she added miserably. "The cottage is in joint names, so I can't sell without Adam."

"But there might be a way round it, Grace—you never know. Just get someone local to check out all the facts for you."

"I will, Mum," Grace replied, pulling an exasperated face at Millie. "I've only been here a day—give me a chance."

"I know, love. We only want to help. Oh, and before I go—James called. He was surprised to hear you'd gone back there, said you hadn't mentioned it."

Grace was riled by her tone. "I didn't realize I had to report all my movements to him," she shot back. Grace and James had been best mates since university, but their relationship had been somewhat strained over the last few years, ever since James had decided not to attend Grace and Adam's wedding.

There was silence on the other end of the line, and Grace immediately felt bad. After all, there was only one reason she hadn't told James she was coming back: she didn't want to listen to him trying to talk her out of it.

"Sorry, Mum, I didn't mean to snap."

"It's okay, love. I understand. Just remember you can call us any time, Grace—day or night."

"I know I can."

As Grace said good-bye, a wave of nerves threatened to swamp her. The phone call had made her all too aware of the distance between her and those who had bolstered her up over the past year.

She shook off her apprehension as she surveyed the living room. Adam's grandparents had been dead for over eighteen months, yet as far as the cottage was concerned they could just be out shopping. The fact that the place creaked and groaned unaccountably might well have been due to the weight of everything inside it. A lifetime spent gathering, Grace thought, looking at the books stacked against the walls, magazines piled in corners, the collection of china bird ornaments that crowded together in the low glass cabinet. It was a long shot that any of these odds and ends would prove revelatory, but she didn't want to overlook them—just in case there was a note propped behind a statuette or a letter misplaced under a magazine that would explain everything.

She began collecting the animal figurines on top of the mantel-piece, almost knocking over an enormous hand-painted vase, which she caught just before it toppled against a brass lamp with a glass shade. In the scramble a wooden box dropped to the floor, falling open to reveal a pipe and a pouch of tobacco inside. The sudden smell brought back the memories of Grace's own grandfather, and the past flew into the present for just a second, disappearing as quickly as it came, leaving a bittersweet sense of longing. She put the box back on the shelf and sighed, a new sense of responsibility dawning on her. Although she was a relative stranger to the old couple, she was now responsible for dismantling the last traces of their lives.

She wished she had more idea of what Adam might have wanted, but they had only had a week together in the cottage before everything fell apart. In those few days she'd noticed that Adam spent most of his time working on odd jobs, putting off anything sentimental. It was clear he was finding it daunting. While he'd been fond of his grand-parents he'd had limited contact with them for most of his life—except for a brief spell when he'd stayed with them for a few months after his mother died. Yet their funerals, so close together, had hit him hard. With their passing, he had lost the last family he had.

Grace had only visited the cottage once while Adam's grand-parents had been alive. She had instinctively liked them, but they hadn't had enough time to move past polite friendliness. The only other occasion they had met had been at Grace and Adam's wedding, which had gone by in a blur of excitement for Grace. But she did remember them: inseparable, looking a little nervous and pale on a rare trip to the south, the subdued black and burgundy hues of their Sunday best in stark contrast to Grace's suntanned parents—her father in his morning suit, and her mother's dress of pink and white swirls topped off by a fascinator that sprouted a large fan of pink feathers from one side of her head. However, Bill and Constance Lockwood had smiled proudly at anyone who caught their eye that day, particularly their grandson.

A year later, Bill had been taken into hospital soon after his wife had been found dead at home; and the stress and grief meant the old man had never returned. When Grace and Adam had first arrived, there had been a magazine on the coffee table, open to a short story. Adam had looked at it in silence for a moment, then told Grace that he remembered seeing his grandmother reading the stories aloud to his grandfather. He'd closed it and gone across to the bin, then hesitated and put it on a bookshelf instead.

Grace looked over towards the shelf and saw the magazine straightaway, exactly where Adam had left it. She bit her lip and put her hands on her hips, as Millie began pushing clothespins underneath the sofa. She barely knew where or how to begin. *One step at a time*, she said to herself. *Just make a start, that's all.*

She had been putting the kettle on, when she heard a knock on the door. Their visitor was five minutes early.

"Michael Muir," said the young blond man waiting outside. "Call me Mike."

He couldn't have been more than thirty, but he had the portly bearing of a man much older, and ruddy cheeks to match. He stuck out a plump hand, which Grace shook obligingly before stepping back so he could come in.

Grace looked on as he began assessing the small entrance hall. "Livin' room this way?" he asked, moving off on her nod. "I'll take a good look round, shall I?" he added over his shoulder as she followed. Then he began to make notes on a pad as he headed towards the kitchen.

Grace let him get on with his assessment while she warmed up Millie's morning milk and prepared her cereal. She was encouraging

Millie to eat when Mike Muir reappeared. "Can we go through this now?" he asked, waving his pad.

She indicated the vacant chair across from her, at the tiny dining table that had been squeezed into the space. Mike Muir contorted his ample frame to fit, sat down, and put his notes on the tabletop.

"Right, then . . . you say you're lookin' at rentin' rather than sellin'?"

"Yes," Grace said, "for the time being."

"And you're gettin' rid of the furniture?"

"Well, I could do—but I don't have to."

Mike Muir looked down at his pad. "Well, I can certainly put a rental advert out for you—see how we get on. However . . . can I give you some advice?" He looked at her hopefully.

"Go ahead."

"Well, as it stands, the place is a bit, er, how shall I put it . . . ?"

"You can say neglected," she replied, smiling.

"Aye," he agreed uncomfortably, his ruddy cheeks darkening to become burgundy splotches. "However, if you made a few renovations . . . instead of looking at long-term tenants—which might cause you some bother out here—you could think about letting it out as a holiday rental instead. We look after a property for a family in the next village who've done something similar, and they're making an absolute killin'. . . . It's got to be at least double what you'd get for a long-term rental, all said and done."

"Really?" Grace felt her mood rising. "So what do I need to do?"

Mike Muir appeared delighted by her enthusiasm. "Well, country getaways like these are quite sought after. But to be canny about it, you need to set it up properly. Keep the best bits of a traditional cottage—your log fires, your wooden beams, and so on—but surround it with modern appliances and some nice furnishins' and you're on to a winner. See, if you took out this wall"—he knocked his knuckles on the wall next to them—"make it open-plan down here, you've got a much bigger area. Right now, it's too cramped. Put new cupboards in here . . . and redo the living room fireplace so it's a bit of a feature. There's not too much you can do about upstairs, but you could up-grade windows, make the bathroom en suite, that kind of thing. You could do a miracle makeover on this place, and it'll be cosy and trendy rather than . . . than . . ." His face colored up again.

"Claustrophobic and drab?" Grace finished for him.

"Aye!" He beamed at her, seeming pleased at how easy this was proving. "And if you do decide to sell down the road, you'll get much more if you've done some work on the place already."

Grace liked the sound of his suggestions. She was turning things over in her mind when he began to get up. "Look, take my card, and give me a call when you've decided what to do next."

"Thanks." Grace ran a finger over the embossed lettering, her mind swirling with possibilities. "You've been great. I'll think it over, and let you know."

She went to see him out, leaving Millie in her high chair banging her spoon repeatedly against her Weetabix with a dull thwack. At the door, Mike turned and the color was high in his cheeks again.

"I remember your Adam," he said. "He played for Skeldale cricket team for a time; he was a crackin' spin bowler. I was right sorry—"

"Thanks," Grace cut in, her discomfort as acute as his, a swift swoop of memories threatening to betray her composure "I'll be in touch," she added hastily, then closed the door, but not before she caught one last sight of Mike Muir's forlorn face looking back at her from the doorstep.

4

There was only one shop in Skeldale, one of the small villages between Roseby and the coast. It was just a terraced house really, no different to its dozen or so neighbors on the narrow lane, except for the sign outside, and notices tacked against the glass of the bay windows. No one else was in sight as Grace hovered in the doorway, casting her eye along the advertisements. She couldn't see what she was searching for.

A cowbell clanged loudly as she pushed open the heavy wooden door. Inside it was dingy, the scant space crammed with paraphernalia. Boxes of fruit lined the shelves to one side of her, precarious towers of tins stacked in the gaps. On the other side an eclectic mix of items were piled in disordered groups—among them, stationery, candles, postcards, and instant noodles. More boxes spilled their assorted contents onto the uneven stone-flagged floor, and in one corner stood what looked like a group of witches broomsticks. Grace peered into some plastic pots as she went past, to see they contained honeycombs, oozing golden liquid from their tiny pores.

The countertop was almost hidden by boxes of sweets, and Millie reached out. Grace pulled her away as an old woman shuffled into view from a door behind the counter. Her dress strained against its seams, and the loose skin hanging in folds under her chin quivered as she swayed towards the desk. "Now then, lass, what can I do for yer?" she rasped.

The shop certainly hadn't been organized with children in mind, and almost everything was within Millie's grasp. The little girl leaned backwards and grabbed a box of matches, which Grace extricated from her and returned to the shelf. The woman watched them impassively.

"I'm after some milk?" Grace asked, unable to see a fridge anywhere.

The shopkeeper pulled a thick grey cardigan tighter around her and disappeared through the doorway again. Grace struggled to keep Millie's eager fingers away from everything until the woman reappeared, a small carton of full-cream milk in one swollen hand. As she placed it on the counter, Grace wondered about asking for semi-skimmed, but decided it was simplest to hand over a five pound note. The shopkeeper took it, rummaged in a drawer behind her desk, and brought out some change. As she held out the coins, the cowbell chimed again, and the woman glanced over Grace's shoulder. Grace thought she saw recognition in her eyes—suspicion even—but the shopkeeper said nothing.

Grace turned to leave, reminding herself to stock up during her trips to town, so she didn't have to come here too often. As she moved, the man behind her stepped aside to let her pass, and Grace looked up briefly in thanks, registering a face similar in age to her own. She was about to open the door when she remembered her other reason for venturing out. She doubted the woman would be of much help, but since she was here she might as well ask anyway.

"Excuse me, but I'm thinking about doing some renovations on my cottage. Do you know anyone local who might be interested in that kind of work?"

The shopkeeper considered her, until Grace thought that the very question must have been some kind of faux pas around these parts, but apparently she was deep in thought, as after an extended silence she said, "Can't think of anyone offhand, like, but I'll put word out. Where's thou at?"

"Roseby," Grace replied after a beat, struggling to decipher the woman's thick accent.

It was as though a key had unlocked the woman's demeanor. Her whole body trembled into alertness as she straightened, and she broke into a grin. "Roseby, are yer now? In 'awthorn Cottage for a guess?"

Grace's heart sank, sure that Adam's name was about to come up again, but, thankfully, the woman kept to the subject at hand.

"Well, like I say, I'll put word out for yer."

"Thank you." Grace smiled courteously. "Shall I give you my number?"

"Don't bother, if I thinks of anyone I'll send 'em round. Yer do right gettin' on with it before the snow comes."

"Okay, thanks." Grace turned to discover the man behind her was studying her. "Excuse me," she said, discomfited by his scrutiny. He said nothing but pulled the door open for her, the bell jangling again at her exit.

There was a low stone wall in front of the shop, and a large black dog lay on the ground in front of it, impervious to the cold, wet pavement. The dog had been resting its head on its paws, but at the sound of Grace's footsteps its ears twitched and its head swung around, two coal-black eyes regarding her solemnly.

Grace usually loved dogs, but this one troubled her, reminding her too much of the black hound of her recent nightmare. Before she could move on, the dog sprang to its feet in excitement and began to nose around her legs, then jumped up to try to sniff Millie's shoes. Grace expected Millie to squirm and turn away, but instead she bent over to peer curiously down at the creature. Grace was trying to ward off the dog with one hand, hissing, "No! Down!" when she heard the cowbell ring again.

"Bess, away!" came a stern male command, and the dog instantly obeyed.

Grace took a deep breath in an attempt to recompose herself as the man from the shop bent over, picked up the dog's leash, then straightened up. He was tall and lean, with features that were chiselled to the point of hollowed. Grace was sure she had never seen him before in her life—but at the same time there was something slightly familiar about him. As their eyes locked, the intensity of his stare left her unsteady for a moment, and she took a small step backwards to regain her balance. His eyes were a deep brown, a few tired lines cutting thin grooves from each corner, before they were absorbed into the paleness of his face.

He ran a hand over his short dark hair. "You're looking for a handyman?"

Grace almost started. His voice was surprisingly soft and low, with just a hint of a northern accent—a similar cadence to Adam's.

"I've done quite a bit of that kind of work," he continued. "I might be interested in the job."

"Okay," Grace replied, thinking fast. He had taken her by surprise, but this was too good an opportunity to pass up. "Well then . . . if you're free on Sunday, perhaps you could come over and I'll show you what I'm thinking of, and we can have a chat about it. I'm open to suggestions, to be honest."

"Great," he replied, though his expression remained serious. "What time?"

"Around one?" she asked. "Millie takes a nap then,"—she indicated her daughter, who had begun to squirm in her arms—"so we'll have a proper chance to talk."

"Fine. I'm Ben, by the way." He held out a hand.

"Grace." She met his grasp, finding his skin warm despite the chill of the morning. "Do you have a number I can call you on if I need to change the time?"

"Sure." He watched as she got out her mobile phone, then pulled his own from his pocket. "What's your number?" he asked. As she reeled it off, he dialed it, and the little screen on Grace's phone lit up. "There you go," he said.

She stored the number. "Thanks."

"See you on Sunday then." He began to turn away.

"I haven't told you that I'm at Hawthorn Cottage . . . in Roseby . . ." she said quickly.

"So I heard," he answered, gesturing to the shop. "I know where Hawthorn Cottage is. I'll see you then."

He set off down the lane, the dog trotting behind him. Grace watched them walk away until they reached a battered black Land Rover. The dog jumped in next to its owner, and moments later the vehicle roared by, the rise and fall of the road soon taking it out of sight.

The return trip to Roseby took about fifteen minutes. Grace drove cautiously along the empty road, the deserted moors spreading out on either side. Approaching the village from this direction, the journey was a stark contrast to the country lanes they had driven on yesterday. Then, at least there had been trees, and patches of grass, and the occasional farmhouse, but here on the moor top it was flat, brown and barren.

She glanced behind her as she neared the crest of the hill that would take them down into the village. Millie had fallen asleep in her seat, her head lolling awkwardly against her chest. Taking the opportunity of a moment to herself, Grace pulled over to the side of the road and switched off the engine. She looked out across the wild expanse and tried to breathe it in, allow her mind to stop, flex itself, and unfurl, rather than chase itself in ever-decreasing circles full of unbidden thoughts.

And yet, she found herself back twelve months, sitting in the cottage answering endless questions about Adam, probing questions designed to find some explanation of his mental health or his circumstances that might have led him to make an abrupt departure from his life. She told them everything; she had nothing to hide. He was happy to have moved here. He was starting work as a supply teacher the following week. He knew the area, yes, from visits to his grandparents and an extended stay here in his teens after his mother died, but he hadn't lived here for almost fifteen years.

But had he ever wandered off before? they'd persisted. Did he have any history of mental illness? Depression?

She had tried to explain Adam to them. That he often sang loudly and out of tune in the shower. That he was fanatical about cricket. That he could quote his favorite Tarantino movies verbatim. That he was always the one offering support to troubled friends, never the one in crisis himself. But whatever she said, the questions kept on coming. And when they found out he had no family left alive to speak of, their doubts had intensified.

The night Adam had gone, Grace had been surrounded by strangers: police, mostly, along with a few locals like Meredith who wanted to help out. Her parents were on their way from France but wouldn't arrive until the next day. Annabel was getting hold of a car and would be there as soon as she could, but had a five-hour road trip from London ahead of her. There had been a sudden flare of hope that they might be able to find Adam via his mobile signal, until she told them that she had already tried the number, and had found the phone ringing in the pocket of Millie's pram.

When her interrogation had finally ended, Grace had briefly gone out into the pitch-black night and stood with Millie held tight in her arms, surrounded by strobing torchlights, listening to Adam's name echoing away in different voices, praying that one of the callers would hear a response. But each call was carried off on the bitter wind to be met with silence. Later she had watched as the search parties returned, shoulders slack, heads bowed. Nothing had explained why Millie had been left alone on the doorstep with no sign of her daddy. Not then, and not since.

Grace's mother and father had arrived twenty-four hours later, pulling their daughter into their arms and letting her sob her helplessness out on them. Grace had seen the horror and confusion on their faces as they watched the police coming in and out of the cottage. But with her family there, Grace had at least felt anchored to the world again. Her parents had stayed by her side throughout the ensuing fortnight as she faced the media, asking for information, then waited for answers that never came. They had helped her search for Adam's passport when the police requested it. To Grace's alarm, none of them could find it, but the police had put out an alert, and there was no record of it being used.

Adam wouldn't leave Millie like that, Grace knew it. But after the police had combed the area looking for him and found nothing, they began to suggest he might have run away. It wouldn't be the first time, they said. New fathers sometimes couldn't cope with the responsibility. And he'd withdrawn a thousand pounds from their account the day before he vanished.

Grace knew about the money—Adam had said he intended to keep it at the cottage, because they were so isolated. Yet she had never found it. The police thought he might have used the cash to disappear. He'd left the baby where he was sure she'd be found, and simply walked away.

But Grace had so many questions. Why not leave Millie in the cottage? Why go without telling her, cutting off all contact? And if he was ready to vanish into the night, then why on earth would he have moved Grace all the way out into the country before he did so? Not to mention the fact that her last memory of Adam before she left for the shops was of him sitting on the floor in front of the television, half paying attention to a morning chat show, his legs crossed and his baby girl cradled within them, her mouth clamped around a bottle. He had appeared so relaxed as he tilted his head up to kiss his wife good-bye. He'd said, "Go on, enjoy the break . . . we'll be fine." No, she knew her husband better than anyone, and the last time she had seen him he had not been a man about to turn his back on the life he appeared to love.

And yet, as Christmas had drawn closer, with no news, Grace's parents had grown more eager to leave every day. They had insisted upon taking Grace and Millie, too; under no circumstances would they leave them by themselves in such a remote part of the world, the antithesis of their beloved, bright and sunny South of France. At the time, Grace had been too upset to do anything but acquiesce, and she was thankful for their steady, guiding hands over the last twelve months. But now she needed to take control. She wanted answers. She couldn't let the insidious suggestion that she was just another duped, discarded wife sneak any further beneath her skin. Because, occasionally, she found herself picturing Adam in an exotic location, laughing, his arm around another woman, with Grace and Millie filed away in some blank, unwanted corner of his mind. She would find herself clenching her fists while forcing those images away, their slow dispersal leaving her shaken. She wouldn't let those beliefs take hold. She didn't want the doubts, or the helplessness that coupled them, to outlast her faith in her husband and their life together. The only way to rid herself of them was to uncover the truth.

Grace jumped as a car flew past, shattering the silence. Her reverie was broken. The moors lay in front of her, bleak and brown under a heavy grey sky. *Stop letting your memories run riot*, she chided herself. *Just keep busy, get things done.* She needed distraction, and was glad that Annabel was coming up this weekend, under the pretext of helping out, even though she knew Annabel was likely to prove useless on that score.

She started the engine again. Halfway down the steep hill that led into the village, they passed an imposing two-story stone house, perched at a point where it could survey the dwellings below, like a patrician parent hovering over its children. After that there was a patch of bare grass, beyond which the remains of a dilapidated row of terraced cottages could be seen in the distance. At the lowest dip in the road stood the whitewashed pub, after which they crossed a small bridge, making their way up the next incline towards Hawthorn Cottage.

She stopped the car outside her gate, observing the Land Rover parked up ahead of them. Then she spotted someone standing at her front door. As she watched, the woman moved to the front window, cupped her hands around her eyes, and peered through.

Grace got slowly out of the car, wondering why *she* should be the one feeling uncomfortable at catching someone else snooping around *her* home. This woman looked totally out of place in an area where the dress code was mostly denim, flannel checks, and tweed. She wore baggy fisherman's trousers and a shapeless stripy sweater, teamed with a beanie in rainbow colors.

As Grace closed the car door, the woman turned, and with absolutely no embarrassment said, "Oh, hello! I thought this place looked occupied." She noted Grace's confusion and laughed. "Sorry, let me introduce myself. I'm Claire, Meredith's daughter." She pointed back the way Grace had just come, towards the big house sitting on the hillside. "Mum saw the car here, and I've been sent round to check it out, make sure you're not a squatter. You must be Grace."

Grace returned the friendly smile. "Yes, I am," she replied. "Pleased to meet you. I didn't know Meredith had a daughter. I'm looking forward to seeing her again—to say thank you. She's done a terrific job of minding the place."

The woman came forward and held out a hand. As she got closer, Grace saw that Claire's eyebrow was pierced through with a small hoop, and her nose sported a ruby gem. One ear had two rings through it, whereas the other one had five, becoming gradually smaller as they ascended her ear.

"Nice to meet you, too," Claire said. "And Meredith hasn't got one daughter, there are four of us, for her sins. And she can't get rid of us either—as one moves out, another one moves back in for some reason or other. I'm the latest refugee. Mind you, Mum loves it. She wouldn't know what to do with herself in that big old house if one or another of us wasn't in need of a hand." Her eyes flickered towards the car. "Is that your daughter in there?"

"Yes."

Claire glanced through the window at the sleeping child. "Ah, she is lovely, Grace, you must be so proud." She remained still for a moment, as though lost in thought, then bent down to retie the laces of one walking boot. As she straightened she continued, "Anyway, I think Mum has decided to adopt you as one of us now that you're back—so she's sent me here with an invitation to lunch tomorrow. Would you like to join us?"

Grace hesitated for a moment, which Claire took as a sign that she needed encouragement. "Please come along, Grace. You'd be very welcome. Mum's had a bit of a rough time lately—I don't know if you heard but our dad passed away a few months ago. It was unexpected, he had a massive stroke and never recovered . . . and . . . well, you know . . ."

Claire trailed off uneasily. Grace understood, as she had grown used to this in the last year. People no longer talked casually of disaster or loss in her presence. Yet she was also set apart by Adam's unexplained disappearance. No one knew quite how to deal with that— including Grace herself.

"I'm so sorry, Claire," she replied. "I didn't know about your dad." She remembered Meredith's husband: he had been in the search party for Adam last year. In particular she recalled his sorrowful eyes, which had conveyed such a depth of compassion that it had reached her through the confused fog of that terrible night.

Grace was unsure of what to say next. She often thought that after the last year she should be able to tackle difficult subjects with ease, but if anything it had made her hesitate even more. She was too aware of what harm a casual slip of the tongue or a careless remark could do to an injured spirit. She'd lost count of the times she'd fielded insensitive questions about Adam's disappearance from well-meaning family or friends. In the end she smiled. "I'd love to come for lunch . . . I was only uncertain because my sister will be here this weekend."

"Oh, no problem," Claire replied, "bring her along, too. Come about midday—we'll see you then." And she walked away down the hill with a wave.

As Grace watched her go, she felt the first spots of rain sting her face. Then she saw Claire move tight against the side of the lane, as a small red hatchback swung into view, bouncing across the bridge. Claire glared after the car, and Grace grimaced. She could always trust her sister to make an entrance.

5

The next day, Grace woke up to a weak sunshine pushing its way in through the curtains. For once the other side of the bed was not an empty hollow. Rather, it contained a person, in a silk nightie with a pink eye mask and bright pink earplugs, snoring softly. Grace had laughed at Annabel as she'd set about blocking the world out the night before. "We're not next to the motorway here, you know. There's nothing out there!"

"I know, but I can't sleep without them now."

Sharing a bed reminded Grace of their childhood. The pillow fights, the pinching and tickling, the risqué novels they had read in whispers by torchlight. The last time Annabel had slept in Grace's bed had been a year ago, when Grace had woken to reality with a painful throb in her chest, on the morning after Adam had disappeared.

She jerked back to the present as she heard Millie stirring, and went to get her. By the time she had made Millie's cereal, Annabel was coming down the stairs. Grace looked around the kitchen doorway to see her sister standing by the window, bleary-eyed.

"Morning," Annabel trilled. "I was completely disorientated when I woke up." She glanced out of the window again. "It's so dismal, isn't it? I couldn't believe it when I was driving here yesterday. It's one long stretch of mud and dead bracken. I'm not sure this place even qualifies as a hamlet—you just live on the road to somewhere else."

The unflinching assessment bothered Grace. But before she could work out why, Annabel flung herself into a chair, saying, "So, what excitement have you got planned for us today then?"

"Well, I thought we could take a look in the attic."

Annabel didn't make any attempt to hide the roll of her eyes.

"It has to be done sometime," Grace persisted. She recalled the police checking the attic after Adam had vanished, and one of them shouting down "Just boxes." Now she wanted to know what was in them. "But," she said to placate her sister, "after that's done we could go for a walk . . ."

At this, Annabel threw back her head dramatically, sighing at the ceiling.

". . . or not," Grace continued dryly. "Whatever, we'll have to be back in time for lunch at Meredith's. And tonight, we could walk down to the local pub."

"That sounds more like it," Annabel said eagerly. "What do we do with Millie, though?"

"We'll take her with us. If I get her ready for bed then she'll sleep in her stroller. It's only a short walk from here."

"I didn't notice a pub when I drove in."

"Then you didn't look hard enough!" Grace replied. "Anyway, come on through here, have some breakfast, and then we'll make a start on the attic."

Annabel followed Grace into the kitchen, where Millie was smearing food over the tray of her high chair.

"Morning, Millie," Annabel said, ruffling her niece's hair gently.

Millie's head swung up in alarm, then she looked at Grace, her face beginning to crumple. Grace was astonished as Millie usually loved her Auntie Annabel. However, after a reassuring glance from her mother, Millie forgot her fears, snatched up her spoon, and began her favorite pastime of beating her breakfast into submission.

Annabel stared long and hard at Millie, then at Grace. As her mouth opened, Grace held up her hands. "I know what you're going to say. She is a serious little thing. I'm working on it." She tried to sound as casual as she could, even though Millie's somber little face regularly plagued her thoughts. She had begun to observe other children of a similar age, and those kids always appeared to be babbling and laughing—or, if upset, they were more animated about it. They seemed to demand that the world bowed before them, whereas Millie was often troubled by anything new—strangers, places, toys, you name it. Grace's mother had reassured her that it was probably a phase, but despite this, Grace had noticed her mother talking to Millie with extra care and precision, watching as the little girl played quietly, and she knew her mother was questioning her own diagnosis. And Grace couldn't help but wonder if Millie's nervousness might be related to her daddy's disappearance. What had Millie seen? Again, her mother had consoled her. "She was only a few weeks old. She'd hardly be aware of it." Grace prayed she was right.

"Hey, daydreamer," Annabel said, bringing Grace back to the room. "I wasn't going to say that actually, I was going to ask if she ever eats anything—every time I see her there's food in front of her that's going anywhere but her mouth."

Grace smiled as she handed a plate of toast to Annabel, then gently took the spoon from Millie, dipped it in the Weetabix, and pushed a dollop into Millie's mouth before she could object. Millie looked taken aback and duly swallowed it, then opened her mouth for more.

"She's not great at feeding herself yet," Grace explained, taking a seat at the table and continuing to offer cereal to Millie.

Annabel studied Millie for a moment then cast a long, appraising look in Grace's direction. "I can't believe you live here," she said, gesturing around her. "It's so . . ." Grace watched her search for the right words. ". . . not you!"

Grace smiled, remembering the enthusiasm with which she'd decorated the London flat she'd shared with Adam—keeping most of the walls neutral and applying careful splashes of color to each room. Now, looking at the intricate floral patterns of the faded wallpaper and carpet, and the mismatched furniture, she had to agree with Annabel.

"Well, this place will be having a makeover soon enough," she replied. "I've got someone coming round tomorrow to give me a quote on renovations." She began to explain what she was hoping to do with the cottage, but could tell that Annabel was only half-listening.

"Am I boring you?" she asked after a while.

"Sorry, no," Annabel replied. "I was thinking about work. It's been manic lately. It's good to get away, even if it's only for the weekend. I love it, but sometimes I wonder what the hell I'm doing. I can't wait for Christmas; I haven't had a week off in a year.'"

"That's what you get for being a high-living, cutthroat journalist," Grace said, rising from her seat and collecting their plates. She had a flashback to her own former busy life: how purposefully she'd marched through the tube tunnels every day clutching Styrofoam cups of coffee; her lunchtimes a breathless assortment of exercise classes; then the rush to get across town to meet friends for dinner, always somewhere new to try. The days seemed to stretch ahead of her now, endless tracts of time.

"Well, actually, I'm applying for a change," Annabel announced. "Hoping to move into features soon, instead of news—slightly less pressured, though not much."

Before Grace could reply, the grandfather clock began to chime.

"Bloody hell!" Annabel pressed a hand to her chest. "That thing keeps making me jump. Can you stop it?"

"I don't know." Grace walked into the hallway and stood for a moment watching the pendulum on its steady arc from side to side. There was something intimidating about this imposing piece of furniture. It stood taller than Grace, looming over her as though on the verge of toppling, while the incessant movement deep in its interior belied the stillness surrounding it. She grabbed hold of the side panels to test its stability, but it was too heavy to move. As Annabel joined her, she twisted the key on the casing, and it swung open. They had a brief look inside. "I don't really want to touch it too much in case I damage it. Adam thought it might be worth something. But I think it should stop itself in a few days—it needs winding every week. Meredith must have kept it going while I was gone."

"It does look old." Annabel ran her fingers along the heavy oak casing. "Are those pictures of places round here?"

Grace followed Annabel's gaze towards the clock face. The circle of roman numerals was set into a wider square, and the space in each corner had been filled by pastel paintings of rustic scenes: a bridge, a lake, a barn, and a stream.

"No idea," Grace said. It was the first time she'd paid proper attention to the motifs. There was a small figure on the bridge, looking over the side into unseen water, the face indiscernible. As she regarded the pictures she shivered. "I'll get it valued and shipped off in the New Year," she told Annabel, turning away.

After breakfast, they settled Millie into her high chair on the landing, where she could safely view proceedings. Then, as Annabel looked on, Grace lugged the stepladder through the cottage and up the stairs. She folded it open, squeezing it into the small landing space, then took the steps slowly until she could push up the attic cover.

Another dark space. She shone her flashlight around, a little wary of what might be revealed. However, as her eyes followed the hazy cylinder of light, her anxiety turned to weary realization. So many boxes. So much work. She gave up counting at a dozen, directing the flashlight into each corner, dust motes dancing wildly as she breathed in the stale musty air.

She climbed back down. "I'll have to get up there properly." She quickly tied back her hair.

"I'll hold the ladder steady," Annabel said, as Grace began her ascent.

When Grace reached the top, she put her hands on the bare boards, pushed hard, and managed to pull herself into the space. Annabel handed up a large lamp attached to an extension cord, and Grace set it down beside her. "Look out for spiders," Annabel called.

"Yeah, thanks for that," Grace muttered.

Now that she could see the space more clearly, she was pleased to realize that there were fewer boxes than she had feared. More than a dozen, sure, but less than twenty. She crawled over the rough wooden beams to the first one. Sure enough, as she tugged at it, a long-legged creature scuttled away into a murky corner. She gritted her teeth, and hefted the box over to the attic opening.

"Ready?" she called down.

There was no answer.

"Annabel?"

Silence.

"Annabel!" she yelled. As she listened, she realized she couldn't hear Millie either.

"For God's sake," she grumbled, half-irritated, half-worried. She turned and let her legs dangle down the hole, and was about to put her weight back on the ladder when she felt two hands go tight around her ankles. She let out a cry and clung on to the rim of the opening.

"Stop kicking!" Annabel cried. "I'm trying to guide you back to the ladder, you idiot."

"Where the hell did you go?" Grace demanded, heaving herself back up into the attic space.

"There was a strange noise coming from your bedroom. I was having a look, but it stopped."

"What kind of noise?"

"Sounded like scratching."

"Bloody hell, don't tell me I've got a mouse to deal with on top of everything else." Grace poked her head out of the attic, upside down. "Is Millie all right?"

Millie was munching on a biscuit, but stopped, astonished at the sight of her mother's disembodied face. "Boo!" Grace said, and her heart soared at Millie's smile, so she did it again, and again, while Annabel looked on, shaking her head. After a few repetitions Millie went back to her snack.

"You're such an idiot," Annabel said. "Are you coming down or what?"

Grace frowned at her. "You don't get off that lightly. I've got boxes to pass to you."

Annabel ran a hand over her forehead. "For God's sake, Grace." She looked at her perfectly manicured nails and sighed. "Come on then." She held out her arms for the first one.

Grace pushed the box to the opening in the ceiling, but had trouble fitting it through the gap.

"I can't manage that!" Annabel shrieked.

Grace tried to keep the exasperation from her voice. "Yes you can. Just step onto the ladder and balance it on the steps as you pull it down."

A moment later she heard Annabel cursing and the box bumping hard down the stepladder. She hoped there wasn't some priceless antique in there. Grace went back across to the rest of the containers and began hauling the next one over.

"How many of these are there?" she heard Annabel call.

"Just a few," Grace lied, but then Annabel's head popped up into the attic space. She looked around and her face fell. "Oh Jesus," she said.

Grace crossed her fingers and hoped her sister wasn't about to bail on her. Annabel glared at her, eyes narrowed, and muttered, "There'd better be lots of wine tonight," as her head disappeared again.

Grace smiled and grabbed the box closest to her. The cardboard that formed the lid had been cut into corners and folded down. As she pulled on it by one of the top flaps, it came open and she found herself looking at a handful of loose photos.

She took them out and shone the light on them, leafing through, then stopping at one of a child sitting alone on a living room floor in the seventies, judging by the garish décor in the background. It was a young boy, his body almost side on to the camera, but his face looking directly at the lens with a surprised smile, as though someone had called his name. He was only about three or four, but there was no mistaking who it was, and Grace felt a painful stab in her chest.

She put the photo to the back of the group she held, and focused on the next one. It was Adam again, in front of a terraced house, his arms around his mother. She wore a long dress and a headscarf, and you could see from the bony sticks of her wrists and the cavernous spaces of her collarbones that she was frail. The cancer must have been advanced by then, Grace thought. Adam would have been around seventeen. His face and frame were thinner than Grace had known, but other than that his outward appearance hadn't altered much over the next two decades. Her heart went out to the boy in the photograph. Only a year or so after it was taken he had been an orphan for all intents and purposes, living with his grandparents over the summer before heading off to university.

Her arms felt heavy as she flicked through the rest of the pictures, before she looked back at the photo of Adam and his mother. Rachel had both arms around her son, while Adam had one arm draped casually across his mother's shoulders, his body towards the camera. What had they been feeling back then? It was impossible to tell from one photo. Or was it? For despite Rachel's smile, she held Adam tightly, as though he were a ballast in the middle of a raging storm, and if she gripped on long enough she might secure him to her. She appeared to be a woman who knew exactly what the future held. Whereas Adam looked like an uncertain young teenager posing for a picture.

"Grace, are you still alive up there?"

She snapped out of her daydream and returned the photos to the box. She would set the personal memorabilia to one side, and sort through it all at once. She didn't want to spend too many days sifting through painful reminders of things that were irrevocably gone.

6

Grace's fingers were stiff with cold as she steered Millie's stroller down the hill, with Annabel trudging beside her. At the bottom, they crossed the small stone bridge and headed for the next incline. "This is the pub," Grace said as they passed a two-story whitewashed building, its chimney puffing grey smoke into the frigid air. "Those are old workers' cottages, back when they had a brickworks here." She pointed towards the tumbledown buildings in a row some distance away, and then indicated the hill ahead of them. "Meredith lives in the house up there."

They could just make out high, grey stone walls. "You didn't tell me we were lunching with the lady of the manor," Annabel said. They began the climb towards it, Grace's arms straining from the effort as she pushed Millie ahead of her. As they drew near, the house towered above them. It was set back from the road at the end of a short gravel driveway, and formed an L shape, a single-story building to their left abutting the double-story house. Four large sash windows were visible at the front, set out in a square, while trailing ivy had formed an arch over the door. A pristine burgundy four-wheel drive was parked by the entrance.

"This place is impressive," Annabel said as they reached the drive. "Why do you think they built it here, on its own?"

Before Grace could reply, a frantic barking began from inside. The door swung open and Grace found herself staring into Meredith's steely grey eyes. Grace was about to speak, when a large black dog bounded out from behind Meredith and launched itself at her.

"Pippa, come here," Meredith commanded, and Grace watched in admiration as the dog immediately scampered back to her owner. Meredith took hold of Pippa's collar and guided her inside, then reappeared a moment later and held the door open for them. She stood straight-backed, as though she had learned to balance a pile of books on her head at a young age and had never forgotten the pose. She hadn't gone for the looser soft perms popular with the older women Grace knew; instead, her hair was close-cropped to her head in a pixie style, and it suited her, highlighting her bone structure, strong lines that would never change underneath the creases of her pale skin.

"Hello, Meredith," Grace said, her warm smile fading a little as Meredith studied her. Grace was sure that on previous occasions Meredith had been affable, but the woman before them exuded a polite coolness, little more. *Don't judge her too hastily,* she chided herself. *Remember, she's recently lost her husband.* She felt a surge of empathy.

"Hello, Grace, it's nice to see you again," Meredith replied, holding out a hand and shaking with a strong, firm grip.

"This is Annabel," Grace said, as they also shook hands.

Meredith glanced at the stroller. "And this must be Millie." She knelt down to look under the shade. "Hello, little miss." Then she straightened again. "Well, come on in."

They were shown along a hallway, past a wide staircase and a few closed doors, before they finally walked into a vast, high-ceilinged room. "Wow," Annabel breathed, echoing Grace's reaction.

In the center, a huge square table was set for lunch, silver and glassware shining atop a pristine cream tablecloth. A three-piece burgundy leather suite was arranged in one corner, the furniture all a matching, gleaming mahogany. But what had really caught their attention was the vast picture window that ran from floor to ceiling on one side, framing a panoramic vista. Before them lay an endless tract of moorland, the unbroken stretch of earth drawing the eye farther and farther away in search of focus. There was little to find except for the occasional thicket, or the odd solitary tree standing sentinel. Without buildings to obscure it, the sky made up the larger part of the picture, and today it was a cloud-spattered backdrop of washed-out blue.

"We had the window put in over a decade ago, when we did some major work on the house." Meredith had followed their captivated stares. "When the heather is out at the end of summer, the whole landscape turns a royal purple—it's quite a sight. Well, come and have a seat at the table. I'm afraid I don't have a high chair . . ."

"Oh, no problem." Grace looked over at Millie. "She'll be asleep for a while, I think." She took in the smell of roasting meat, and her mouth began to water. "Can we do anything to help?"

Annabel set a bottle of red wine in the middle of the table. "We brought this. Would you like me to pour?" She set about opening the bottle, while Grace marveled at how easily Annabel made herself at home wherever she was.

Meredith was heading out of the room. "Thank you. I'll just go and check on lunch."

While they waited, Grace guided the stroller into a corner and took a seat at the table. It was set for four, glinting silver cutlery laid out in perfect symmetry, next to side dishes that featured a delicate motif of apples and oranges. Annabel took Grace's glass and poured her a generous amount of red wine, as Meredith returned from the kitchen bearing a tray of Yorkshire puddings the size of dinner plates.

"In Yorkshire we always serve the puddings first." She used a pair of tongs to put a pudding on each of their plates. "Claire should be down in a minute."

"She said she was living here at the moment?" Grace asked, as she accepted the large jug of steaming gravy Meredith held out.

"Yes," Meredith replied as she sat down. "She's been on her gap year for as long as I can remember. It seems holidaying is her occupation, and work is what she does to fill the time in between."

"It's not holidaying, Mum," Claire said merrily as she entered the room. "It's seeing the world. And I work while I'm away, too, you know." She came and took her place at the table. "Hi, Grace," she said, without waiting for her mother's response. "And you must be Grace's sister. Annabel, is it?"

Grace began eating her pudding as she listened to the introductions. "These are delicious, Meredith."

"Mum's been making them since time began." Claire looked fondly at her mother. "She's got it down to a fine art. She may not sound like a Yorkshire woman, but she definitely cooks like one."

Meredith gave her daughter a wry glance, then turned to Grace and Annabel. "My father's side is Yorkshire through and through, but the war changed things here. He went down to London during his conscription, and brought my mother back with him. She loved the countryside, but wasn't so keen on the accent. She worked hard to make sure I spoke 'the Queen's English,' as she used to say. She did the same to all the children she taught; caused a few rifts with the locals around here."

"My father built the schoolroom," Claire explained. "The long building on the left as you come towards the house. There's quite a history to this place."

"Did you go to the school here when you were a child?" Annabel asked Meredith.

"Yes, when I was small. When I got older I went to Ockton."

"And what was it like, having the school on your doorstep?"

"Not much fun, actually. My mother didn't want anyone to think she was favoring me, so she was horribly strict—she came down on me much harder than the other children. She wasn't averse to using a cane."

Meredith's tone didn't invite further questions, and an uneasy silence fell while everyone finished their puddings. As Grace laid down her knife and fork, her gaze was drawn to the mantelpiece opposite her, which was full of photo frames. Claire saw that something had caught her attention and twisted around to look.

"That's an old school photo of me and my sisters," she said, getting up to collect one of the larger pictures, and passing it over for Grace to see.

The colors of the photograph had faded. Grace looked at the four brunettes in school uniform, their similar elfish faces, three of them with long hair, one sporting a back-combed crop with red streaks through it.

"That's me," Claire chuckled, leaning over and pointing to the short-haired girl. "I thought my hairstyle was brilliant. And Mum loved it, too, didn't you, Mum?"

Meredith snorted as she began collecting their plates.

Annabel moved closer to look. "That's Veronica," Claire said, her finger resting on the tallest girl at the back of the group, who was posing confidently. "The oldest, and the bossiest. Always was, and still is. Married to Steve the lawyer now, with three boys, lives a very respectable life in Ockton." She motioned to the girl next to Veronica with wavy dark hair and a shy smile. "Next to her is Elizabeth. Liza for short. She's a year younger than me. Moved down to Leeds eighteen months ago when her husband Dan changed jobs. They've got a baby on the way. And then there's Jenny—" She pointed to a sweet-looking girl with flame-red hair, sitting at the front of the group. "She's the baby—though she turned thirty this year so I don't think I can say that anymore. She's only recently moved back to the area after spending ten years working down south. She teaches at a primary school—she's crazy about kids, that one. She's had some rough luck with relationships, but she's just started seeing someone, so I'm told, which means I'm the only one left on the shelf."

"Perhaps you wouldn't be if you took out that nose stud," Meredith cut in. Claire rolled her eyes at Grace and Annabel, and Grace warmed to her further.

"Take these plates, will you, Claire," Meredith said, "and you can help me bring the roast through."

Claire stood up, and the two of them disappeared. While they were gone, Grace glanced across at the other photos. There were a few of Meredith's husband, including a faded one of their wedding day. She noticed photographs set on a smaller side table, too, and got up to have a closer look. They were mostly babies and toddlers, presumably Meredith's grandchildren.

Soon after she sat down again, Claire and Meredith returned—Meredith bearing a platter of meat and a dish of steaming roast potatoes, while Claire carried two more bowls of assorted winter vegetables.

"This looks magnificent." Grace only wished she could cook like this. She waited while everything was laid out, then Meredith began ladling potatoes onto her plate. "Meredith, I owe you an enormous thank-you for looking after the cottage so beautifully. I was expecting to return to a place that felt unlived in—but you've kept it so homely. I am so appreciative, I can't begin to tell you . . ." She stopped as Meredith began waving away her words.

"It wasn't a problem. I was glad I could be of use. It helped me to keep busy after Ted died." Before Grace had time to express her sympathies, Meredith added, "So what are your plans now, Grace?"

Everyone fell silent, waiting for Grace's answer. She felt her face growing warm under their collective gaze. While her thoughts tumbled around the notion of finding Adam, she wanted to keep this to herself. She wasn't willing to be diverted by their reactions or opinions.

"I can't decide whether to head back to London or start afresh somewhere else," she said eventually. She could tell Annabel was listening closely as she added, "But before I can think about anything else, there's a lot to sort out in the cottage. So first of all I need to do that."

As she finished, she tried her best to ignore the little voice that kept hounding her, yearning for a return to her former life. *It doesn't exist anymore*, she reminded herself. *You can't jump into your own shadow.*

"I can assure you she's quite civilized to have around," Annabel said, a sparkle in her eye. "She was always the one trying to talk me out of holding wild parties while our parents were away."

Claire smiled, but Meredith didn't, as she looked across at her daughter. Claire briefly raised her eyebrows and returned her attention to her meal.

Meredith observed Grace thoughtfully for a moment. "Well, you have done a brave thing coming back here. I didn't think you would. It's not an easy place to be with a small baby, especially in winter, what with the snow causing all sorts of chaos." She took another bite of her lunch, leaving the comment hanging, so that Grace felt obliged to reply.

"I wanted to sort through the cottage myself, not leave it to a stranger. Whatever else, I feel I owe Adam's grandparents that much, for Millie's sake."

"Besides, Mum, you raised a family out here," Claire added.

"Yes, Claire," Meredith replied. "But I've lived here all my life. It's different."

Grace wondered what she meant by that. Was Meredith implying that Grace might have problems adapting to life in the sleepy village? Or was there something troubling about the area itself? Because Grace was already finding the unbroken silence unnerving, the way nothing moved except at the will of the wind—but she kept telling herself that she would get used to it.

Now Claire was speaking to her. "So there's been no word then—about Adam?"

His name hung heavily in the space between them all. Claire's face was filled with concern, and Grace noticed out of the corner of her eye that Annabel was casting her sister a worried glance.

"No," Grace said, breathing deeply. "The police have filed him away as a missing person . . . but, I don't know . . . I can't believe that he just walked out . . . Oh, I'm sorry, do you mind if we don't talk about it?" She could feel her breath tightening in her chest.

Annabel cut in. "So, Meredith . . . when you say you've lived here all your life, you surely don't mean in this house?"

"I do indeed," Meredith replied. "All my life. My grandfather built the original house, and my parents added various extensions to make it what you see today. When my father was a young man, Roseby was very different. There was a brickworks operating a few hundred yards from here, and there were more small tenements. Most have fallen down—there are only three left, ramshackle now, you've probably seen them from the road. When the brickworks closed, everyone left. There weren't enough children to need a school, so the area went wild again. Just a few families stuck it out."

"Don't you find it isolated?" Annabel asked.

Meredith shrugged. "This house contains so many memories, it's never occurred to me to leave. I belong here."

Annabel glanced at Grace.

"Don't judge us too hastily, Annabel," Meredith said, laying her knife and fork slowly to rest on the edges of her plate. She interlaced her fingers and propped her chin on her hands, looking from Annabel to Grace. "I can honestly say I have never seen any place as beautiful as it is here. Desolate, yes, particularly in winter, but watch it come alive in spring when the lambs are born and all the birds return from their migration. And it's glorious when the heather crowns it late in the summer. This place has more life to it in one square meter than there is in a square mile of the concrete sprawl so many of you are keen to call home nowadays."

Annabel raised her hands. "I think you've misunderstood. I'm a journalist. I'm instinctively curious, that's all." But Grace knew what Annabel had been trying to convey with her eyes. *She belongs here, Grace. You don't.*

There was an uncomfortable pause, then Claire said, "Our dad was a farmer. My sisters and I grew up playing in the ruins of the workers' houses and the remains of the brickworks. It was fantastic— like having our own little make-believe village to run around in."

"Then they used them to hide in while they drank and smoked their way through their teenage years," Meredith added, a glimmer in her eye as she glanced at her daughter.

"If you say so." Claire laughed. "Did Adam never tell you about them, Grace? He joined in for a while, in the few months he was here. He was a big hit with us all, I can tell you—new blood around here is extremely rare . . ."

Meredith's eyes lingered on her daughter for a moment, then she looked down at her plate. "Remember that he was only here for a short time, Claire. It might not have felt like a big part of his life, not in the same way you remember it."

Claire considered that. "You're probably right. At the time I thought we were great friends, but when he left for university I don't think I ever heard from him again. He didn't even come back for a visit—did he, Mum?"

Meredith didn't reply, but Claire's comments were making Grace think back. When she'd first known Adam he had kept in touch with his grandparents by phone, but he'd never seemed keen to make the journey up from London to see them. "It's a hell of a way," he'd told her, "and there's nothing to do up there. They're lovely people but we're not all that close—I only saw them now and again before Mum died, and I didn't stay with them for long before I went off to university." But she recalled how deeply touched he had been when his grandparents made the long trip south to see him get married. So after their wedding, he'd taken Grace to visit. There hadn't been room to stay in the small cottage, so they'd booked bed and breakfast at a local farm. She remembered how much he'd enjoyed showing her around. It must have been then that his love for the area had been rekindled.

While caught up in her distraction, she had missed the change of topic. She began to listen again as Meredith said, "Emma and Carl . . . they live next door to Grace. Didn't think they'd last when they first came—but they appear to have settled in. Their son prowls around the area, doesn't say a word to anyone. Jack lives next door to them . . ."

"Uncle Jack," Claire cut in.

"My late husband's older brother," Meredith explained. "Ted and Jack were originally from Skeldale, but Ted took over the farm from my dad after we were married, and Jack moved here a few years later to help out. So he's lived here for over thirty years. Never married. Keeps himself to himself now. You'll be lucky if you catch sight of him."

"And the house at the top?" Annabel asked.

"Another relative," Claire chuckled. "It's so incestuous here."

Meredith cast her a withering glance. "Hardly. They're a couple about your age, perhaps a bit older. Distant cousins in the family, yes, but a few times removed. When they heard the house was vacant they snapped it up. It seems to suit them. They have also taken on one of Pippa's siblings. Our dog Rosie had pups a few years ago, so we kept Pippa, and Holly and Bess went up the road. Rosie died last year, so now we've only got Pippa."

"That's why I keep seeing black dogs everywhere!" Grace said. "I was worried it was some kind of omen. I even dreamed about one the other night—with bared teeth and slavering gums—horrible."

"Well now, that could have been a barghest," Claire said. "There's a legend of a black dog around here. Some say it's Dracula's dog—though I think it was actually Dracula himself who turned into the black beast that jumped off a ship in Whitby and raced away into the night."

"Whitby is only ten miles or so over the moors," Meredith added.

"However," Claire continued, warming to her subject, "others will tell you that the barghest appears to people just before the death of a local." On seeing Grace's horrified face, she laughed. "Don't worry, Grace—I've lived here on and off for the best part of thirty-two years and I've never seen one shred of evidence to support the stories. They're folktales. You had a nightmare, that's all."

Grace looked at Meredith for confirmation, but Meredith only gave her a stiff smile. "The moors are full of ghostly apparitions, Grace. Surely Adam told you that? We even have one of our own." She glanced from Grace to Annabel. "In here." She waved her hand around the room.

"His name is Tiny Tim," Claire added, nodding to show her mother was telling the truth.

"Are you joking?" Annabel was gaping at them like they'd announced that the house was a spaceship and liftoff was imminent.

"No, not at all." Meredith's face was solemn. "Though Tiny Tim is the girls' nickname for him. He's a little child. He's only been spotted a few times, but he gets up to mischief now and again, banging things around during the night. We've learned to live with it, and it doesn't happen all that often—hardly ever since the kids grew up."

"You've got to be kidding." Annabel's eyes were ablaze with curiosity. "Who's seen him?"

"My eldest, Veronica, once said she'd seen him watching her from the end of the bed. Our youngest, Jenny, used to talk about playing with Timmy upstairs, when we moved her into Liza's old bedroom. Neither girl was scared. He's pretty harmless. I think he only appears to children—as far as I know, no grown-ups have ever seen him. We just hear him now and again."

"I can't tell if you're winding me up," Annabel said after a beat.

Meredith looked slightly offended. "I can assure you we're not. I've researched it. An eight-year-old boy called Timothy was killed on the road near here, back in the twenties. We're pretty sure he's the one who lives with us."

"Jesus Christ!" Annabel looked at Grace. "You don't have any ghosts in the cottage, do you?"

"I . . . I don't think so," Grace replied. She didn't think she believed in ghosts, but she was momentarily very aware that Adam's grandmother had died there—probably in the bedroom Grace was sleeping in.

"Hawthorn Cottage is one of the older dwellings, been here since before the brickworks," Meredith told them. "But I've heard most of the local tales and I don't remember a ghost ever being mentioned there. I think you can both rest easy." She picked up a napkin and gave her lips a dab.

"Ghosts wandering everywhere out there, though." Claire gestured at the moors beyond the picture window. Grace saw that the corners of her mouth were turned up, and there was a flicker of amusement in her eyes.

"Really?" Annabel sounded excited, and Claire's enjoyment seemed to wane a little. Grace smiled to herself—they didn't know Annabel yet. While she complained and squealed a lot, her fascination with ghoulish tales overrode any fears she might have. Annabel was more likely to organize an exorcism and then clutch at everyone throughout the event rather than run away.

"There's plenty of folklore, that's for certain." Meredith got up from her seat and held out her hand for Grace's plate. "Now, would you like some dessert?"

Once Meredith had left the room, Grace stared out of the picture window, only dimly aware of Claire and Annabel's conversation. There was nothing out there, she reassured herself, except a bare expanse of nature. Ghosts made good stories, that was all.

Meredith returned bearing an apple pie, which she deftly sliced up, placing portions into bowls. She passed around a jug of cream, and they all ate heartily again. Grace's stomach was uncomfortably full, but the pie was too delicious to resist. As they ate, the only sounds were the scraping of their spoons against the bowls and the whining of Pippa, hoping to be let into the room to join them.

"So how long are you staying, Annabel?" Meredith asked when she'd finished eating.

"A couple of days," Annabel said, a spoonful of dessert halfway towards her mouth. "Then back next week for Christmas. I've been helping Grace pull down boxes from the attic all morning," she told them, making a face at her sister.

Claire rested her wineglass against the tip of her chin. "I hope we never have to sort this place out. Nightmare."

"You will when I die," Meredith replied.

Grace didn't know how to react to that, and neither did Annabel by the look of her, but Claire laughed. "I think we'll probably all die before you do, Mum." She pushed away her empty bowl with a sigh of satisfaction and rubbed her stomach. "She's made of extremely tough Northern stuff, my mother," Claire explained to the others.

Meredith smiled, and Grace thought it was perhaps the most genuine response she'd seen from the woman all afternoon. Then Millie began to wriggle in the stroller. Without even asking, Meredith walked across, unbuckled the child, and lifted her up. Millie stiffened, then stared around the room at them all. Grace smiled at her, and Millie held her arms out to her mother, her little face crumpling as she began to cry.

"There, there," Meredith said, jiggling her up and down as she walked across to Grace. "No need for that." She handed Millie over. "They're so clingy at this age, aren't they? I much preferred mine as they got a bit older."

Grace felt defensive but didn't reply. Meanwhile, Millie leaned into the hollow of Grace's arm and looked around at them all from her place of safety.

"Can we help you clear up?" Grace asked, as she rocked Millie gently.

"Not at all." Meredith began collecting plates. "You have your hands full there. Claire and I are more than capable."

Annabel got up to help anyway, and Grace went to sit in one of the armchairs with Millie. The little girl had woken up irritable, and squirmed to be free. As the women filed back in from the kitchen, Grace stood up. "I might have to take her home, Meredith. I'm sorry to rush off after such a lovely lunch."

"I understand," Meredith replied. She went across to a tall dresser, rummaged in a drawer, then strode over to Grace. "Here's your spare key back. Now, why don't you come again during the week—I have a portable crib I keep for the grandchildren that Millie can use. Or why don't you come at five, when she's up? I'll make you another meal and we can get to know one another better."

"Yes," Claire added, "come and eat here, Grace, don't sit in that cottage by yourself."

"Thanks," Grace said, taking the key. "That would be lovely." She was grateful for their hospitality, despite Meredith's severe manner. And next time she could ask more about Adam's family without arousing Annabel's suspicions. It might be a long shot, but she was buoyed by a renewed sense of purpose. That was reason enough for her to look forward to returning, just so long as Tiny Tim didn't make one of his rare appearances that night.

7

It had been dark for hours by the time they finished emptying the attic. There were now seventeen boxes of various sizes stacked precariously against the banister on the upstairs landing, which Grace had to squeeze around to get to the bathroom and Millie's room. With each box added to the pile, Grace's enthusiasm for the task had diminished. There was an awful lot of work here, and she had an unwelcome feeling that she would be decluttering rather than finding the answers she craved. But now that the attic was empty at least she wouldn't have to venture up into the roof space again. She had prized open a couple of lids to discover a real mishmash of items, and decided that going through everything was a job for another day. She was ready for a break, and didn't want to push her luck with Annabel.

Instead, they got ready for their trip to the pub. Grace put on some jeans and a sweater, while Annabel emerged in a short black dress, smart blazer, and heels. Grace thought of where they were heading and tried not to giggle. When Adam had taken her into the pub a year ago, the predominant fashion had been flat caps and pipes.

They put a sleepy Millie into her stroller, and then set off on the short walk down the hill. The moon was lost somewhere behind the clouds, so the only light to navigate by came from the windows of the pub. As a result, there was a faint, irregular glow over small sections of the road ahead of them, but the rest lay cloaked in heavy shadow. A strong wind lashed their faces, whipping Grace's hair in all directions, sending it in stinging slaps across her skin. As she concentrated on keeping the stroller steady, she waited for Annabel's first complaint. It didn't take long.

"Hey, slow down, I can't go that fast in these shoes."

Grace slackened her pace. "I'd love to see you trying to get down this hill when it's frosty. You'd be on your backside in five seconds."

"We don't all want to live in UGGs, you know," Annabel answered, then stumbled and gripped Grace's arm. "Bloody hell, I can hardly see the road. I feel like I'm skating over a black hole."

"Stop moaning," Grace laughed, sucking in her breath against the wind, the sharpness of it making her teeth chatter. As she bent her head, a fast-moving dark shape low to the ground caught the edge of her peripheral vision. She felt a twinge of fear in her chest and peered at the blackened space, but there was nothing moving now. The barghest flashed into her mind, and she quickened her pace over the little stone bridge, moving at speed towards the entrance of the pub. "Here we are."

Annabel held open the door, a blast of warm woodsmoke greeting them as Grace wheeled the stroller inside.

The interior of Roseby's only drinking establishment was as quaint as Grace remembered it. The main sitting area was basically a decent-sized living room. Two men standing side by side would have taken up the whole width of the bar in the corner, but that probably didn't matter much here, as there weren't enough patrons for a queue. When Grace had been in with Adam, he'd found his grandparents on a few of the old pictures that were hung around the walls, and pointed out the dartboard in the corner, saying his grandfather used to come down every Friday for a game.

Tonight would probably be deemed a busy night for the elderly couple who ran the place, as they already had three customers in, and as many dogs. That was what she'd seen, Grace reassured herself. Someone's dog had been nosing about outside. After all, it seemed everyone in the area owned a dog.

"My round!" Annabel trilled cheerily, and headed straight to the bar.

As Grace unwound her scarf, she glanced up to see a man studying her from a dingy corner, but he quickly looked away. Grace had the unnerving feeling that she should recognize him—what was it with familiar faces around here? She studied his broad back as he hunched over his pint, trying to place him, but he didn't look in her direction again.

"Grace!"

At the sound of her name, she turned to see a middle-aged couple seated in the opposite corner by the fire, wearing matching thick green sweaters. Sitting stoically to the side of them was yet another Labrador, its black fur glowing in the firelight. The woman leapt up and came over, pulling Grace into a hug.

"It's good to see you, Emma," Grace said, as the woman stood back.

Emma kept hold of Grace's arm. Her face had a rosy sheen to it, her highlighted blonde hair giving way to dark roots. "Grace, how are you? Any news . . . you know?"

"No, nothing." Grace felt her eyelids prickle.

"Oh Grace," Emma said, patting her arm. "It's the strangest thing I've ever heard happen, I still don't understand it."

Annabel came up to them holding two glasses of red wine. "Unbelievable prices!" she said. "Are you sure those two wouldn't like to relocate somewhere nearer London?" She gestured towards the publicans, perched together on bar stools, engrossed in a quiz show on the small television set high above the bar.

"Len and Joyce come with the pub," Emma replied, grinning. "It's been a package deal for, oh, at least half a century or more. I'm Emma. You must be Grace's sister—I think I remember you."

"Emma and Carl joined in the search party last year," Grace reminded her sister. "They live next door to me. Emma and Adam worked together baling hay in the summer Adam lived here."

"That we did—we had a right laugh," Emma said. She flicked her head towards their table. "Come and sit with us." She led the way over to her husband.

"Now then," Carl greeted them as they sat down. "It's good to see you back, Grace." He shook Annabel's hand.

"How's your little one?" Emma asked kindly, gesturing to the stroller.

"She's fine," Grace replied. Her memory jogged again. "Weren't you . . ."

"Pregnant!" Emma finished for her. "Sure was—size of a house when you saw me last. She's nearly one now—how wonderful she'll have a little playmate next door."

Grace winced, wondering whether to explain that her plans were not long term, but instead she asked, "And how's she doing?"

"The baby's grand!" Carl cut in good-naturedly. "It's the teenager that's the trouble." Close up, Carl might have been Emma's twin—ruddy cheeks that matched his solid frame, wholesome without looking fat.

Emma gave her husband a nudge with her elbow. "Hush, that's your free babysitter you're talking about."

"True, true," Carl agreed, taking a sip of his pint. He looked at Annabel as he set down his glass. "So are you here for a visit?"

"Yes, just for the weekend," Annabel replied. "Then back next week for Christmas."

"So where do you live?" Emma asked.

"London," Annabel answered happily, and Grace listened with a deep pang of longing as her sister launched into an enthusiastic spiel about the capital. It was all there for her if she wanted it: the busyness, the bright lights, the never-ending movement that wouldn't be halted for any reason, great or small. Where only a short tube ride separated the huge global department stores that Annabel lived in and the tiny hidden markets that Grace adored. Where she could meet her friends at restaurants down cobbled lanes that served exotic dishes for next to nothing. She and Adam had been ice-skating at Hyde Park a couple of years ago, their arms around each other as some people whizzed past and others grabbed onto them laughing as they struggled for balance. In London you were whipped into the cacophony of the city—and how vibrant and alive that could make you feel. Here, you had no choice but to stop and let the tranquility enfold you. Perhaps she should go back to the south. Perhaps it wouldn't be so different after all. She and Millie might fit right in as though they had never been anywhere else. But, she reminded herself, she couldn't recapture the London she had known with Adam. And she knew that if she tried to throw herself back into her old hurly-burly life for the wrong reasons, the chaos of the capital might easily overwhelm her. Besides, daydreaming was all very well, but there was unfinished business here to deal with first.

"Are you ready for Christmas, Grace?" she heard Emma asking.

"To be honest, I haven't thought about it too much," she admitted.

"Not a bad idea," Carl said. "My sisters have it planned like a military campaign—with spreadsheets and everything. I know I sound like an old git when I say this, but when I was young we loved the carols and the tree and the stories as well as the presents." He caught sight of Emma playfully rolling her eyes and gave her a rueful smile. "All right, I'm off my soapbox. Come on then, our lass," he gestured to Emma's drink, "let's get home and kick the lad off the Internet before he can cause too much damage."

Emma drained her glass then stood up, smiling at Grace. "Just let me know if you ever need me to mind Millie," she offered. "I know how hard it is without a babysitter in these parts."

"Thank you so much." Grace doubted she'd have a reason to take Emma up on the offer, but it was generous nonetheless.

They watched Emma and Carl leave, then Annabel motioned towards Grace's empty glass and asked, "Another one?"

Grace glanced over at Millie to check she was still sleeping.

"Come on, Grace, I need to get a bit drunk so I can spend another night in your cottage after listening to ghost stories all afternoon."

Before Grace could speak, Annabel was already on her way to the bar. When she returned with two large glasses of wine, Grace sat back and listened to her sister talk, growing ever more tired as Annabel became increasingly animated. She wanted to get a good sleep, aware of how much she had to do at the cottage, and was debating how she could get Annabel to hurry up and finish her drink when the wind wailed abruptly into the room, then the front door was sucked back with an almighty bang.

Everyone's head whipped around towards the noise. A man in his early thirties stood by the door, his coat collar pulled up so high around his neck that his head appeared half-buried within it. He approached the bar with a wariness that made Grace feel on edge, though his posture wasn't particularly menacing, and she couldn't imagine anyone bothering to hold up a pub that was probably lucky to get to three figures in the night's takings. As he reached the bar and spoke to the old couple seated behind it, the woman shrank back, while her husband moved slowly forward and leaned his hands on the countertop. Glowering up through bushy brows, Len said something short and sharp, but Grace was too far away to catch it. "No!" the old man shouted a second later, as he banged his hand down on the wooden bar top with a force and speed that belied his age.

The younger man backed away with his hands held in the air as if in surrender, then turned on his heel and was gone. The couple retreated to their perches, muttering to one another, until their attention was gradually pulled back to the TV and they fell under its trance once more.

"What the hell was that about?" Annabel asked, her cheeks flushed.

"God knows," Grace replied, her heart hammering, one eye on the door.

"Well, if that's how they deal with potential robbers here it's most effective." Annabel chuckled a little nervously to herself as she took a big gulp of wine. "God, I never told you about Julie getting her bag snatched right off her shoulder in the Sail and Anchor, did I? We all gave chase and the bastard obviously got scared, as he dropped it with everything still inside—one for the girls, hey! She sends her love, by the way."

Grace smiled and gave responses where required as Annabel

continued to gossip away. Her head was somewhere else, however—remembering the man who had stood briefly by the bar. As he had turned she had recognized Ben straight away.

In the morning he would be coming to the cottage. And she knew absolutely nothing about him.

8

An hour later, Grace and Annabel walked up the hill, their breaths sending clouds of mist into the icy air. The wind had dropped, but Grace's head was swirling, both from the wine and the commotion.

Away from the pub, the darkness became a blindfold. Grace's other senses began to heighten in the absence of vision. She was acutely aware of the weight of each step, the rustle of her coat as she moved, the wool of her gloves rubbing between her fingers and the padded stroller handle.

A high-pitched shriek of torment suddenly tore into the night. Both women stopped, frozen, then reached out for each other. "Jesus," Annabel cried, "what was that?"

"I heard it the other night, too. It's probably a bat or something."

"Oh for God's sake." Annabel quickened her pace. "It scared the life out of me, whatever it is. Let's get inside."

As they reached the cottage and Grace unlatched the gate, she automatically looked back down the road towards the pub. A man was standing outside, silhouetted by the light from the open door. She couldn't see his face at all, only the outline of him, but she was sure he was watching them.

"Look," she hissed at Annabel.

A moment later, the man wheeled around and they heard the distant creak and slam of the pub door.

"That was odd," Annabel said. "Do you know who it was?"

"No idea."

Annabel gave a visible shudder. "This place is creepy, Grace. Why on earth did you and Adam move here?"

Grace didn't want to dwell on that right now. "Emma and Carl were nice enough, though, weren't they?"

"Yes, thank goodness," Annabel agreed, and her mood seemed to lighten. "Right, get that little one into bed and we'll crack open another bottle."

Grace was about to say that she was tired, but before she could speak, Annabel gave her a look. Grace knew she wouldn't be let off easily. "All right, just a glass. You do realize Millie will probably be up at dawn."

By the time Grace had settled Millie into bed, Annabel had poured the wine. Grace was about to take a sip when both of them suddenly jumped as someone banged hard on the front door.

"What the hell . . . ?" Annabel spluttered on her drink.

Before Grace could even reply, there was another bang. She got up, opened the curtain a fraction and peered towards the door. She could make out a shadowy figure. Annabel joined her, pulling the curtain further back. "He doesn't look like an ax murderer," she said thoughtfully.

"Do ax murderers knock?" Grace whispered. They looked at one another and burst into nervous laughter.

As Grace turned again to the window, trying to get a better look, the man glanced across, staring straight at her.

She stepped backwards in shock. It was the man from the pub, she was sure of it. And now she could see his face, her memories shifted, forming an old picture. She had opened the same door to him twelve months earlier. She could still remember how her hands had trembled as she let him inside.

"It's okay," she told Annabel. "I recognize him." She headed through the hallway and opened the door.

The man on the step was short and thick set, his face red from the cold, his eyes watering in the wind.

"Now then, Grace."

"It's Niall, isn't it?"

"That's right." He looked pleased that she remembered. "Can I come in for a minute and have a word?"

Grace turned to see Annabel brandishing an umbrella, as though ready to use it as a weapon. Her stance jolted Niall into understanding.

"I'm sorry, love." He ran a hand over his face. "I didn't mean to scare you. I was caught unaware when I saw you at the pub. I couldn't place you right away, but when I realized who you were I reckoned I'd better come up and see you." He held out a hand to Annabel. "Constable Edwards, call me Niall."

He was much smaller than Grace remembered, but perhaps the uniform he'd worn when they'd first met had made him more of a presence. His eyes were the same, though—extending an unspoken compassion that Grace found as unbearable now as she had a year ago. In his presence it was impossible to pretend that nothing was wrong.

She realized they were waiting for her to speak. "Come in," she said, and stepped back to let him through. "Annabel, this is the policeman who came round first on the night Adam disappeared."

Niall waved away Annabel's offer of a drink. He sat on the edge of his chair, his hands clasped between his knees. "How's your little lass doing?"

"She's fine," Grace replied. "She's asleep upstairs."

"That's good." He looked pleased. "I've often thought about you two, you know. I have to say I didn't think I'd see you back round these parts."

Grace stiffened. "There are things that need sorting out. I want to tie up the loose ends, so Millie and I can move on with our lives."

"Well, that's fair enough. I kept an eye on the investigation, and I don't think much has changed . . . ?"

"No." Grace looked into her wineglass, swirled the liquid, and took a large sip. "I haven't heard from the police recently."

Niall's sigh was sympathetic. "It happens, I'm afraid, when there are no new leads, and new cases coming up all the time. Everyone scurrying about, overworked, and underpaid. Did you have a Family Liaison Officer?"

"Yes—Ken Barton."

"Have you told him you're back?"

Grace shook her head. "No. Should I?"

"Wouldn't hurt. But listen, I won't keep you." He got to his feet, then fumbled in his pocket and pulled out a piece of paper. "Have you got a pen handy?"

Grace found one for him. He scribbled on the paper. "If I can be of any help to you, while you're here . . ." She looked at the mobile number scrawled on the scrap he'd handed to her.

"Thank you."

"I've two lasses of my own, and I've always found it hard to believe that your husband just ran off that night, leaving your bairn on the step like he did."

Grace's jaw felt tight as she replied, "I know, I can't believe it either . . ." She wanted to add more, but couldn't find the words.

Niall nodded. "Well, I'll leave you be then." He turned for the door.

After they had seen him out, Annabel considered her sister for a while, then said, "Are you going to tell me?"

Grace frowned at her. "What?"

"Come on, Grace, something is bothering you. Spit it out."

"It's nothing." Grace ran a finger round the rim of her glass.

"Well why don't you explain, and then I can decide that for myself."

Grace looked squarely at Annabel. "It's just—the day before Adam disappeared, he went out for a few hours. He said he was going to watch the Arsenal match at the pub in Ockton, and do some Christmas shopping afterwards. But then, while I was in France I heard Dad grumbling about how many games Arsenal had at the end of the season, because of all the ones cancelled for bad weather around Christmas. I went on the Internet—and the game had been cancelled that day."

"Right. So . . . ?" Annabel looked uncertain.

"Well, he didn't tell me that."

"Perhaps he just went shopping instead."

"Maybe. But he didn't come home with any bags. There was nothing on our credit card. I never found any presents hidden away."

"Why didn't you say something earlier?"

"Dad convinced me it was nothing—said he probably watched another match instead. I rang Ken Barton as well, but he sounded as skeptical as Dad. There was a big local derby on that day, apparently, which went ahead, and all the pubs would have been showing it."

"But you're not sure?"

"Oh, I don't know. They're probably right. But seeing Niall reminded me of it, that's all. And I keep racking my brain—looking for anything suspicious—and that's the best I can come up with so far."

They sat in silence for a while, drinking their wine.

"You could mention it again when you next speak to Ken Barton," Annabel suggested.

"I will," Grace agreed, but doubted she'd be taken seriously. Anyway, her dad was probably right. It was such a tenuous lead, and she had to be careful not to embellish her memories with meanings made from hindsight. Her mission was daunting enough as it was.

9

Annabel left early the next morning, keen to avoid the Sunday afternoon traffic on the long journey to London. Soon after she had gone, heavy rain had begun to pound the windows, and so far showed no signs of slowing. When Millie was settled for her lunchtime nap, Grace sat down in an armchair and began to reflect on everything that had happened since she'd returned. Gradually, the fizzing of her mind abated, and she fell into a half-slumber.

An insistent banging catapulted her awake and sent her springing from her chair. For a moment she was confused, before she realized with a rush of relief that it was only someone knocking on the door. It would be Ben, calling about the renovations.

"Hello," he said, taking down his large black umbrella as she opened the door. Bess sat next to him, droplets shimmering at the tips of her wet, clumpy fur, her tail wagging. "Can I leave Bess here?"

"Of course."

Ben led the dog underneath the porch, and Bess shook herself, water spraying from her coat. "Bess!" Ben cried in exasperation, jumping out of the way. The dog wagged her tail eagerly, and he laughed and gave her ears an affectionate scratch. "Stay," he instructed, and Bess immediately lay down.

Grace was still a little wary of Ben after what she'd witnessed at the pub, but as she watched him with the dog her concerns dissipated, and she stood back to let him in.

"So, what are you planning for this place?" he asked as he followed her through to the kitchen.

Grace pulled out Mike Muir's drawings, and a few rough sketches of her own. "These are really basic," she said as she gave them to him, half-embarrassed by her simple designs. But Ben sat down and began studying them carefully.

"Ah, I see what you're thinking. Knock out this wall," he banged the wall next to him, "and you've got a nice cozy area. And sort out the bathroom upstairs so it's en suite. This looks like a good plan." He glanced up. "Want me to do some proper drawings for this, and then figure out the best way to go about it?"

Grace had gone across to the kettle. "Well, we'd better talk money before we get too much further. I've only begun thinking about this recently, and I need some idea of how much it would cost."

Ben folded his arms and looked down at the sketches for a while without saying anything. "I'll tell you what—let me do the plans for nothing, and we'll figure it out from there."

Grace was taken by surprise. Ben's expression was unreadable, but not unfriendly. As she looked at him she noticed that his eyes were framed by grey circles, and there was a melancholy aspect to his face that struck her as almost tragic. *A Heathcliff*, she thought, and couldn't decide if the current that ran through her was fear or something else.

"You don't need to do that," she said.

She thought he might smile, but he just said, "I know," and began to browse through the papers again. "To be honest you're doing me a favor. I'd be grateful for a project to keep me busy at the moment." He raised his eyes to meet hers. "Okay?"

Grace felt off-balance, his suggestion sweeping her ideas along much faster than she'd intended, and she faltered under his direct stare. "Well, if you don't mind."

"Can I take these?" He held up the loose sheets of drawings.

"Of course. Would you like a drink?"

Ben shook his head as he got up. "Don't worry about that. Why don't you give me a quick tour of the place, then I can get out of your way."

"All right, then," Grace murmured. *He came for work,* she reminded herself, *not to pass the time of day.* She showed him the upstairs rooms, careful not to wake Millie. As they came back down the stairs, Ben gestured towards the corridor and said, "What's in your cellar?"

Grace spun round. "What cellar?" she asked in confusion.

"Er—" Ben had diverted his course, heading for a small wooden door behind the stairs. "This cellar," he said as he rapped on it.

"I thought that was a cupboard," Grace answered. "Are you sure it isn't?"

For the first time since he'd arrived, he smiled. "Pretty sure. You've never looked inside then?"

"No," she said. "It's locked." To be certain, she lifted the old-fashioned latch and pulled, but the door didn't budge. "I've never seen the key."

She tried to recall what Adam had told her. She was sure he hadn't contradicted her when she'd asked about the cupboard under the stairs. He'd said it was locked, and they needed to find the key. That was as far as they'd got before he disappeared. She'd told the police that it was a cupboard when they searched the place. They'd wanted the key. But they must have forgotten.

"Do you want me to pick the lock for you?" Ben offered.

"Ha ha."

"I'm serious."

"Misspent youth, hey?"

He smiled again, and this time it was briefly echoed in his eyes. "Something like that. I need a paper clip or a safety pin."

Grace went to find a paper clip. Ben inserted it into the keyhole and slowly moved it around. There was a click, then he twisted the handle and pulled open the door.

"There," he said, holding it ajar.

Grace looked past him. Sure enough, steps led away from her into blackness.

"Have you got a flashlight?" Ben asked as he felt about for a light switch.

"Yes," she replied, but she didn't move. The thought of what might be down there had caused panic to spring up from nowhere. She felt sick.

"Want me to take a look?" he offered, seeming to read her mind.

"Yes, please." She ran through to the kitchen to get the flashlight. When she returned, Ben took it from her, flicked it on, and headed down the stairs.

She didn't release her breath until he called up, "It's mostly boxes." Giddy with relief, she peered down to see a beam of light illuminating what looked like pile upon pile of odds and ends. "Come and see," he suggested.

Tentatively, she moved inside, letting the door swing shut behind her. Then she began to make her way down carefully, hands pressed against the walls that closed in on her from either side of the staircase. When she reached the bottom, she said, "Ben?"

"Hang on." His voice was alarmingly close, but the flashlight was flitting over the wall. She remembered the old couple's faces in the pub last night, how scared they had looked, and her mouth went dry. Had she misread him completely? What was she doing down here with this man she barely knew?

Another flash of panic overtook her, and she blindly whisked around to head back up the stairs. As she did so, light flooded the room. "I thought there had to be a switch," she heard Ben say to one side of her. "Why the hell did they put it down here?"

She swung to face him. Ben caught her expression before she could recompose herself, and she saw his astonishment fade into something more like disappointment. He switched off the flashlight and put it into her hand without meeting her eyes. "I'll wait for you at the top," he said, then took the stairs two at a time, his upper body tense.

She surveyed the small room, now lit starkly by a white bulb dangling overhead. It seemed like it should have a chair in the middle, with someone tied to it being interrogated, but the reality was far more mundane. And wearying. Because everywhere she turned she saw junk—spilling out of boxes and cupboards, oozing from shelves. Just piles of assorted debris and dusty rubbish. She grimaced, hands on hips, considering the amount of extra work she had found in this one small space. Then, taking note of where the light switch was, she pressed it and used the flashlight to guide her back up the stairs.

Ben was leaning against the corridor wall, waiting for her. "You okay?" he asked, his tone kind. She threw him a guilty smile, feeling silly for panicking, and grateful he was being so gracious about it.

"I think I've just found a few months' work," she said dejectedly.

"You might be right. It looks like they literally threw stuff in there. What a state."

"I know."

"You could always lock it again and tell everyone it's a cupboard."

She tried to laugh but could only manage a weak smile. "It's tempting. Still, at least I know what I'm up against now."

As the conversation died away, Ben seemed to decide that it was his cue to leave. "Right, I'll take a look at all this," he waved her notes in the air, "and come and see you again in a day or two when I've got something to show you."

"I really appreciate it." Grace followed him to the front door. "Are you sure I can't get you a drink?"

"I'm fine, thanks," he said. As he opened the door, Bess got to her feet. "I'll see you soon, Grace."

Then he was gone, with Bess trotting next to him, and Grace was left staring at the empty garden path.

She went to make a cup of coffee, before deciding to investigate the cellar again. This time she grabbed a couple of heavy books, using them to keep the door ajar. As she headed down, she wished she could afford to pay someone to empty the place and save her the stress, but she didn't want to spend money on jobs she could do herself, especially now that her savings would be stretched with the renovations. At least Annabel would be back soon to help out, although she imagined that Annabel might have convulsions if she saw the state of this place.

On reaching the bottom of the stairs, she moved swiftly over to the far corner. Something had caught her eye there earlier—two battered cardboard boxes she thought she recognized. She hadn't wanted to check them out in front of Ben, but now she opened one of them and stared miserably inside. They were Adam's mementos: a cricket statue; an old T-shirt with handwriting all over it, the jokes and scribbles of teenagers elated at their impending freedom from school; and a collection of Arsenal programs. The problem was, Grace had seen these things before. They had been in the London flat she and Adam had shared; she remembered him packing them up. Which meant he'd brought them down here last year. So it looked like he had known there was a cellar, after all.

Damn you, Adam, she cursed aloud.

As soon as she'd spoken, a distant noise began, as though in response. She paused, listening. It was the long, determined creak of a door moving towards its latch.

Grace dropped everything and raced towards the cellar steps, taking them two at a time as the shaft of landing light quickly diminished. If the latch clicked into place she would be stuck—there was no handle on the inside—and she had a flash of horror at the thought of Millie alone upstairs. She reached the door when only a fraction of light remained, pushing it back, giving a cry of relief when it moved obediently. The books she had used to hold it ajar had moved slightly, and she set them back in place and added two more, before sprinting down to turn off the cellar light then racing back up again. The door's weight had pushed the books away, she told herself once safely back in the corridor, gradually recovering her breathing. The timing was spooky, that was all. However, there was no way she would be going down there again on her own.

10

The day's events weighed uneasily on Grace's mind as she sat in the living room, watching Millie's little hands slowly turning the pages of a picture book. Why hadn't Adam told her about the cellar? Did he have something to hide? Her father was convinced that if Adam had been about to vanish, there would have been warning signs, but Grace had always been adamant there weren't. Adam had been his usual self on that last morning, joking around, his face glowing with pride each time his glance fell on Millie. It was a new look in his eyes, one that Grace was still getting used to, but it was already among her favorites. He was minding Millie for the afternoon, while Grace did some shopping in town. It was the first time she had left Millie for so long, and she was both excited to be going and reluctant to leave.

By the time she got home, laden with bags, Adam had taken Millie out, leaving her that strange, serious note. And she had never seen him again. She had always imagined that something drastic and shocking had occurred that day; but what if her husband had been hiding the truth from her all along?

The boxes in the cellar were her first real indication that Adam had deliberately misled her. And if he had lied about them, what else might he have told her that wasn't true? Her memories were beginning to splinter. The Adam she had known and loved, the man who could read her moods and raise her spirits with a few perfectly chosen words, was becoming overlaid with another Adam whose sincerity was deeply questionable. Were his jokes designed to divert her attention? Were his reassurances a calculated method of keeping questions at bay? And were his oversights, his omissions of important information, a deliberate ploy to deceive her?

The more she thought this way, the angrier she became towards both of them—him for being so callous, herself for being a fool. But was it true? It was all too easy to think the worst of Adam when he wasn't here to defend himself or explain. If only . . .

She bit back the longing that made her lip tremble, before it turned into distress. She needed to shake off these cloying fears, go down to the cellar, and explore further, but as she thought of its dim, dusty corners, and recalled the sound of the door slowly closing, she knew she hadn't the nerve for it. She wished Annabel were here to lighten the atmosphere and talk her out of these ridiculous thoughts. Instead she listened as the rain turned to ice, the hailstorm hammering on the windowpanes in cracking staccato bursts. All around her the shadows of the room languidly stretched themselves out, resettling as the darkness grew. She jumped as the upstairs landing creaked, another of the cottage's strange nocturnal echoes, and turned on all the lamps so that cozy light filled the room.

She sought to tear her mind away from its never-ending loops of questions by taking Millie up for a bath, then getting her ready for bed. After Millie was settled, Grace headed downstairs and switched on the TV, wanting distraction. She avoided the inevitable horror stories on the night's news, grateful to come across an old film until she realized it was *Rear Window*. Even though she'd seen it before, tonight she needed something safe, so eventually she settled for a few old episodes of *Friends*. After they finished, she switched off the TV and was left looking at her reflection in the blank screen. She was slouched on the sofa, a blanket over her legs. She looked like an old lady, slumped there alone.

She made her way up to bed, got undressed, and settled down under the duvet. She flicked off the light, then waited for sleep to come and claim her. But, as she feared, nothing happened. So she switched the light back on and read some more of *Rebecca*, imagining the second Mrs. de Winter sitting under a chestnut tree, contemplating the fickleness of time. For a while, Grace was there, too, breathing in the scent of fresh-cut grass, hearing a bee buzzing close to her ear, the sea murmuring in the distance. She grew drowsy, so put the book to one side, switched off the lamp, and closed her eyes. Against her will, her ears attuned to the noises in the cottage. Every now and then an unexpected creak would startle her. She could also hear a faint scratching, and feared she really did have a mouse. She didn't know if she could bring herself to set traps, and decided to ignore it, concentrating instead on the ticking of the grandfather clock. Its steady rhythm slowly infiltrated her mind, lulling her into a slumber.

And then the clock stopped.

She opened her eyes to the darkness. Listened more intently. But all stayed silent.

It had just wound down, she told herself. But the hush had distorted the atmosphere. She closed her eyes again, but she couldn't relax. After a while, her ears began to ring from the effort of straining when there was nothing to hear.

My grandfather used to call it the heartbeat of the cottage.

She rolled over and snapped on the light. For a second her vision quavered, the walls shifting slightly before settling. Then the room was there before her, just as it always was. . . . Why had she expected it to be different somehow? She peered round from behind the covers, but nothing moved, yet the atmosphere felt full of energy, a living current swirling around her, willing her to get up and go downstairs.

She opened the door to the landing. She snapped the light on and edged along to the next bedroom, to see Millie soundly asleep, face to the wall.

She looked down the stairs, thinking fleetingly of the cellar two storys below. She decided she'd go and turn on the television again, find some company that way, and so she made her way down to the living room and switched on both the fire and the TV. Then she went and closed the curtains so that not a tiny crack of darkness could peek through. She needed to fortify her surroundings, to make believe that she was in a different room, somewhere else. London at night sprang into her mind. The brilliant neon glow of it, the electrifying bustle. People always passing by. Sometimes she felt that this place was the dream, and soon she would wake up and find herself in their old flat, listening to the distant thumps of music, the regular rumble of traffic, and she would only need to turn over to see Adam asleep beside her.

There it was—the familiar spasm of pain at the thought of him. She shook off the fantasy and flicked through the channels until she came across a late-night music program. She tried to concentrate on the soothing rhythm and blues, but found that she kept turning down the sound on the remote, checking to see if she could hear anything. Finally, she stomped back into the hallway in frustration, and stood before the grandfather clock, their faces level, its pendulum still. The air around her was so chilly she could see her breath. It hadn't been that cold before, surely?

She had imagined that it would be a blessing once the clock

stopped, but now she knew what Adam's grandfather had meant. Without the incessant ticking, the cottage was too quiet, too still. She sighed. And as though in reply, the pendulum suddenly moved and the clock gave a loud *tock*.

She jumped backwards in shock, disbelieving, holding her breath. But when the noise came a second time, she fled upstairs, crawling rapidly under the covers and clamping a pillow over her head.

11

The next morning, when Grace looked out the window she saw snatches of blue beyond the sheet of bright white cloud. Instead of frost, the hedgerow was covered with shimmering droplets of fresh dew. A robin perched on the garden gate. It bounced this way and that, flicking its tail, before it sensed her watching, was frozen for a moment and then took flight.

Despite the fact her sleep had come in stolen, shallow snatches, nothing looked terrifying today. Rather, the small garden, with its trellis arch and flagstones, sundial and pond, was a picture-postcard image of country life.

She heard Millie stirring and went to get her, walking past the grandfather clock, which was now keeping up a steady beat as though nothing had happened. When they'd had breakfast Grace decided that the washing up could wait: it would be good to get outdoors while they had the opportunity, to give Millie some fresh air without snow or rain to impede them. So she put Millie into her sturdy stroller and set off up the hill.

She found herself slowing as they approached the redbrick house where Ben lived. Grace studied it from the opposite side of the road as she drew closer, remembering what Meredith had said, and tried to imagine what Ben's wife would be like. She hurriedly put her head down as the front door opened, but she couldn't help a few sidelong glances in that direction. At the far end of the garden path, a woman with long red hair in a thick woolen coat had emerged through the front door. Ben was behind her, and she turned back to pull him into an embrace. As Grace looked on, Ben wrapped his arms around the woman for a brief moment, before she walked down the path with Bess trotting behind her.

Grace hurried away to avoid being spotted, and continued up the hill. A few moments later a large estate car roared past.

Grace continued following the road, enjoying the fresh air as it rushed into her lungs. As she walked, she found herself relishing the peace and quiet. There was little movement around her, just a few wet sheep huddled together next to a low stone wall. She leaned over the top of the stroller to see Millie sitting forward, surveying the surroundings. It was nice to be just the two of them, tackling the next phase of their life, striking out together. She couldn't wait until her daughter started to talk, but Millie only made strange sounds at present, and hadn't really begun to babble. Grace didn't know whether to be worried about this or not, since she had no benchmark by which to compare Millie's progress. As soon as they were settled, they could join a playgroup, so that Millie could meet children of a similar age and grow in confidence. Grace had heard her friends talk about playgroups, where people endlessly compared their children's developments. It sounded exhausting, and while Grace had been pregnant she had imagined all the playdates and coffee mornings she'd be going on with a mixture of enthusiasm and trepidation. However, it seemed all those emotions had been a waste of time, since in the end life hadn't worked out that way.

Grace kept up a steady pace as her thoughts flitted from one thing to another, and when she eventually refocused on her surroundings she found they were some distance from the cottage. The day was beginning to lose its color as the clouds swelled and darkened. "I guess we should go back," she said, leaning over the stroller again to find that Millie had fallen asleep. She smiled at the sight, and headed for home.

When the row of dwellings came into view, she saw that Ben was leaning over the open hood of the Land Rover. He glanced up at her approach, an oily rag in his hand, and then bent over the car again. For a moment Grace thought he was going to ignore her, but as she got closer he stood up, using another cloth to wipe his hands clean.

"Grace! I'm glad I've seen you." His voice was loud and deep against the silence of the morning. "I did some work on those plans last night. Come in for a moment and I'll show you how far I've gotten."

He held open the gate for her, and she wheeled the stroller down the path. "Do you want to leave her here?" he asked as they reached the porch. He began to open the front door, saying, "No, Bess," as a large black nose poked eagerly through the gap.

Grace looked behind them at the empty road and felt her nerves clench at the idea of Millie out here alone. "I'd rather she was inside," she said. "Can we lift the stroller in?"

Ben helped Grace carry Millie's stroller into the hallway. Grace checked her daughter was still asleep, then followed Ben, as he took hold of Bess's collar and led them both through to the kitchen. The countertops looked scrupulously clean—unlike the cottage right now, she thought, with its scattered crumbs and half-empty mugs. Bess settled herself on a large square pillow in one corner, while Ben went across to a drawer, pulled out some papers, and laid them on the bench in the center of the room.

"These are only rough ideas. I'll need to get measurements of everything, of course. Would you like a drink?"

"Just some water, please," Grace replied, as she began studying the papers. On some, he had done a few simple line sketches, but on others he had gone further, drawing the entire living room so she could clearly see how his suggestions would work. It was amazing, she thought, that he had remembered so much detail after one visit. The fireplace had become the central feature of the main sitting area, while the wall between the living room and kitchen was replaced with a benchtop that could also be used as a breakfast bar.

Ben brought over a glass of water and put it down in front of her, glancing at the papers. "This area is multifunctional," he said, tracing the detail in one of the drawings, "but it will make the space downstairs a lot bigger. You could leave the outer stone walls as a feature, rip out the carpet, and put in a really nice wooden floor with a big rug. I'd suggest wooden floorboards for the downstairs hallway, too—and then replace the carpet on the stairs with something a bit more luxurious. Rebuild the fireplace so that it's a real feature of the living area, and get a flat-screen TV so that it doesn't take up unnecessary room." He pointed to another corner of the living room. "That nook there, full of books—you could also make much more of that by putting in a few decent shelves with downlights, and adding some ornaments. Fit a seat into the bay window at the front with a few cushions, and the same upstairs. Repaint the hall banister—easy— and then tile the bathroom, too, if you can stretch your budget. The big thing upstairs is adjusting the bedrooms so that the master is at the back, with the better view, and has en suite access. Then it's just fixtures and fittings, and sorting out the furniture."

Grace was trying to keep up with him as he flicked through the various sketches. After he'd finished, he looked at her.

She shook her head. "I don't know what to say—this is . . . amazing. I can't believe you've gone to so much effort and got so far with it already. I'd barely got my head around knocking down the kitchen wall!" She beamed at him. "It's brilliant! I love it, I can picture it all so well—looking at how you've laid it out I couldn't fail to! I'm completely sold. When can you start? Oh god, please tell me you're not horribly expensive."

He laughed, a deep, rich sound Grace hadn't heard before. "Don't you want to check out some other options first?"

"Not anymore!" Grace smiled. "But I really have to pay you something for all this work, so include it in your price, will you?"

"No, I said I'd do it for free. As for the rest, I'll work out the estimated cost for materials. Then how about a hundred pounds a day for the labor? For a full working day, I mean," he added. "This will all take a good few weeks, so I'm happy to get started as soon as possible."

Grace was dumbfounded. She remembered the expressions of the old couple in the pub, and stalled for a moment, finding his gaze inscrutable as he waited for her response. Despite what she had witnessed, her instincts detected nothing overtly threatening about him. It was a generous offer; one she would be foolish to turn down.

"That sounds like an absolute bargain," she replied. "I think perhaps you should take a bit of time to think about it, work it out properly."

Ben's face became serious again. "I have," he said. "That's my price. I'm looking forward to doing it, so when do you want me to start?"

"Well, I guess as soon as possible after New Year's, if that's all right?" she ventured.

Ben seemed confused. "I thought you were keen to get on with it? It's only the middle of December."

Grace was taken aback. "Well . . . yes . . . but I assumed you and your wife would be busy over Christmas. New Year's will be fine. I've got lots of boxes to go through anyway—you saw the state of the cellar . . ."

Now he appeared astounded. "My *wife*?"

"Oh . . ." Grace floundered. "I . . . erm . . . Meredith told me that you and your wife lived here. And I thought I saw her this morning? The woman with the long red hair?"

His expression changed immediately to understanding. "No, that wasn't my wife you saw. I think Meredith must be confused. I'm house-sitting for the owners—they've gone overseas for a while and they wanted someone to look after the place, what with Bess and all . . ."

"Oh . . ." Grace said. "Oh . . ." *Say something else*, she cajoled herself. *So you don't look like an idiot.*

As she searched for the words, Ben began to gather together the papers. Grace went to move her glass of water out of the way, but fumbled and sent it flying towards the drawings. In a panic she reached out and managed to tip the glass away from them, only to knock it towards herself. The water splashed the front of her coat, while the glass shattered on the tiles.

"Oh no," she said, staring in dismay at the jagged slivers on the floor. In the hall, Millie began to cry. Grace looked at Ben, her cheeks blazing. "I'm so sorry, I'm such a klutz."

"Don't worry. I've got a dustpan and brush somewhere."

She hoped he would smile, but his face was solemn as he began searching in cupboards. Bess got to her feet, wagging her tail and looking curiously at the kitchen floor. "Stay, Bess," Ben told her sternly. Meanwhile, Millie wailed louder.

"Sounds like you need to go," Ben said, and he grasped Bess's collar and guided her out the back door. "I'll clear this up in a second, after I've helped you out with the stroller."

Grace hurried down the corridor to Millie, her face ablaze with embarrassment. Ben was right behind her. He opened the front door, and helped Grace carry the stroller down the step. When he'd finished he knelt down and smiled at Millie, stroking her cheek briefly with one hand. At his touch, Millie quieted, eventually giving him a shy smile in return. Grace watched them both in astonishment.

He straightened up as he said, "So, how soon do you want me to start? I could probably knock down the kitchen wall before Christmas, if you like?"

"Really?" To Grace, the task looked onerous, yet he talked about it as though it would be simple.

"Can I come round in the morning and take another look at it? Check it's not a bigger job than I think it is. But, yes, I reckon it's manageable, if you're prepared to live upstairs for a few days."

Grace thought about it for a moment. This was decision time. Her last chance to run away, before she made a proper start on things before she got other people involved, and would have to see it through. Then she felt the courage she had been cultivating for the last year rising firmly above her fear, and she smiled at Ben and said, both to him and to herself, "Right, then. Let's get on with it."

12

That night, after Millie was safely tucked up in bed, Grace was finally able to continue her search. Adam's omissions were piling up like stones in the stream of her convictions. He hadn't told her where he'd put the money, or where he'd been the day before he vanished, and now it transpired that he'd kept the cellar a secret, too. Was this all circumstantial, or an indication that she didn't know him as well as she thought? These worries were hard to bear, and the only way to combat them was action.

She wanted to return to the cellar, but she needed company before she dared to tackle it again. In the meantime, if she would be living upstairs for a few days then it would help to get through some of the boxes on the landing. She carried one of them down, set it in the middle of the living room, and kneeled on the floor in front of it. Opening the lid, she began plucking a few things from the top at random.

Out came clothes. Old-style blouses, a couple of dresses, a christening gown.

At first she handled things carefully, one at a time, but after a while she stood up, heaved the box onto its side, and spilled all the contents onto the floor. Then she picked through the mound in front of her, examining each item before putting everything except the christening gown back into the box they had come from. After she'd finished, she found a pen in her bag and wrote "Charity" on the lid.

One down—in half an hour. *Why have I avoided this for so long?* she asked herself, then went to get the next box.

This one contained books. She pulled out the top layer so she could turn over the box, then tipped it upside down, searching through, glancing at titles and authors. There weren't many names she recognized, and they all looked dated. Besides, she didn't need any extra reading when there was a bookshelf of classics upstairs. She put one or two aside, and began to pile the rest back into the box.

When she had finished, she moved to the little alcove set into the living room wall, where, in addition to a small glass duck and sprigs of dried heather, there was another row of books: crossword dictionaries, field guides for bird-watching, and a few gardening encyclopedias. They all went into the box with the others.

She paused as she came across a slim hardback covered by a dull grey dust jacket with raggedy edges, a black and white picture on the front of it. She read the title: *Ghosts of the Moors.* The photograph featured a tall stone cross in the foreground and a shadowy stone bridge visible in the distance, across a strip of moorland. The photo looked like it had been taken in twilight, so that the bridge was dimly lit, the low-lying hills behind it little more than shadows.

She opened the book and began to read the introduction:

The North Yorkshire moors. A place of many souls: those unborn, those departed, and the few who dwell in the scattered villages and wander the old monks' paths. People come and go, their lives ebbing and flowing like the river that cleaves its way through the valley. Yet, beneath their feet, the moors themselves are timeless—soaked in the love, grief, happiness, and despair that saturates the air and weeps down past the heather into the thickly layered earth. This place is one that ghosts wander to and through, since the untended, patient land embraces both the living and the dead, as the seasons spin perpetual circles within time's sticky web . . .

Grace shuddered, and turned the page, thumbing through the rest at random. The book was full of short chapters, with titles like "The Hob on the Hill," "The Witches' Knoll," and "The Knights of Freeborough." Towards the back, she came across "The Barghest." She read the first few sentences: *A fearsome hound with razor-sharp teeth and claws. Seen shortly before the death of a local.*

She remembered the dream she'd had on her first night back. She could vividly picture that contorted face, smell its hot, meaty, panting breath. *The death of a local.* Grace hastily closed the book and put it inside the charity box. She would be rid of that one as soon as possible.

"Just checking in," Annabel said brightly the next morning when Grace answered the phone. "What's new in no-man's-land then?"

Grace laughed despite herself. "You'll be pleased to hear I'm making some progress—and I'm getting the kitchen wall knocked down this week."

"So you're going ahead with renovating?"

"Yes—I'm not sure how much I'll do, but I'm really tempted to try and rent it as a holiday property, and it'll work much better with one big room downstairs."

"Sounds good," Annabel said, then her tone changed. "Hang on, are we going to be living in a dust box all Christmas?"

"Don't worry, Ben says he'll have it all sorted by then. It might not be too pretty, mind you."

"Ben said so, did he? And who, tell me, is Ben?"

"He lives up the road—I told you he was coming over on Sunday about the work. He's done a great job on the plans."

"Grace, please tell me you've checked out his credentials?"

Grace immediately felt defensive. "He showed me heaps of drawings. It's obvious he knows what he's talking about."

"GRACE!" Annabel shrieked through the phone. "For God's sake—he's about to knock down a wall in your home. Unless you want the whole ceiling to come crashing in, then I suggest you ask to see some references. Honestly, what are you thinking?"

Grace was relieved she hadn't told Annabel that it was Ben they'd seen in the pub last Saturday, being unceremoniously told to leave. However, she knew her sister had a point. She had agreed to let Ben do the job without being thorough. She'd been grateful to find someone so easily, someone who talked like they knew what they were doing, and who could be left to get on with it.

"Grace, are you listening to me?" Annabel was saying. "Before you let that man into your cottage with a large hammer, I want you to ask him for some background information. References, qualifications, experience—and I mean *relevant* experience. Promise me?"

Grace knew Annabel would never leave her alone until she'd agreed—or, worse still, would phone their parents. So there was little option but to say, "Fine, I promise."

Ben was at the door soon after breakfast. Grace waited as he wandered around downstairs making notes, then began to study the wall that divided the kitchen and living room. Millie sat on the floor, inspecting him closely.

"As I suspected, solid stone," he said. "I'll check upstairs, but I don't think it's load-bearing. I can always put a beam in for extra support if need be." He looked at the furniture. "Anywhere we can move this to?"

Grace thought for a moment. "I suppose we could stack it in the cellar."

"Well, you can leave that to me. If you clear those shelves in the corner and pack away everything in the kitchen, then I'll cover it all up and get cracking. I plan to have the wall down by Thursday, and spend Friday clearing up. It might not be pretty over Christmas but you'll have a lot bigger area, and you'll be able to think more about what you might do with it next. . . . Does that sound good to you?"

As he waited for her reply, Grace knew it was now or never. "Ben, I'm sorry, I know I should have asked you this earlier . . . Do you have any references or qualifications you can show me?"

He looked surprised rather than offended. "I'm really sorry, Grace, but I don't have anything with me. You know that I'm house-sitting, and I'm a long way from home right now. I can reassure you that I once worked as a laborer, even though it's been a while, and I'm a qualified architect. However, I can't actually prove anything without troubling people to go into my empty house and send me documents." He sighed. "I completely understand why you're asking, but it might take me a while to get these things to you . . . particularly with Christmas around the corner. Would you rather find somebody else? I understand if you want to—it might be better for your peace of mind?"

Grace's thoughts raced as he stood waiting for her answer. What should she do? The possibility of going back to square one appalled her, particularly when everything had fallen so easily into place. There weren't many alternatives around here, and she needed the help. Annabel was only worried because she didn't know Ben. He might be reticent, but he was kind to her and Millie, and so gentle with Bess.

"I'd still like you to do it," she said decisively.

"Okay then." Ben picked up his coat. "You're putting your faith in me, I appreciate that, but you've got nothing to worry about."

As he spoke, Millie pulled herself up against the sofa and tried to reach Ben's papers. "No Millie," Grace said, hurrying over. But Millie ignored her and snatched them, flinging them aside and watching as they floated to the ground.

Grace began picking them up, and Ben joined in. As they got to their feet, Grace handed over those she'd collected, and caught Ben's eye. They were standing far too close, and he was looking at her so directly that a shiver ran through her.

"Do you have any more questions before we get started?" His voice was a deep susurrant burr.

Grace stepped back. "No, I don't think so."

"Then I'll be over tomorrow." He moved past her, heading for the door.

Grace saw him out and went back to Millie. As they began to play together, numerous questions about Ben ran through her mind, but few had to do with the cottage.

13

By Wednesday evening the downstairs of Hawthorn Cottage was a shambles. Ben had saved Grace from any thoughts of returning to the cellar by moving a pile of furniture down there to clear his workspace. Meanwhile, the fall of night had brought with it a howling wind, so this time Grace decided to drive up to Meredith's. She was glad she'd accepted Meredith's offer of a meal now that her own kitchen was unusable.

Grace was standing on the schoolhouse driveway, unbuckling Millie from her seat, when the front door swung open. "Come in," Meredith said, ushering them both out of the cold. They could hear Pippa barking in another part of the interior.

She followed Meredith through to the dining room. The curtains to the picture window were open, but night had fallen and there was nothing to see beyond them this time, not even a light on the horizon or a star in the sky.

"Thank you so much for inviting us again." As Grace looked around, she noticed that the table was less extravagantly furnished this evening, with only two place settings. "Is Claire here?" she asked, her spirits waning at the thought of trying to make conversation with Meredith on her own.

"No, Claire's gone to collect Jenny and bring her home for Christmas," Meredith replied. "All my girls will be here this year— although Veronica, my eldest, is staying in Ockton. This place is big, but it's not large enough for her brood and everybody else as well." She indicated the sofas. "Please take a seat. I'll go and dish up."

Grace began to play with Millie, showing her the toys she'd brought, though it was obvious that Millie wanted to crawl away and begin investigating this interesting new space. Grace glanced around the softly lit room, with its thick chintz curtains and polished furniture. Everything looked precisely positioned, as though she had found herself on a stage set rather than in someone's home. She wondered if this room was singled out and kept pristine for entertaining, or whether the whole house was like this. Judging by how well Meredith had looked after Grace's cottage, it was probably the latter, she thought.

She heard footsteps getting louder, and then Meredith reentered the room, carrying two plates piled high with vegetables. "I've managed to borrow a high chair," she said as she set down the food, "so you can bring Millie over. Will she eat some roast chicken?"

"It might be messy," Grace warned, picking up Millie.

Meredith motioned to the polished wooden floor. "It's easy enough to wipe."

They took their places at the table, and Meredith chopped up a few pieces of chicken and some vegetables, then presented them to Millie on a child's plate with a plastic knife and fork. Millie ignored the cutlery, and picked up the meat with her fingers, looking thoughtful as she tested it with her teeth.

Meredith took a sip of water. "So, Grace," she said, "how are you getting on with the cottage? Found anything interesting?"

Grace speared a perfect golden roast potato with her fork. "I haven't gotten very far yet. It's been lots of books and clothes so far, but most of them mean little to me, I'm afraid. It's very odd sorting through people's belongings and making decisions when you didn't know them very well. Since I'm unaware of the history behind anything I'm looking at, I always have this feeling I might be missing something important."

"There's not really much we own that is all that important, though, is there?" Meredith looked around the room, her eye falling on the mantelpiece of photographs. "I would be a lot less cluttered if it weren't for my girls—they practically handcuff me every time I suggest having a clear-out. They don't want to live here anymore, but I think it gives them a sense of security to know that their childhood home is still here, the same as it always was. They come here to feel safe."

Grace put down her cutlery for a moment to encourage Millie to try her vegetables. She recalled the contents of the boxes that she'd sorted through so far, debating what Meredith might find interesting. "You know, I did find a book about local ghost stories."

"Let me guess—*Ghosts of the Moors*."

"Yes," Grace said, surprised, "I'm sure that was the title."

"And did you notice the author?"

When Grace shook her head, Meredith got up, went across to a bookcase, pulled a slim volume from the shelf, and handed it over.

Grace recognized the cover, and now she looked at the author's name: "C. Romano?" She regarded Meredith blankly. "Should I know who that is?"

Meredith nodded and waited, but on seeing Grace's confusion, she said, "That's Connie Lockwood, maiden name Romano. Adam's grandmother."

"Oh." Grace looked down again at the slim volume in her hands. Millie's great-grandmother had written this. She supposed she had better take it out of the charity box.

Meredith took the book and returned it to the shelf. "She presented all the villagers with one, when it was first published, back in the eighties."

"Why did she use her maiden name?"

"I'm not sure, but Connie was fascinated by the legends around the place. She grew up in a village nearby, but moved here with Bill in the early 1950s, once they were married. It took them a long time to have children—Rachel came late in life for them, and was unexpected, I think, but they doted on her. Didn't Adam tell you any of this?"

As Grace shook her head, Meredith echoed the gesture sadly. "You know, it's such a shame these stories get lost. Why are we so careless that we let our own histories die without even noticing?"

Grace thought of the little she knew about Connie and Bill. After hearing this small snippet of their lives, she couldn't help but picture them differently—as a young couple struggling to build a life together after the war. Her sense of responsibility towards them grew stronger—and she wasn't sure she welcomed the feeling. Thank goodness she hadn't thrown away the book.

Meredith was studying her closely. "Do you like it here, Grace?"

The question was asked offhand, but Grace felt the air around them thicken with the anticipation of her reply. Not wanting to offend, or lie, she hesitated before saying, "I can't tell yet, to be honest. I'm sure I would like it a lot more if the circumstances were different."

Meredith nodded as she thought. "You know, I often wonder whether this place—the villages, the moors—has a certain mystical quality that draws people back—or one which won't let them go. Perhaps I feel like that because it's where my family are from, where we belong. But people often return here. And I don't know why—since we're obviously well away from most of civilization. You and Adam, for instance . . ." She looked at Grace carefully. "Why did you decide to come here?"

Grace began to cut up more of her dinner to give to Millie, who had wolfed down her first portion and was banging her plate on the table. "Adam thought it would be good for us to get out of the rat race for a while—try something different. We *both* thought so," she amended.

"Well, it's certainly different to London," Meredith said. "I often think about what will happen to the village when my generation dies out. Will people stick it out here, ignoring the lure of the big cities, or will it be abandoned? I have a feeling it'll become an out-of-the-way holiday destination, and these old houses steeped in history will be nothing more than the temporary homes of travellers."

Grace bit her lip. It was probably best not to mention that she was considering renting out Hawthorn Cottage as a holiday home.

"How long was the school open here?" she asked, hoping to move to a more comfortable topic.

"It closed down in the late sixties when there were no longer enough children to sustain it. My brood had to get a bus over the hill to Ockton. Did Adam not tell you anything of the history of the village?"

Grace shook her head. *I imagined he'd have plenty of time to show me around*, she added to herself. "I'm not sure how much he knew," she said. "I don't think he ever came here until after his mother had died."

Meredith seemed somber. "Rachel was only eighteen when she

left—there were five years between us, but we were good friends," she said. "Since we were the only young girls in the village, we leaned on each other. I was shocked when she vanished without warning—although we hadn't seen as much of each other since I'd gotten married and had Veronica. Then, all those years later, Adam was back here with his grandparents. I hadn't even known that Rachel had a child. But, as I said, if you've a connection to this place it draws you back in, one way or another. Of course, Adam wouldn't have lived here that summer if Rachel hadn't died." She paused, then shook her head as though clearing unpleasant memories. "Adam was a rather intense young man, I remember that . . . but I put it down to grieving rather than character. He was terribly young to be without his mother." Meredith looked intently towards the picture window as she spoke, as though something was visible to her in the darkness.

Grace felt her curiosity growing. "Did you know Adam's father?" Adam hadn't talked about him much—the topic was obviously painful so she had never pressed it.

"Yes, I knew him." Meredith's mouth tightened into a grim line "Jonathan Templeton—he lived on a farm not far away. Everyone around here knew him—he was quite the catch. Rachel was madly in love with him. From what I've learned since, I gather he got her pregnant just before his family emigrated to Australia on one of those ten-pound tickets. So he fled from the responsibility. And afterwards she ran away . . ."

"Adam didn't know much about him," Grace confided. "He knew his name, and that Rachel ran off to stay with some friends in York when she was pregnant; gave birth to Adam there. When Adam was two she began a love affair that lasted the rest of her life—although she never married the man; they never even lived together. He was well off, apparently, and took care of Rachel and Adam financially. It was only after Rachel died that Adam found out the man already had a wife and two children. Adam never spoke to him again after that."

Meredith had stopped eating to listen, as Grace trailed off. Had a new baby and their return to the cottage triggered unpleasant memories for Adam? He had been so in love with Millie from the first moment he held her. But he must have wished that his mother could have seen her grandchild. And he surely would have dwelled on what it meant to him to be a dad, having never known his real father, and feeling ultimately betrayed by the man who had taken on the role instead. What were his deepest feelings about fatherhood? Where might they have driven him to?

Grace put down her knife and fork, her pulse beginning to race. She picked up a napkin to wipe Millie's hands, trying to hide her distress, when Meredith set her cutlery down on her empty plate, placed her arms on the table, leaned forward and said, "Actually, Grace, there's something I want to talk to you about."

Grace stopped what she was doing, wary of Meredith's purposeful tone.

"I'd like to buy Hawthorn Cottage."

"Oh," Grace answered, astonished. She let go of Millie's hands and sat back. "The thing is, I can't sell it right now, even if I wanted to. Adam put it in joint names, so there are legal issues while he is missing . . ."

"I suspected that might be the case," Meredith said, without missing a beat. "But if you're interested in my proposition, my son-in-law Stephen is a lawyer—I can ask him to look into it further, see if there's anything you can do. I'd be happy to make some sort of arrangement. Perhaps rent it now, in hopes of buying it in future."

Grace had been caught completely off guard. As Meredith held her gaze, she wondered if these meals had been ploys to butter her up. She'd thought that Meredith was being friendly, but perhaps there had always been more to it.

"Why would you want to do that?" she asked.

"Well, I'd like to sell this place eventually. None of my girls want to live here, and it'll be too big for me to manage on my own as I get older. I'd enjoy a bit of travelling with the extra money, but I've lived in this village all my life—I want to stay put. Hawthorn Cottage would be just right for me. I could sublet it until I'm ready to move in myself."

This seemed an entirely reasonable explanation, but Grace still didn't want to be rushed into any promises she might regret. "I appreciate the offer, but I'm not sure what I want to do yet . . ." she said. "Let me think about it."

There was an awkward lull in conversation, as Meredith got up without a word and began collecting their plates. She disappeared through to the kitchen, and Grace waited uneasily for her to come back. A moment later, Meredith returned with a large bowl of trifle. She sat down and began to ladle a portion into a bowl, her spoon repeatedly striking the china with a harsh clang. "I'm sorry, Grace, I didn't mean to put you in a difficult position. Perhaps I shouldn't have brought it up. I had imagined you wouldn't want to stay around—I thought I might be doing you a favor . . . maybe I presumed a bit too much. But think about what I've said, won't you, and let me know if you'd like to discuss it further."

"Thank you," Grace replied, accepting the bowl of dessert that Meredith held out to her. "You took me by surprise, but I'll certainly consider it."

"Right, then." Meredith was all brisk and businesslike now. "Would you like a cup of tea?"

As they finished their meal, Meredith's interest in Hawthorn

Cottage hung in the air between them. Grace felt wrong-footed, all too aware that she was alone in this big old house with only this austere woman and a resident ghost for company. Meanwhile, Meredith kept up a steady stream of conversation about local concerns: the extension of the railway line, the ridiculous price of oil heating, her fight with the council to get the one streetlight in the village working again. Grace half-listened as she turned Meredith's words over in her mind.

Millie had been taken out of her high chair, and for a time she sat on the floor playing with her toys contentedly, but as the evening progressed she began to cling to her mother's legs more and more, yawning and whining.

"I think I should get her to bed soon." Grace set down her empty cup. "Can I help you clear up?"

"No need," Meredith said. "It was nice to have the company."

Grace collected the toys and lifted Millie onto her hip. She felt she should reciprocate Meredith's generosity with a meal invitation, but her culinary skills were nowhere near as good, and anyway the kitchen was out of action at the moment.

Meredith showed them to the door and held out a hand. "Thank you for coming, Grace. And remember to consider my offer, won't you?"

"I will," Grace assured her. She walked to the car, put Millie in her seat and clicked the buckles together, then had to spray the windshield with deicer before she could start the engine. While she did all this, Meredith stood motionless in the doorway, her body backlit by the lights behind her so that all Grace could see was her silhouette. As Grace began to back out she waved, but Meredith didn't move as they drove out of sight.

14

On Saturday morning, Ben arrived at the front door, toolbox in hand, to clear up the final debris from knocking down the wall. The last couple of days had been difficult for Grace—Millie hadn't been napping well, which made it hard for Grace to get things done. And she missed the kitchen. She'd eaten instant noodles for two nights in a row, and was desperate to cook herself a meal. She was glad the work was started, but was already looking forward to the break for Christmas.

Meredith's offer kept running through her mind, although she had made it without knowing of the renovations underway. Perhaps it wouldn't stand now anyway. But what if it did? In that case, did Grace really need to be here, resurrecting the past?

She had had a restless night last night. No demonic dogs had appeared to her, but instead, she had dreamed of Adam. He was trying to tell her something, his face frantic, sometimes with worry, sometimes with fear. He looked to be shouting the words, but there was only silence. At one stage he had raised his arms and Grace had seen that he was behind thick glass as he banged his hands on it, over and over.

She had woken numb with cold, to a darkness so absolute that she couldn't see her fingers held an inch from her face. For a moment it felt as though she no longer existed at all. Shaking, she fumbled frantically for the bedside light switch. The room lit up. Everything in place, at rest.

She had taken long, deep breaths, and when she felt calmer had picked up *Rebecca*. Soon she was engrossed, getting through almost a hundred pages before she fell asleep again. In her dreams, for a while she lay among bluebells, with a cocker spaniel running through the meadow. But then she was no longer amid flowers but on bare brown earth, and she had scrambled up to see Meredith's schoolhouse towering above her, windows blazing with light. Shivering uncontrollably from the freezing night air, she rushed towards the brightness and warmth, peeping through a large window to find a dance taking place—couples whirling, a blur of color—and while she stood there, a woman to one side in a white dress, hat in hand, turned slowly towards the window, caught Grace's eye, and her mouth opened in the stretched O of a scream.

Grace had woken up sweating this time. The scream lingered beyond her dreams for a moment, frightening her further before it died away. She found she was still clasping the book, and threw it onto the floor before scrambling out of bed, flicking light switches and going to splash water on her face. She had registered herself in the mirror, but looked away before she could catch her own reflected eye. When Ben arrived, he began to fill her in on his progress, but she barely listened, still caught in her reverie until he put down his toolbox and reached out, gently touching her arm. "Grace? *Grace?* Are you all right?"

Grace focused on him, and they were still for a second, their eyes locked, before Ben dropped his hand.

It took Grace a moment longer to recover. She took a breath. "Yes, of course," she said, bending down to rescue Millie, who had crawled over to Ben's toolbox and was trying to pick up a hammer.

Half an hour later while Millie was napping, Grace heard the crunch of gravel as she was tidying upstairs. She peered out the window and saw Annabel climbing from her car—an obvious city girl in her sparkling knit top and jeans teamed with knee-high boots. Ben was downstairs, somewhere, clearing up and doing some preliminary work on the fireplace. She ran down to the front door to make introductions, and got there in time to see Annabel stop halfway along the path, dragging an enormous suitcase, her mouth dropping as Ben opened the door ahead of Grace, carrying a bag of rubbish.

"Annabel, this is Ben . . ." Grace said behind him.

Annabel glanced towards her sister, her face full of wry amusement.

"He's helping with the renovations, remember?"

"Ah." Annabel grinned. "I do remember, Grace," she said, looking at Ben and offering him her hand. "It's very nice to meet you."

Annabel's flirtations were never subtle, and Grace watched on with resignation as Ben took hold of her slender fingers. "Same here." He smiled civilly. "Would you like me to take that for you?" He motioned towards her case.

"Yes please!" Annabel looked delighted.

As soon as he'd gone, Annabel came close to Grace and said in an undertone, "You didn't tell me he was so good-looking. Finally, this place has something to offer. I might have to buy myself some shiny new wellies and come and visit more often."

Grace rolled her eyes as she followed her sister inside. Annabel claimed she didn't have time for romance because of her career, but apparently she had no qualms where flirting was concerned. Grace's friend James regularly joked that it was Annabel's favorite sport. At the thought of James, Grace felt guilty. She hadn't even let him know that she was back in Yorkshire. She knew she was putting it off, in case he questioned what she was doing here. The problem was, despite their recent differences, he still knew her too well.

While in the hallway, she heard Millie beginning to stir. She went to collect her daughter, finding her yawning and needing her nappy changed. By the time they got back downstairs, Annabel was curled up on the sheet-covered sofa, steaming mug cradled in her hands, observing Ben as he worked by the fireplace.

"I was just asking Ben about his Christmas plans," Annabel said as she spied Grace. "And he hasn't got any, as it turns out. So I've invited him to join us—the more the merrier, right?"

As Ben faced them, Grace saw that his cheeks were slightly flushed. "Look," he began, "I hadn't actually—"

"Ben, it's fine," Annabel chided, "it's the least Grace can do when you've spent all week working on the cottage. Come on, I promise us Taylor girls know how to have a good time—don't we, Grace?"

"Of course," Grace agreed. "Annabel's right, you're very welcome to join us."

"In fact we'll be completely offended if you don't," Annabel added cheerfully.

Ben looked unsure, but said, "In that case, thanks," and moved back to the fireplace, continuing to take measurements. Millie struggled out of Grace's arms and crawled over to Ben, putting her hands on his knee and pulling herself up to inspect what he was doing. Ben turned to her and smiled, and she gave a shy smile back.

Grace watched them, wondering what it was about Ben that Millie found so intriguing.

"I thought that thing was supposed to have wound down by

now?" Annabel was looking beyond the living-room doorway towards the grandfather clock.

Grace immediately tuned into the steady ticking and shuddered. "Actually, you're right, it should have. I thought it had stopped last weekend, but it started again . . ." She remembered the fright it had given her, then frowned, "I think it's been going ever since."

That doesn't make sense, she thought, beginning to feel hot with panic.

"Did you want to let it wind down?" Ben sounded apologetic. "I'm sorry, I didn't realize. It stopped on Wednesday while I was here, so I wound it up again for you."

Grace let out a sigh of relief. "It doesn't matter," she said, relieved that there was a rational, ordinary explanation. *What has gotten in to you?* she scolded herself. *You didn't believe in ghosts before, there's no reason to start now.*

Then her focus shifted to her sister, as Annabel cried, "Guess what, Grace, I've got some great news." She nearly spilled her tea as she bounced up and down on the sofa. "I pitched a piece about living with ghosts to my editor, and she loved it! So I'll be able to do some research while I'm here for Christmas!"

"Oh, right." Grace was unable to match her sister's vivacity. "When did you decide to do that?"

"On the drive back from here. I couldn't stop thinking about what Meredith and Claire said. I can't believe they're so glib about living with a ghost. . . . If there really is a ghost in the house, of course. Perhaps they're fibbing and that's why they don't care. But, whatever, readers will lap it up, it'll make a great story. I'm going to try to persuade them to talk to me, and see what else I can uncover of the local spirit population. I can see the piece now, all moody black-and-white photographs. I haven't quite got the angle yet, but it'll come."

Grace had kept her eye on Ben and Millie as Annabel talked. He was holding a tape measure along one side of the mantelpiece, but he wasn't moving, and she was sure he was listening to them.

Annabel hadn't noticed. "I'm actually quite excited about it. Who would have believed that a bit of frosty old countryside would fire up my imagination!"

"Yes, it's great," Grace agreed, trying to be supportive. Then a thought came to her. She went across to the boxes, rummaged around, and returned with a book.

"Adam's grandmother wrote this." She passed it over. "I've been meaning to rescue it from my charity pile—it should help you with the piece."

"Wow, *Ghosts of the Moors*. This is perfect," Annabel said as she began flicking through it.

Grace knelt down on the floor beside Millie. She spent a few moments showing her daughter how to stack her blocks to make different shapes. In the silence, Ben kept his back to them, ostensibly making notes, but Grace wasn't convinced.

Annabel continued leafing through the book with interest. "Looks like most of my research has been done for me. God bless you, Granny Lockwood," she cried, waving the book in the air as though Connie were floating above them in the room.

"Are you related to Adam Lockwood, by any chance?"

Both Grace and Annabel looked at Ben in astonishment. He had gotten to his feet. His brow was furrowed, his eyes full of interest.

"Yes," Grace replied. She took a breath, summoning up the courage it took to explain. "Adam was—is—my husband. He went missing this time last year, just after we'd moved in here. I've come back to sort through his grandparents' belongings, decide what to do next with the cottage . . ."

Ben's eyes were wide as he listened, his mouth agape. He seemed lost for words. Grace felt herself flushing under his stare.

"Did you know Adam?" Annabel asked.

The question drew him out of his stupor. He blinked rapidly and shook his head as he answered, "No, not really, but I know the name."

"It made the news last year," Annabel said. "When he disappeared."

"I didn't see that. I've lived in Australia for a long time. But I grew up not far away."

"Australia—fantastic!" Annabel exclaimed. "So what the hell are you doing here?"

Ben didn't reply. He and Grace were staring at one another. Grace was full of questions; while it appeared as though Ben were seeing her in a completely new light—and she wasn't sure whether she liked it. He broke away first, picking up his notepad and tape. "I've got what I need. I'll leave you both to it."

As he headed for the door, Annabel followed him. "Hang on a moment, Ben. If you know the area, can you take me out one day on a ghost hunt?"

Grace expected him to decline, but he answered, "If you like."

"Great! I'll pop by later and we can plan a trip." Annabel looked at her sister and winked. "You don't mind, do you, Grace? I won't distract him for long."

Ben was already in the hallway, and Grace was glad that he couldn't see her face as she replied, "Of course not."

15

"So," Annabel said a few hours later, looking around the living room, "shall we loll here getting drunk, or shall we dive into a few of these boxes?"

"How about both?" Grace suggested, surprised and grateful for the offer, as she went over to the kitchen area, returning quickly with a bottle of red wine.

"Great idea!" Annabel grabbed a glass and held it out. Once it had been filled, she knelt by the boxes. "So, how do you want to go about it?"

"Well, I've been tipping them out one at a time and sorting everything into three piles: keep, throw away, and give to charity."

"Right-o," Annabel said, grabbing the box closest to her and dumping its contents onto the carpet before Grace could object. "Lots of clothes here."

"Thanks, Annabel," Grace said dryly. "I've actually been through that one already."

"Oh my god, what is this?" Annabel cried, ignoring her and holding up a long dress printed with large purple, green, and orange daisies. "Flower power or what! Hang on, I have to try this on!" She wriggled out of her blouse and jeans and pulled the dress over her head.

"How do I look?" she asked, and at Grace's giggles she rushed out of the room and up the stairs, undoubtedly heading for the bedroom, where there was a full-length mirror. Grace heard the excited exclamations from where she sat, and winced, half-expecting Millie to wake up and counter them with a shriller reply of her own. Annabel's footsteps came rushing down the stairs again, but there was no other sound to be heard, and Grace silently offered a prayer of thanks.

"Hilarious!" Annabel pronounced. "Right, you have to put something on from this lot—let's see, what about this—" She pulled out a cream blouse with outlandish ruffles, and then delved back into the box until she produced a pair of bright purple corduroy flares. "Come on, get them on!"

They weren't going to get much done, but Annabel's enthusiasm was infectious. Grace sprang up and put down her wine. Soon she was wearing her own ensemble, and Annabel had found the closest thing to seventies music she could in Grace's collection—the *Moulin Rouge!* version of "Lady Marmalade." They began trying to remember as many of John Travolta's *Saturday Night Fever* moves as they possibly could, and Grace was doubled over laughing, when they were interrupted by a sharp knock on the door.

"I'll get it," Annabel sang, and boogied her way out of the room. "Meredith! Claire!" Grace heard her cry, and she felt her lightheartedness vanish.

"You two look like you're having fun," Meredith said, coming into the living room. Annabel was behind her, swinging her hips and clicking her fingers, flicking an amused glance towards Grace. Claire followed at the back of the group, smiling, yet from Meredith's expression, Grace felt like a child caught doing something she shouldn't. She went over and switched off the music. "It's lovely to see you both. Would you like a drink?"

"No thanks," Meredith replied. "We won't stop if you're busy."

"We came to let you both know about the ball at Freeborough Hall on Christmas Eve," Claire explained. "It's a bit of a local event and we thought you might enjoy it."

"Sounds great," Annabel replied, going across to the counter-top to replenish her wineglass, and returning with the bottle in her other hand. She poured more into Grace's glass as she added, "We'd love to."

"I don't think we can actually," Grace demurred. "Because of Millie . . ."

"Didn't Emma volunteer to babysit for you?" Annabel interjected.

"Yes, but . . ."

"But nothing, Grace. You need a break now and again. Let's ask her, and if she's free then we'd love to come."

"Okay, then." Meredith took hold of Claire's arm and turned to leave. "We won't keep you. Just let us know if you want tickets—I'm on the committee so it won't be a problem." She stopped in the doorway. "You know, they look like Rachel's clothes," she said, staring hard at Grace before she left the room. Claire raised her hand affably, then followed her mother.

Annabel saw them to the door, then returned and looked perplexedly at Grace. "Well," she said, "there's a woman who knows how to kill a mood. And who the hell is Rachel?"

"Adam's mum." Grace threw herself into one of the armchairs. Now she felt awful about prancing around in a dead woman's clothes, as though she were dancing on her grave. Maybe she did need Meredith to help her sort through these things.

"Oh, I see." Annabel went across to the sofa and sat down. "Well, don't feel bad. I'm sure Rachel would rather we were dancing in her clothes than we left them festering and moth-bitten in a dusty old attic."

Grace smiled at her sister and tried to rouse her spirits. She went to put on her pajamas, and when she returned, Annabel had changed the music and was back in her own clothes. Together they emptied another box onto the floor.

"So tell me about Ben," Annabel said a little while later, as she sorted through a pile of linen.

Grace kept her eyes down as she replied. "I'm not sure I can. I don't know much about him other than the fact he knows how to knock down a wall. You got more out of him today than I've managed to in a week."

"He lives alone in the house at the top of the hill?"

"Yes, I think so." However, as she spoke, Grace remembered the woman she'd seen leaving early one morning. She opened her mouth to tell Annabel about the redhead, then closed it again, deciding not to. "He's house-sitting, and he said he's an architect, but other than that he keeps himself to himself." In fact, she thought, he was particularly good at answering her questions without actually telling her anything.

"Don't worry, I'll find out all about him when he takes me out," Annabel said confidently.

"Well, good luck. He's painfully difficult to talk to."

Annabel laughed. "God, I'm used to that in my line of work." She put the last of the linen into another charity box. "Can we call it a night now?"

"Let's just do this one," Grace suggested, and moved to a small box in the corner, pulling out what looked like a photo album. She opened it, and her breath caught painfully in her throat.

It was Grace and Adam's wedding day. She had looked at their official photos many times, but she'd never seen these before. They were simple snapshots. Adam waiting outside the church. Adam with his arms around his grandparents. Then Adam and Grace at the church after they'd been married. She turned the pages—to see Adam and Grace with his grandparents; Adam and Grace with her parents; with Annabel; with her extended family; with their friends. *Adam and Grace* . . .

She had to summon all her willpower to swallow the emotion that began to rise in her throat. She searched their faces for some clue that their love story was destined to end abruptly, that they weren't as happy as she had imagined—but all she could see were joyful smiles and laughter. That night, as they had gone to sleep in a four-poster bed, Adam had whispered his love in her ear, telling her he'd had the greatest day of his life. And when he'd first held Millie in his arms he'd promised he would do everything possible to protect his family. He'd said it with such gravitas . . . Too much gravitas? How would she ever know? Could she really live the rest of her life with all this doubt? But what choice had he left her?

She'd forgotten about Annabel until she moved closer. Grace leaned her head on her sister's shoulder and Annabel wrapped an arm around her. "I don't get it . . . ?" Grace's voice began to break. "Why would he just go . . . ? He couldn't. It isn't right, Bel . . . But I don't know . . . What if he—"

"Enough," Annabel insisted, taking the album from her, putting it back in the box, and then closing the lid. "You're drunk and emotional, Grace. Here . . ." She took Grace's glass and poured them both another wine.

"Remind me, how will this help?" Grace asked, before she put the full glass to her lips.

"Medicinal purposes," Annabel replied assuredly, and took a great gulp of her own drink.

By the time they went to bed they had both drunk far too much. For Grace this normally meant that she would sleep solidly until morning, but tonight her rest was fitful, with blurry visions running into one another: strange shadows on hilltops; indistinct figures walking towards and then away from her; Adam's face close to her own; an empty bed; a stone bridge; a stream; then finding herself standing alone in a glade of trees, a voice calling her name. Chasing it, only to hear it echoing behind her. Twisting and turning, trying to find its source, but never catching up. She woke with a start numerous times, settling down when she heard Annabel's soothing snores beside her, but each time she fell asleep again her dreams only tormented her more. In the morning Grace woke up groggy and dazed, and when she moved to the window, she saw that overnight the landscape had been transformed by a pure white covering of snow.

16

"I've got a surprise for you!" Annabel said. She had disappeared briefly midmorning, but Grace had been too busy with Millie to notice where she'd gone.

"And what would that be?" Grace asked, helping Millie with her drink.

"I've just seen Emma next door, and she says she'll be happy to babysit on Christmas Eve—so we can go to the ball Meredith was talking about!"

Grace swung to face Annabel, hand on hip. "I can't believe you did that without asking me first."

Annabel glared at her. "Oh lighten up, Grace. They live *next door*! Emma's the most convenient babysitter you'll ever find. She's even coming round here so you can put Millie down in her own bed. The most she might do is use a tea bag or eat a packet of crisps. Could you please live with that, and stop being such a wuss?"

But Grace wasn't going to be talked down. "No, Annabel, that's not the point. Where Millie's concerned, I make the decisions. I'm going round to apologize, right now."

She picked up Millie and went outside, stomping down the garden path before heading next door. She rapped hard on the door and waited.

Moments later, a teenage boy answered. His face was so white that if Grace hadn't heard Emma and Carl mention a son, she would have suspected that this was the resident ghost of next-door's cottage. His blue eyes and ruby mouth looked strangely artificial against the rest of his flesh, like they had been colored in—and she was sure his eyes were rimmed with black eyeliner.

"Is your mum in?" she asked politely.

He left the door open and skulked off, his shoulders hunched.

Emma came to the door a moment later, tea towel in hand. "Grace! Come in!" she said cheerily. "Don't worry about Jake—he's going through his Goth phase! And hello little lass." She reached out and took Millie from Grace. "Now, you," she said to Millie, "are just in time to sample some of Auntie Emma's cupcakes—they're still warm!" And she carried Millie down the hallway.

Grace followed her through to the kitchen and launched straight into her apology. "I gather Annabel asked you about babysitting Millie—I'm sorry, she got a bit ahead of herself, and I hope it didn't look rude. She spoke to you before consulting me. You'll surely have other plans on Christmas Eve."

"Oh, don't be daft," Emma said. "I'm happy to, I told you at the pub. We're staying home this year so I'll get everything sorted in the afternoon. Then Carl can stay in with our bairn and I'll come round a little early so you can tell me where everything is. I'll be glad to leave this place for a while; truth be told, it's all moody silences from the lad and bursts of irritation from Carl at the moment. If it's just me and the baby it's like a little holiday, so I won't know what to do with a few hours to myself! I'm quite excited about it!" She stroked Millie's hair, and as Millie put her fingers towards Emma's mouth, she pretended to bite them. Millie let out a joyous squeal, making both women laugh.

Emma went across to a tray of cakes, then looked back at Grace. "Is she allowed?"

"Yes, that's fine."

Millie took one eagerly, then Emma turned on the kettle and came and sat down with the little girl on her lap. Millie looked at her treat happily, before biting into it with satisfaction.

"So, what time do you want me then?" Emma asked.

Grace recalled Annabel's excitement, and considered how contented Millie appeared to be with Emma. She reminded herself how long it had been since she'd had a night out, and made her decision. "About seven, if you're sure."

"Grace—relax, it's absolutely fine," Emma insisted. "Now, you must stay for a cup of tea and tell me what you've been up to since I last saw you. I gather you've been busy, what with all the banging this week?"

"Oh no, I hope the noise hasn't been bothering you . . ." Grace said contritely. "I've had the wall knocked down between the kitchen and the lounge—I'm trying to make it a bit less poky downstairs."

"Don't worry about the noise, it hasn't been bad," Emma reassured her. "I'm looking forward to seeing what you've done. I'm sorry I haven't invited you round sooner—I've been so busy with the kids and getting ready for Christmas. I hope you haven't been lonely?"

Grace shook her head. "I'm fine. Annabel's staying till after Christmas now, and I've had a couple of meals at Meredith's."

"Really?" Emma looked intrigued as she handed Millie back to Grace and went to pour the tea. "How did that come about?"

"She invited me."

"Well, I'm amazed. We've lived here for five years and we've never been invited over once, let alone twice. What did you do to deserve Meredith Blakeney's hospitality?"

"I think it might have been because she's interested in renting the cottage," Grace admitted.

"Is that right?" Emma put two mugs on the table, along with a carton of milk and a pot of sugar. "What would Meredith want with your little cottage when she fancies herself the lady of the manor in that big old house up there?"

Grace didn't know how to reply, since she was asking herself the same question.

Emma mulled it over, then sat back. "Don't be bullied by that family, Grace."

"Why do you say that?" Grace asked uneasily as she poured milk into her tea.

"Oh, I've heard a few rumors . . . they sound like a mixed-up lot."

"Really? What have you heard?"

Emma shook her head. "Perhaps that's a bit unfair of me. They've been through a hard time lately, what with Ted passing away like he did . . ."

But Grace was too curious to let it go. "Still, is there anything I should be aware of?"

Emma took a sip of her tea. "Oh, I don't have that much to tell. I only know Meredith in passing, but I've caught a bit of gossip about her—usually people saying that she interferes with her daughters' lives too much. She's caused some mighty spats between her children, so I'm told, and one of her son-in-laws, Dan, seems to dislike her intensely—often bad-mouths her if you come across him in any of the local pubs. Mind you, he's not exactly a saint—he used to be a policeman but there was a big scandal last year, something to do with him turning a blind eye to a mate dealing drugs. He got kicked out of the force, and apparently it was Meredith who found him another job in Leeds, something to do with security. Just as well since his wife's expecting a little one shortly. From what I gather, if Meredith's daughters have a problem they run straight to their mother and she sorts it out for them. You know that one of them is staying there right now . . ."

"Yes," Grace said. "I've met her. Claire—she seems really nice. Says it's just a stopgap."

Emma looked surprised, then chuckled. "Grace, you probably know more about them than I do. Now, tell me what you've got planned for the rest of your cottage . . ."

Grace began to fill Emma in on the renovations. After a while, Emma noticed that Grace's mug was empty. "Another cuppa?"

Grace checked her watch. "I'd better not. I should be getting back. Annabel will be waiting for us."

Grace began to get up, and Emma went across to the countertop, returning with a Tupperware container full of cupcakes. "Here, take these. I always make far too many."

Millie snatched the box gleefully before Grace could say anything, and they laughed.

"Thank you," Grace said, following Emma along the hallway. "Now . . . are you sure . . ."

"Grace! Go and have some fun. Millie will be fine with me."

"Well, I owe you one." As Grace started down the path, she glanced to her right, to see next door's chimney puffing away. Emma stood on the step behind her and followed her gaze.

"Have you met Jack yet?"

Grace shook her head.

"You'll be lucky if you do. We hardly ever see him. His chimney goes almost twenty-four hours but he never switches on his lights. You only come across him when he's feeding his birds."

Something clicked in Grace's mind. "Oh—is that where the noise is coming from? I've heard a few screeches, it's pretty unnerving at night."

"Thought the spirits were out, did you? No, it's just the owls next door. Jack's obsessed with them—people round here call him Feathery Jack. I think he's got two at the moment, though he's had up to half a dozen. And not just owls, either, he takes everything from kestrels to crows. We only know this because sometimes the birds are out in the front garden when you go past. Carl says he's meant to have licenses for them, but it looks like he's tending injured ones back to health, so no one's going to report him."

"I haven't seen him or the birds." Grace surveyed the cottage with its smoking chimney. In London her neighbors had included two accountants and an aspiring model. How times had changed.

"Don't worry, he's harmless enough," Emma reassured her.

Grace turned and smiled. "Thanks again, Emma. I'll see you soon." Then she headed home. So the screeches were from owls that lived two doors away, she thought as she walked down the pathway. There had been no need for all the anxiety about unknown noises. She had to stop worrying about everything and loosen up a bit. Over the next few days she would keep searching, and by the time Christmas arrived she would surely be closer to answers.

17

"What an incredible afternoon," Annabel said, coming into the living room and flinging herself onto a chair. She ran her fingers through her damp hair. "It's snowing," she explained as she noticed Grace glaring at her. "Ben says it's meant to get bad after Christmas. We might be stranded," she added, sounding absolutely fine about that.

Grace could barely resist the urge to run over and pull her sister's hair, as she would have done when they were younger. In the past three days, she had barely seen Annabel. While Grace had put on old clothes and begun sorting through the cupboards and drawers, listening to endless crappy Christmas music blaring from the radio and wishing away the time, Annabel had been out every day. First of all she'd gone to Leeds to "finish my Christmas shopping," returning with copious Harvey Nichols bags in the trunk of her car. Next, Ben had fulfilled his promise and taken her roving over the moors; then yesterday evening Annabel had announced that they were going out again. Grace was still feeling slightly disgruntled that neither of them had thought to invite her and Millie. But much worse was that she had uncovered absolutely nothing of significance concerning Adam. She was beginning to question the wisdom of returning to the cottage in the first place. She couldn't wait for Christmas and the excuse for a break.

Annabel began to waffle on about their visit to Whitby, saying she was still full of their famous fish and chips, and describing a severed hand that Ben had shown her in the local museum. "It's called the Hand of Glory," she said, "though it's more gory than glory. It's an actual hand that's been pickled to preserve it—and there are all sorts of legends around it to do with paralyzing people or sending them to sleep. It's pretty grim."

Grace decided never to go near that museum if she could help it, while Annabel continued talking. "This place is fascinating, you know. All over the moors there are these tall stone crosses with different names, like Fat Betty and Old Ralph. I thought they were gravestones at first, but apparently there are different reasons for them—many function as memorials, religious icons, or old signposts—in many cases I don't think it's even known for certain why they're in place. And we also went to this little pub in the middle of nowhere with a 'ghost chair' in the corner—it's cursed, supposedly, so that anyone who sits in it will die soon afterwards."

"For God's sake . . ." Grace said, not wanting to hear any more.

"I know, it's brilliant!" Annabel cried, misreading Grace's mood completely. "And then, to top off everything, it began to snow when we were coming home, and it's taken us ages to get back. The snow is incredible in the dark, you can't see anything, it's like jumping into the white noise on the TV. I don't even know how Ben managed to stay on the road, it's utterly disorientating. He was telling me about one of the locals who got caught in a blizzard and tried to walk home, and got lost. He collapsed and died in the snow, and when they found him he was only a few meters from his front door. I wouldn't have believed it if I hadn't just seen what it's like with my own eyes." She leapt up.

"We're really cut off, aren't we," she said, with a visible shiver. "Have we got everything we need?"

Grace went over to the window and peered outside. The porch light cast a short dome of illumination over the garden, which was white with the snow that fell thickly. Beyond that, there was nothing to see except blackness. She pictured Millie upstairs. What had she brought her to?

A flash of movement caught her eye. Something was out there. She squinted, looking harder, but now she couldn't see anything. Perhaps the ceaseless fall of the snow was playing tricks on her vision.

But then a figure came into view just beyond the low garden wall. A man wearing a padded jacket and gloves, his head down, a thick scarf around his neck. He pushed at the gate a few times as though the latch was stuck, but finally freed it. As he hurried down the path, he lifted his head, causing Grace to cry out in amazement.

She rushed into the hallway and flung open the door. "James! What the hell are you doing here?" She threw herself into his embrace, feeling absolutely safe as he wrapped his strong arms around her.

"What a welcome!" James stepped back, his face glowing.

Grace heard Annabel behind her. "Well, well, well . . . look what the cat dragged in." When she looked around, Annabel was smiling.

"Happy Christmas, Grace!" James said.

"Did you know about this?" Grace demanded, grinning at Annabel.

"She invited me," James confirmed, as Grace looked from one to the other.

"I don't believe it." Grace hugged James again. While she kept telling herself that things would work out, with James here she felt more confident about being right.

Grace had only seen James a couple of times since he'd headed off to Switzerland to work in a bank. His departure had been hasty, and Grace knew she was partly to blame for that. She vividly recalled that night in a London bar when James had introduced her to Adam as a friend of a friend. The way he'd watched them as they'd hit it off. *Now* she could see his face dropping. *Now* she could see the tension in his arm as he repeatedly lifted his pint to his mouth. Back then, she had completely missed it—right up until the time, a year later, that she and Adam had held their engagement party and James had gotten horribly drunk, stormed out, and thrown up on the pavement. That night, he had told her that he loved her, and that he had been waiting patiently in the background for Grace to figure out that she loved him, too.

It was as though she had never known her best friend. She realized he'd never had a girlfriend that she could remember, only a few one-night stands. "Why didn't you say something much, much earlier?" she'd admonished. He'd been too scared of rejection, he'd admitted. Instead he'd hoped to see something in her face one day that meant she had discovered her own feelings for him. After that, he'd buried his face in his hands.

Once James was in Switzerland they had never spoken about it again. Neither of them wanted to risk saying or doing anything that might finally sever their bond.

Nevertheless, James had come to France in the aftermath of Adam's disappearance. He had held her tightly while she sobbed herself to sleep. Taken her out to try and distract her. And shown her a picture of his new Swiss girlfriend—"taken from a magazine," Annabel suggested slyly behind his back. However, later on they had visited Grace, and James had looked very proud as he'd put his arm around Natasha and introduced them.

"I'm surprised you made it through the snow," Annabel was saying to James, as Grace tuned back in to the conversation.

"You're telling me!" James said as he took off his coat and shoes. "Where the hell is this, Grace? The drive here has been crazy—I've hardly been able to see more than ten meters. I've practically been hallucinating—I was half-expecting to come across Santa's cottage and find him tending his reindeers and filling up his sleigh . . ."

They all went back through to the living room. After they had plied James with wine and he'd warmed up a bit, he explained, "I called your mum and dad, as I actually fancied a beautiful French Christmas, and that's when they told me you'd locked yourself away in the wilderness up here with nothing but a toddler and a list of things to do for company—oh, and a minx of a sister . . ." he added, looking across at Annabel.

Annabel pretended to punch his arm. "Bet they didn't tell you she's got a hottie helping her with the cottage."

"Which is probably the only reason Annabel's actually staying here," Grace put in, "since *I* have been working my butt off, and Annabel is actually a one-woman tour group, distracting my *employee* and roaming the moors with him under the pretext of researching an article that I've seen no sign of her writing."

"Now, now, ladies," James said, settling back on the sofa with his wine, "I can see I arrived just in time to stop you two from pulling each other's hair out."

"How's Natasha?" Annabel asked.

James's face fell. "It's over." Resignation propped up his smile as he added, "Drifted apart."

Grace moved towards him, but he held up a hand. "No sympathy needed. I knew she wasn't 'the one.'" He leaned back. "So, what's the plan for Christmas then? Aside from Millie getting her Santa loot"—his smile was genuine now—"I can't wait to see her." He reached for Grace's hand and gave it a squeeze.

Unaccountably, Grace felt herself begin to well up. "You'll be amazed. She's changed so much."

"She tries to bite you now if you annoy her, so watch out," Annabel added.

"Really?" James looked at Grace in amusement.

"It's a recent phase, sadly. Anyway, how long are you planning to stay?"

"Just a few days. My boss wants me straight back after New Year's."

"That's great. But you do know I haven't got a spare room?" Grace glanced worriedly about the place. "We're a bit cramped here."

James patted the sofa. "Seems comfy enough. Unless this is your domain, Bel?"

Grace snorted. "Not likely. She's practically pushed me out of my own bed, the amount of space she takes up."

"Yeah, yeah," Annabel said. "Who's for more wine?" She got up and plucked the bottle from the side, refilling their glasses without waiting for a response. "Now you're here, perhaps we can get you into tomorrow's excitement," she told James.

"And what might that be?"

"A ball!" Annabel squeaked with delight.

"Where?" James asked, the corner of his mouth turning up. "The local cow shed? And with who? There's no one here, guys, just miles of empty space. Is it just us and a flock of sheep ready to party?"

"There's a local hall," Annabel replied knowingly. Grace sat back and listened, sipping her drink, well aware that she was unlikely to get a word in. "A very posh hall, by all accounts. And the local riff-raff have a Christmas Eve ball—it's a tradition that started a decade ago, and everyone loved it so much that they've done it every year since. A rich aristocrat owns the place, and lets them use it. They raise quite a bit for charity."

"How long have you lived here, Annabel?" James said, a twinkle in his eye as he looked at Grace. "You really are in the right profession, aren't you. Is there anything you don't know after you've been somewhere for five minutes?"

Grace laughed, while Annabel feigned indignance. "Well, it's a ticketed event, so I don't know if we'll get you in."

"Ignore her," Grace chuckled. "We'll get you a ticket. I'll call Meredith in the morning."

"But I haven't got a suit, let alone a tux . . ." James said. "Presuming I can come, of course," he added sarcastically to Annabel.

"There's probably a shop in the next town." Annabel looked thoughtful. "We'll check it out tomorrow when we go and get the supplies for Christmas dinner."

"What would I do without you, Bel?" James replied, raising an eyebrow at Grace, before he settled back onto the sofa and closed his eyes.

Grace smiled as she watched him, thinking that it had made her Christmas simply to have him here.

As Grace made her way downstairs with Millie the next morning, she expected to find James still asleep. However, he was up and fully dressed, seated at the small dining table with a coffee, looking over some papers.

"Hi," he said on seeing her. And then, "Hello Millie. Wow, you've grown so much!"

Millie whipped around and hid her face in her mother's neck.

"She's always a bit shy," Grace explained apologetically.

"Understood. Not to worry," James replied. "Actually, I've got a present for her." He went across and pulled a large brown teddy out of his bag, then jiggled it around, trying to coax Millie to play, but she gripped on to Grace even more tightly. Grace took the teddy and attempted to give it to Millie, but the little girl snatched it and threw it on the floor.

Grace was embarrassed. "She takes time to respond to new people and new toys," she reassured James, noticing that he was crestfallen despite his efforts to hide it. "Ask Annabel, she's had the same treatment." Yet Grace couldn't help but remember Millie holding her arms out to Ben, and kneeling by his side.

James sat down again, and Grace strapped her daughter into her high chair, then went to put Millie's morning milk into the microwave. Once it was ready she shook the drink before giving it to her daughter, who used it as a security barrier from which she could inspect James further.

"My god she's like you," James said.

"Really?" Grace smiled. "In what way?"

"Well, big eyes and long legs for a start," he replied immediately.

Grace laughed. "Most people tend to see Adam in her, since she's got his coloring and his curly hair."

"Yes, well, perhaps it's more indefinable than hair color, but I definitely recognize something in those baby blues peeping at me." He stuck his tongue out playfully at Millie, but she looked worriedly at Grace.

Grace moved over and stroked her hair. "Well, you're probably the only person who sees it."

"Perhaps it's because I know you a lot better than most," James replied.

Millie broke the charged silence that followed by dropping her cup on the floor, and they both laughed. "I'll get it," James said. And when he bobbed his head up above the table again, things were back to normal.

"Shall I make you scrambled eggs for breakfast?" Grace asked as she flicked on the kettle.

"That would be great, I'll help you in a sec." He glanced once more at the papers in front of him. "I hope you don't mind—these were lying here, so I was taking a look at your plans."

"Of course I don't mind." Grace sat down opposite him. "So, what do you think?"

"It's a really good idea. But it could be a lot of work. Are you all right out here, really? Because this might take quite a while."

"I'll be okay. Besides, I've got Ben helping me out, so hopefully that will speed things up."

"Ah, yes. Ben." James put down the papers. "Tell me about Annabel's hottie—has she seduced him yet?"

Grace ignored the unease she felt at the question. "I doubt it. He's very reserved. He's been a godsend to me, though, as I was worried it would take weeks for me to find someone to work on the cottage. Although Annabel has been monopolizing him a bit of late, for her 'story.'" Grace made speech marks in the air as she said the final word and James chuckled. "They've been roving all over the moors with him telling her spooky tales. But that's all, I think."

"How romantic," James commented dryly. "Trust Annabel."

"Trust Annabel what?" said the woman herself, appearing at the door.

"I was admiring your dedication to getting a good story," James laughed, then spluttered on his coffee as Annabel clipped his head with her hand as she went past. "Ow."

"You deserved it."

"So, what's the plan for today then?" James asked. "There appear to be all sorts of exciting possibilities around here." He got up and gestured out at the white sky and the bare expanse of the moors, now pockmarked with last night's melting snow.

"You're as bad as Annabel!" Grace went across to the worktop and poured her sister a drink. "Tell you what, let's go for a walk while the weather holds, see if we can get you two city slickers to actually enjoy a bit of fresh air."

"Whatever," Annabel murmured, leafing through a magazine as she accepted the mug Grace handed to her.

James winked at Grace. "Good plan." She smiled back at him, but faltered for a moment at the expression in his eyes before he looked away.

18

As Grace strapped Millie into her stroller, she listened to Annabel and James on the doorstep, both complaining about being outside in the bitter cold.

"Are you sure this is a good idea?" Annabel asked doubtfully, rubbing her arms with her gloved hands.

"It's only a walk, Annabel, it won't kill you, Grace retorted, surprising herself. In London, she had regularly grumbled about the distances between bus, tube, and destination, but now she found herself looking forward to these long countryside rambles. "Come on." She pushed Millie's stroller towards the gate, the others falling in step behind her.

To reach the moorland path, they headed up the steep road past the other cottages. "Who lives in these places?" James asked, breaking the hush of the frosty morning.

Grace looked across at the row of cottages as she replied. "Emma and Carl are next door to me. They're lovely. Apparently an old man called Feathery Jack lives in that one"—she pointed to the cottage with smoke rising from the chimney—"but he's reclusive by all accounts. I've never seen him. And Ben lives in the house at the top." She motioned towards the redbrick dwelling standing incongruously beside its stone neighbors.

"Feathery Jack?" Annabel repeated. "What's that about?"

"He keeps birds, apparently—owls."

"That's actually pretty cool," James said.

Annabel raised an eyebrow at him.

They continued walking in silence, following the tarmac road to the summit, leaving the houses behind. At the top, they turned down a path marked only by flattened grass and occasional groups of uneven stones. They made their way along until they reached another peak, and as they crested the hill the moors spread out before them.

"There's not a lot of green about, is there," James said.

"That's because it's winter," Grace snapped, lifting Millie out of her stroller and hoisting her onto her shoulders so she could take in the view. "Here," she instructed the others, "before you both start gabbling away, shut up for a moment and look at this place, will you, and breathe it in. It might be deserted, but it's absolutely pristine."

Annabel glanced across at Grace and tutted, but then did as requested. James turned obediently, but with his arms folded as though he doubted he'd be impressed. Grace surveyed the desolate expanse, mottled with melting snow, wondering why she'd felt so defensive when James had spoken. There was something beautiful about this place, she thought—in daylight, the raw, untouched vista had the power to stop your mind for a moment. Here, you didn't have to look up to see the sky, it came right down and met you, ever-present beyond the ceaseless shifting of color, clouds, and light.

Briefly, the void inside her was filled with something close to peace. She remembered standing in a similar spot with Adam, holding hands, their tiny daughter in a sling against her chest. She recalled the sense of belonging she had felt; the contentment in Adam's face. Even though he wasn't here, this place linked them. So should she indulge her occasional crazy notions about staying here and trying to carve out a life for herself once the cottage was renovated? Of course not, she told herself hastily. She was a city girl. But she was all too aware that she had never known London as a single mother, and she wasn't daft enough to think it would be the same for her now.

So what choices did she have? She sighed. Nothing much was clear to her at the moment. Nothing except Millie's mittened hands clutching her mother's ponytail. When she looked at her daughter she felt a resolve of purpose beyond herself, and at present that was enough to keep her going when everything else seemed so uncertain.

She let her thoughts drift away, coming back to her surroundings. The chilly air filled her nostrils, fresh and slightly sweet. As she breathed in, a gust of cold wind nipped at her face, setting her teeth on edge.

"It is beautiful, in a rugged, remote sort of way," Annabel said, breaking the spell. "But still, you shouldn't hide out here for too long, Grace . . ."

Grace felt stung by the remark. "I'm not hiding, Annabel. I'm doing what needs to be done."

Annabel and James caught each other's eyes, and Grace had to breathe deeply to stop herself from yelling at them. She put Millie back in her stroller, then barked, "this way!" and walked off without checking to see if they were coming with her.

No one spoke as they followed the rough stone path, the fresh, clean air rolling over the hills and bursting into their faces. The wind was a puppeteer, bending the trees to its will and making the dead leaves and twigs dance and scuttle along the ground away from them. Grace tried to concentrate on pushing Millie along the rocky path, but her mind insisted on drifting back to what Annabel had just said. Was she hiding? Was that really why she had come back?

She attempted to distract herself, watching a flock of fieldfares dart overhead, and Millie shrieked with delight as they spooked a grouse into noisy flight. But for the most part there was nothing except a glorious expanse of nature at its barest, and for Grace the solitude and silence were settling. Out here she didn't feel so lost, or overwhelmed, or alone.

They reached a patch of open ground with a cluster of large flat boulders, which overlooked the train line that followed the curves of the valley. As they slowed, Annabel cried, "Oh my god, that's Lover's Leap." She pointed to a place a little farther on, where the rail track crossed a steel bridge suspended above a small gorge, partially hidden from view. "I read about it in your book, Grace, and Ben mentioned it as well. It's probably the most haunted place in the area. People have been going over the edge since time began, apparently—usually because of unrequited love."

James shook his head. "Love makes people do the strangest things," he said, gazing into the distance.

Grace couldn't bear this conversation. "Can we keep going?" she asked them, hurriedly getting up.

The other two got to their feet and followed her. Grace tried to imagine Ben telling Annabel stories of the moors, unable to picture him conversing so freely. Then her mind switched back to Adam, wandering along this same track with her, his arm slung over her shoulders as he told her about his plans for the cottage, for their new life.

All at once, she couldn't bear her constant reminiscing. She stopped and swung round, startling James and Annabel. "Where the hell is he?" she cried. "What happened? I mean, he wouldn't just disappear. And he wasn't the kind to jump off cliffs."

She glared at them, hands on hips, demanding that one of them answer her.

"He might still come back," Annabel said uncertainly.

"Why the hell would you say that?" Grace shouted. She caught Millie's eye, and as she registered her daughter's alarm she made an effort to calm herself down. "Don't you see, I can't think like that anymore. Because how long am I meant to wait? There are no rules as far as I can see. What's the proper time for this? Two years? Five? Ten? I could spend the rest of my life waiting—what kind of miserable existence is that?"

There was silence, then James said, "Grace, I'm not sure that staying here is good for you if it's making you feel like this."

Grace threw her hands in the air. "I *KNOW* that, James! But what choice do I have? I have no major assets except a damned cottage I can't sell, and I have to sort everything out properly for Millie's sake. Adam did care about his daughter, whatever anyone says, and I want her at least to have some things of her father's to remember him by. And that's as far as I can think about it without going crazy."

Annabel came over and began to rub Grace's arm. "Let's not talk about it anymore. Let's help you do what you need to, and try to enjoy Christmas. Time to move on, eh?"

Grace saw that Annabel was upset now. Her sister's heartfelt sympathy took the fight out of her, and she buried her face in her hands. "I miss him," she said, confused and defeated, feeling her eyes filling with tears; at which point James and Annabel both wrapped their arms around her, taking her weight, even if only for a moment.

19

Millie sat on her mother's lap, as Grace turned the pages of a book and pointed to the pictures. Her mood was low, and she wondered if it would have been better had they gone to town with James and Annabel. But she needed to stop for a while and rest, particularly as she was heading out this evening. And she also wanted to spend some proper time with Millie. Grace knew she was physically meeting her daughter's needs, but her mind was often elsewhere, and meanwhile Millie grew and changed every day. Grace wanted to absorb as much of this sweet little toddler as she could.

As she closed the book, there was an unexpected knock on the door. She jumped, startling Millie. "Who's that?" Grace asked as Millie stared impassively at her. She set the little girl on the floor with the book and went to find out.

Opening the door, she was greeted by a Christmas tree standing alone in front of her, its branches flailing in the wind. "Did you knock?" she asked the tree, then couldn't help chuckling to herself.

"Yes, we did." Ben peeped around from behind it. "I thought you might like this. If you don't want it I'll put it up instead, but I think it would go better in here. And I heard that you'd knocked down a wall to make room for it."

Grace beamed at him. "That's a great idea. Thank you!"

She stood back as Ben lifted the tree and swung it over the threshold, pushing it towards the front room. Millie looked up in awe, and Grace went to pick her up, while Ben asked, "Where do you want it?"

"There is fine." Grace pointed towards a bare corner, and Ben maneuvered it into place. "It's a shame I don't have any decorations for it, though."

Ben dusted off his hands as he studied the bare branches. "Are you sure you don't?" he asked. "You've got a lot of boxes in this place, perhaps one of them has Christmas stuff in it?"

"You're right," she said as she cuddled Millie. "I'll have a look in the tops of them, see if I can find anything. I don't think they'd have been in the attic—but perhaps there might be something in the cellar . . ."

They walked through the hallway to the cellar door. "Do you want me to take a look?" Ben offered.

Yes, please, she thought, but she steeled herself, not wanting to look wimpish. "No, it's fine. I know where the light switch is now."

"Shall I take Millie for you then?"

"You can try," Grace replied, not really anticipating that Millie would allow it. But to her astonishment the little girl went willingly to Ben.

"Right, then," she said, ruffling her daughter's hair. "I won't be a moment."

She made her way down the steps. At the bottom she felt along the wall for the light switch and flicked it on. The place still depressed her, with its piles of debris and stacks of boxes, but she began to hunt around.

It was so cold down here. Everything she touched was icy, and Grace felt the chill creeping up her fingers and beginning to crawl along her arms. She came across Adam's mementoes again, and remembered that he had brought them down here unbeknownst to her. After what had happened last time she found herself reluctant to touch them, but she briefly hunted through. There was nothing surprising, just a jumble of souvenirs.

"Any luck?" Ben called.

She was aware of him waiting. Turning away, she spotted tinsel poking from the top of a small box. "I've got something!" she called as she pulled it from the shelf, finding it was lighter than she'd expected.

There was no reply from Ben as Grace went across to the stairs. She switched off the light and headed up, holding the box awkwardly in front of her and navigating by the strip of illumination coming through the doorway at the top.

Suddenly, the door slammed shut with a loud bang and she was plunged into blackness. Shock made her drop the box, and she heard it tumbling away down the stairs. Panic seized her, and she scrambled blindly up the rest of the steps until she felt the wood of the door solid against her palms. She pushed hard, but it didn't move. She began to hammer on it with her fists, until it swung open.

Ben and Millie stared worriedly at her frightened face.

"Grace, are you all right?" Ben asked, as Millie reached out for her.

She clutched the door frame as she gulped in air. "I'm fine," she said, taking Millie. "The door slammed and gave me a fright."

"Sorry." Ben sounded contrite. "I'd taken Millie outside to say hi to Bess, and I heard the bang—the draft must have blown it closed." He noticed her empty hands. "You didn't find anything?"

"There's a Christmas box, but I dropped it." She wavered, reluctant to go down there again.

"I'll get it." Ben headed down into the darkness.

Grace stroked Millie's hair while they waited, saying, "Mummy got a fright, but it's fine now," as Millie clung tightly to her.

A moment later, Ben reappeared. "Here you go," he said, carrying the box through to the living room. He set it down on the floor and stood up, dusting off his hands.

He was getting ready to leave, and Grace realized how much she didn't want to be alone.

"Would you like to stay while we decorate the tree?" she asked. "I have beer."

Ben smiled. "That would be good, but I don't want to leave Bess out in this weather for too long . . ."

"Bring her in, then."

"Are you sure?"

"Of course."

Ben went to the front door and a moment later Bess bounded inside and began sniffing at everything in sight. To Grace's surprise, Millie struggled to be free, and once on the ground the little girl gawked at the dog in amazement, and even chuckled briefly when Bess licked her face. Grace knelt down and patted Bess, feeling herself warming to the dog. She couldn't be too nervous of an animal that could make her daughter giggle like that.

When Annabel and James arrived home they found Bess curled up in front of the fireplace, looking on as Grace and Ben put the final touches to the Christmas tree. Millie sat beside them, playing with an assortment of baubles that she had commandeered.

"What are you doing here, Ben?" Annabel asked as she began pulling off her gloves.

"You told me you didn't have a Christmas tree," he said. "So I brought you one."

Grace felt her face fall as she saw Annabel's light up. She'd thought the tree was for Millie's benefit. *Why do I care?* she asked herself, as she began to help them with the bags.

"I think we've got enough food to feed the whole village," Annabel announced as she went across to give Bess a stroke. "You should have seen the town, Grace, it was like one of those Olde World postcards—the market was on a cobbled street, everyone was wearing Christmas hats, and all the shops were decorated with multicolored twinkling lights and streams of tinsel."

As she listened, Grace noticed that the two men were eyeing each other, waiting for introductions. "James, this is Ben."

They shook hands. "Been hearing a lot about you," James said.

"Oh?" Ben looked wary.

James smiled. "All good, don't worry. Annabel's been telling me about your day trips. Local, are you?"

"Used to be." Ben went across to get his coat. "Not lived here for a long time now, but I know some of the old stories."

"Are you coming to the ball tonight?"

"No." Ben shook his head. "Not my thing. Come on, Bess."

The dog sprang to her feet.

"I'll see you all tomorrow then?" Ben looked around the room at them before he turned to leave.

Grace went to see him out. She wished he were coming to the ball. She enjoyed his unobtrusive company, and wanted to get to know him better.

"Thanks again for the tree," she called after him belatedly as he neared the gate, with Bess trotting behind him.

He didn't turn, just waved a hand in reply.

20

Freeborough Hall loomed sturdy and imposing at the end of a long circular driveway, lights blazing from the downstairs rooms. Grace grasped the skirt of her long black satin dress so that it wouldn't trail along the wet ground, and headed towards the ornate doorway with the others.

Annabel had borrowed a sparkly silver number that Grace hadn't worn in years, while James had managed to rent a tuxedo in town. He fiddled with his cufflinks as they made their way up the steps. At the top they were greeted by two elderly women, in similar royal blue knee-length dresses that looked more appropriate for church than for a ball.

After parting with their tickets and entering the raffle, they headed along a wide corridor in the direction of voices and music.

"Look at these," James said, as he glanced up at the large disembodied head of a stag, its beady eyes glaring malevolently down at them—one of a number of animal trophies that were mounted between various works of art.

"I'd rather not, thanks," Annabel replied.

They entered the large function room to see the party in full swing. Multicolored balloons were bunched at regular intervals around the wall, streamers trailing from them. The stage and the bar area were well lit, but the rest of the light came from small lamps on each table. People milled around, or sat in groups holding animated conversation, while a few had already taken to the floor, dancing to a swing band. Grace glanced at the double bass player, his eyes closed as he plucked fiercely at strings, and wondered what it would be like to be that absorbed in something. When was the last time she had lost herself like that? She couldn't remember.

"Where the hell did all these people come from?" James murmured.

They bought drinks and found an empty table, but it didn't take long before Annabel began cajoling them all to dance.

"All right then," James muttered crossly as Annabel pulled him from his seat. "Come on, Grace, you, too."

But Grace shook her head as they got up and moved to the dance floor, and after a few attempts at waving her over to join them, James gave up. Annabel began sashaying around with her arms in the air, while James did his best impression of a swing king, leaning forward and clicking his fingers to each side of his knees, nodding his head enthusiastically. Grace was laughing at them when she heard someone saying her name, and felt a hand on her shoulder. She swung around to see Claire.

"Hi, Grace." Claire was smiling. "My family are over there—come and say hello."

Grace got up and followed Claire across the room to a large round table. "Everyone," Claire announced, "this is Grace."

Conversation drifted away as all eyes fell on her. On the far side, a burly, shaved-headed man had his hand placed proprietorially on the thigh of the woman next to him. The woman was observing the dance floor, and Grace saw that she had a pretty elfin face and dark hair piled high on top of her head. Nearest to Grace, a woman with long auburn hair had turned to stare, her face somber. Last of all, Grace spotted Meredith in a dim corner close to the wall, one elbow on the table, the heel of her palm elegantly propping up her chin as she coolly regarded the dance floor.

"These are my younger sisters, Liza and Jenny," Claire said, gesturing to the women as she spoke. "And over there is Liza's husband Dan."

"Hello, Grace," Meredith said from her shadowy corner, her mouth barely moving. "Claire, can I talk to you for a moment?"

Claire moved across to her mother, leaving Grace on her own. As she looked around, her gaze fell on Jenny, whose long red hair was familiar. Then she realized: this was the person she had seen leaving Ben's house when she'd been out walking. Perhaps Ben was the "someone" Claire had referred to when she'd said Jenny was in a new relationship. She realized too late that she was staring, and Jenny was regarding her with a frown. Grace averted her eyes.

Dan got up and held out a hand. "Nice to meet you," he said without smiling. "So you're living in Roseby? Claire said you're from London—the change of scene must have taken a bit of getting used to?"

"Yes, it has." She shook his hand, expecting more conversation, but he sat down and began rolling a cigarette. Grace remembered Emma telling her about him, and tried to picture him as a policeman. His manner was both abrupt and slightly menacing, and she was grateful that it was Niall and not this man who'd been sent to help her on the night Adam disappeared.

"How are you getting on at the cottage?" Liza asked. "Mum says you're busy sorting through everything?"

Grace wondered if they knew about Meredith's interest in the place. "Yes, but I'm enjoying the break for Christmas."

Before Liza could say any more, Jenny leaned across the table and said something to Dan. He looked down at the tablecloth and let out a short bark of laughter, and Grace saw Jenny's eyes flicker to her, then away. Grace began to feel uneasy, but was saved as the music stopped and it was announced that the raffle was about to be drawn.

"Good to meet you all," she said, glancing around to find Meredith's eyes fixed on her. Claire began to move towards her again, but Grace pretended she hadn't seen, and hurried away.

Annabel and James were already back at their table. "Where did you go?" Annabel asked accusingly. "You left my purse on the chair, it could have been stolen."

"I'm not here to babysit your handbag," Grace retorted. "Look after it yourself."

"All right, calm down." Annabel glared at her.

Their attention shifted towards the stage as the raffle was drawn. Grace glanced at her tickets, then screwed them up. Then the lights were dimmed again, the music resumed, and everyone went back to their conversations. Trying her best to absorb the carefree atmosphere, for a while Grace chattered inconsequentially to Annabel and James over another glass of wine, but she felt as though she were alone in an invisible bubble. "Time for another dance," Annabel announced a little while later, and James agreed, saying, "This time you're coming, too, Grace," but dancing was a step too far for her tonight, in front of all these people, particularly when she couldn't shake the feeling that she was being watched.

She decided she would go for a walk rather than sit by herself next to the packed dance floor. She thought she might find a moment's solitude in the ladies' bathroom, but when she arrived there was a queue of women gossiping animatedly while they waited for a cubicle. So she headed back beneath the leering parade of hunting trophies, towards the main doors of the building. The old women who had welcomed them were no longer there, and she leaned against the cool stone wall, breathing in the frigid air, feeling the chill of the night seeping through her skin and into her bones.

"Grace?" a female voice said.

Grace whirled around. One of Meredith's daughters was standing behind her, contemplating Grace nervously.

"Liza, isn't it?" Grace asked.

"Yes," the woman replied, a small jewel in her brown hair glinting in the soft light. "I need to talk to you. Alone. It's about Adam."

21

As Grace stared at Liza, she noticed that Liza's stomach protruded in front of her like a perfectly rounded egg. Grace's whole body had stiffened upon hearing Adam's name, but before she could speak, Liza said, "This way," and headed down the steps. At the bottom she glanced back and beckoned Grace to come with her.

Grace followed in a daze, as Liza made for two soaring oak trees whose trunks stood set apart but whose branch tips bent to join each other in a delicate embrace. There wasn't much light to navigate by, but between what little moonlight had managed to penetrate the clouds, and the glow from the hall, Grace could make out a small lake in front of her. Liza had turned right and disappeared, and as Grace came through the trees she saw there was an ornamental gazebo a little farther along. Creeping plants had spun a web of stems over the wrought iron railings, and there were a few steps leading into it.

Liza waited inside, looking out across the lake. As soon as Grace joined her she said, "I'm sorry to bring you out here like this, but I didn't know how else to speak to you on your own. And I need to tell you something . . ." She searched Grace's face for reassurance.

"I'm listening," Grace told her quietly.

Liza took a deep breath before she spoke. "I saw Adam in the library in Ockton, the day before he went missing. I'd nipped in there to browse while I waited for a bus, and I was amazed to bump into him. We recognized each other straightaway, even though it's been, what—over fourteen years. . . . But during the summer he spent in Roseby, my sisters and I saw him all the time—he made life far more interesting for a while, I can tell you. Anyway, it was really lovely to catch up. He told me about you, Grace—said he was married and had a baby girl—he looked really proud."

Grace felt a searing pain in her chest. She went across and leaned on the railing, studying the ink-black lake. Patchy light illuminated small parts of its glassy surface, and highlighted the dark outlines of plants and bushes surrounding it.

Liza came closer and put a hand on her arm. "I'm sorry, Grace. I can only imagine how difficult it must be—"

"Why the hell didn't you come forward at the time?" Grace interrupted, anger sitting low in her voice.

"I didn't know that Adam had gone missing right away," Liza explained, withdrawing her touch. "And when I found out, it was complicated . . . for reasons I don't want to go into, but which have nothing to do with Adam. Anyway, at the time I didn't think our conversation would be relevant—but when I heard you were back, I knew I should talk to you, just in case . . ."

"What else did he say?" Grace demanded impatiently.

"Well, he was sitting at a computer when I saw him, with the phone book open next to him, and when I asked him what he was doing, he appeared kind of sheepish and said, 'Looking for my dad.'"

On hearing those last four words, Grace froze. Liza didn't notice, and carried on.

"I was taken aback by that. When he'd stayed in Roseby after his mother died, the main things I remember about him were first of all that he pretty much chain-smoked, and secondly that he talked a lot about how much he hated his father for abandoning them. So I wasn't sure what to say, but he added, 'I'd just like to hear his side of the story.' And then I'm certain that we began talking about something else—that's all I remember him saying about it anyway. But I recall him telling me that very clearly, because he'd obviously had such a big change of heart."

Grace was trying to imagine this conversation taking place. "Adam rarely talked about his father to me," she told Liza. "He seemed to have dealt with the trauma of his early life. He was one for always looking forward, not backwards."

"Well," Liza said, "he had changed then, because he used to be obsessed with his dad. And that's probably a good thing, actually, because although I didn't really understand at the time, it wasn't very healthy the way he talked then. But he had only just lost his mother—he needed someone to direct his anger at, I guess. The way he spoke in the library struck me, because that hate wasn't there anymore—he was quite matter-of-fact about it."

Grace swung round. "I want to tell the police about this," she said. "In case it makes a difference. I wish you'd said something at the time."

"Grace, I understand how you must feel, but I'm asking you—begging you, in fact—not to get me involved." Liza sounded frightened.

"Can I ask why?" Grace persisted.

Liza shook her head. "I can't say, I'm sorry. Please—I've told you all I know. Leave me out of it now."

Grace made a noise of frustration and looked back across the lake for a while, lost in thought. When she turned round, she was alone in the gazebo.

All at once, the cold was unbearable. She looked through the trees towards the lights of the hall. She wasn't ready to go back there yet. Her thoughts tumbled over one another as she tried to make sense of what she had heard. While Liza had been talking, half of Grace had been listening attentively, but the other half had been picturing Adam's earnest face and trying to figure out why he hadn't told her what he was doing. She had a disconcerting feeling that she might know the answer. While Grace was pregnant, she had asked Adam if he'd thought about tracing his father. He had seemed agitated by the suggestion, and had given her a big speech about how the past was best left alone. If he'd changed his mind, and decided to do some research while they were at the cottage, he might well have put off telling Grace, knowing what he'd said before, reluctant to admit his change of heart.

She remembered his note now, with a shudder of disquiet: *I have to talk to you when I get back, don't go anywhere.* As she sighed, a cloud of mist formed in the frosty air. Surely this was it—he had meant to tell her about Jonny. So why had he chosen that moment? Had he found something in the library?

She watched her breath dissipating. This was all supposition—who knew if it even had any bearing on why he'd disappeared. She recalled Liza and her family at the table tonight. Meredith's indifferent stare. Perhaps they were trying to unnerve her, make her feel that her husband had been keeping secrets from her, maneuver her out of the cottage so Meredith could take it over. Well, if that was their intention they were going to be disappointed.

It was time to get back inside before she caught pneumonia. She left the gazebo and moved hurriedly along, careful not to trip on the long undergrowth next to the murky water. As she walked through the car park, she pictured Millie's sleeping face, and rummaged in her small bag to phone Emma.

"I've been expecting you to call!" Emma said as she answered. "And she's fine. Not a peep out of her. Enjoy yourself while you've got the chance. I'm not expecting you back until way past midnight."

"Thank you, I really appreciate it," Grace said.

"Don't you worry, I'm sure we'll be needing a favor from you at some stage."

As Grace hung up, she registered the sounds of the ball again, and wondered if James and Annabel had realized that she was missing. *Annabel probably won't even notice if I'm not in the car on the way home*, she thought, *since she's likely to be both drunk and exhausted by then.*

Grace's mother had always urged her to be a responsible older sister and look after Annabel, even though they were only thirteen months apart. She had once done so willingly, yet nowadays, at times, she resented her sister's devil-may-care approach to life. "Grace was born responsible," her father used to say proudly. And so it appeared. Was this what she was doing now by moving back to the cottage— putting herself through all this because of some questionable notion about what "the right thing to do" might be? What if she didn't want to be responsible anymore? Perhaps that should be her New Year's resolution, she decided, with a surge of defiance.

There was an unexpected movement behind her. She whirled around, peering back towards the trees, and saw a familiar figure vanishing behind one of them, a tall man with dark hair.

She shook her head briefly to try to reestablish reality, but it was no use—that short glimpse had stung her so hard that she broke into a run, screaming as loudly as she could, "Adam!"

22

At the sound of her cry, the man spun on his heel. "Grace!" Ben said, a mixture of astonishment and worry on his face. "What are you doing out here?"

For a moment she had imagined it was her husband, and nothing else had mattered except catching up to him. Now, bitter disappointment derailed her.

"Why the hell are you creeping around?" she shouted. Ben appeared to wince at her loud voice, and glanced uncomfortably towards the trees and the car park and hall beyond, but there was no one visible, only the faint sound of music.

"Grace, I'm so sorry, I didn't mean to scare you—I didn't know anyone else was down here."

"But what are you doing here?" she demanded, still angry. "You said you weren't coming."

"Well, I changed my mind. A few times, actually. I was wondering if this might be—" He stopped, as though reluctant to go on.

"Be what?" Grace insisted.

Ben shook his head. "Never mind, it doesn't matter." He came closer. "Here," he took off his jacket and held it up to drape over her shoulders, "you must be freezing."

Grace became aware of how tightly she had wrapped her arms around herself, and how hard she was shaking. She let him lay the jacket over her, and as the fight left her, tears began to form in her eyes. She looked down.

"You should go back inside, Grace, where it's warm."

She kept her focus on the ground. "I'd rather not, for a minute."

"All right then, come and sit in my car for a while and get warm."

He led the way to the Land Rover, slivers of light from the hall reflecting off the bonnet. Grace climbed into the passenger seat and laid her head back against the headrest, while Ben got into the driver's seat and started the engine.

"Where are we going?" Grace asked, alarmed as the doors automatically locked with a loud click.

"Nowhere," Ben said, "I was just switching on the engine to get the heat coming through properly."

Grace looked at the bright lights of the hall, and pictured the cheerful celebrations inside. Right at this moment she wanted to be far away from it all. "Actually, can you take us for a drive?"

Ben didn't say another word, but put the car into gear and began to reverse.

Once they were heading slowly down the gravel driveway, Grace nestled into her seat. The silken lining of Ben's jacket was soft against her arms, and she pulled it closer around her, breathing in the unfamiliar scent of his aftershave on the lapels. The dark sky formed a backdrop to the sable silhouettes of trees as they sped along. Nightfall made everything an illusion. The small red and blue lights on

Ben's dashboard were comforting, reassuring little beacons of safety; the car their small enclave on the unfamiliar roads.

She roused herself as Ben slowed, to find that they were caught in a traffic jam.

"What's going on?" she asked, intrigued.

"They're heading for midnight mass."

Grace looked towards the church in the distance, then at the cars pulling up. "I've never been," she said. "Have you?"

"Would you like to go now?"

Grace considered the unexpected offer. "Yes."

Ben pulled to the curb without a word. They got out of the car and made their way through a small lych-gate, then along the church-yard path towards bright, welcoming light. Grace hadn't been to a church service since she was a child. Her parents used to attend every week, until her father had found a new religion called golf.

They slid into an empty pew at the back, and Grace looked around. The church was long and thin with an ornate high ceiling. The organ droned in the background as the congregation filed in, then struck up with a renewed vigor as the clergy proceeded slowly down the aisle.

When the service began, Grace let the words wash over her, the vicar's voice rising and falling in prayer. When she was asked to kneel, she pressed her face against her hands and let her tears come in silent relief, acknowledging how helpless she felt, and sending out a plea that the coming year would be brighter and happier for Millie and for herself.

When the service ended, she felt lighter. She hadn't so much as looked at Ben since entering the church, but now, as people began to wish one another a Merry Christmas, he turned to her with a smile.

"Happy Christmas, Grace." She smiled in reply, enjoying the snatched moment of tranquility. Then she glanced at her watch.

"Oh no, I've got to get back. Annabel and James will be going mad . . . and I need to get home for Millie."

"The ball doesn't finish until one," Ben reassured her. "They might not have even registered that you've gone."

But Grace had no doubt that they would have noticed by now. "Can we go quickly?" she asked as they hurried out of the church, saying a brief Merry Christmas to the vicar before rushing back to Ben's car.

Ben unlocked the doors as he went swiftly around to the driver's side. "Don't panic, Grace, we'll be there in ten minutes," he said as they climbed inside.

During the journey, Grace jiggled her knees up and down impatiently. But as they came onto the long gravel drive she was distracted from her worry as Ben said, "Look, why don't I leave you all to have Christmas dinner on your own. I don't want to intrude."

"Ben, you're not intruding—really," Grace insisted, keen for him to come after he had been so gently supportive of her tonight. "We'd love to have you. Annabel will grumble all day if you back out now . . ."

"Well, all right, if you're sure."

For some reason his detachment infuriated her, and she twisted in her seat to face him. "Ben, why are you house-sitting in the middle of nowhere on your own? What's going on?" Jenny's wary face and long auburn hair flashed through her mind. What role did that woman play in his life?

Ben lapsed into silence for a long moment, his features grim, before he said, "I have some unfinished business, like you."

"You skirt around giving straight answers every single time, do you realize that?" Grace demanded, irritated.

She saw his jaw tighten. "Grace, I can assure you, this is not a Christmas Day kind of conversation."

She sat back in her seat with an exasperated sigh, unable to think of a reply.

When they reached the end of the drive, instead of going right to the car park, Ben pulled up on the grass beforehand.

"Will you be all right from here?" he asked.

"Yes, of course," she said, puzzled. But before she could turn away, he slowly leaned towards her, and she felt her heartbeat skitter as his face drew close to hers. She smelled his aftershave again, studied the taut line of his jaw, and when his face was almost touching hers, she looked into his eyes. He was watching her curiously.

She had forgotten to breathe. Then she heard the latch of her door as he opened it for her, and he straightened back up into his seat, even though he was still scrutinizing her.

"Ben," Grace began as she let go of her breath, forgetting that anyone was waiting for her now. She sensed she might not get another chance at such intimacy with him. "You can trust me, you know."

Ben leaned back, staring at the car roof. "I know," he said. "I know that, Grace. I just don't want you to think . . ." He stopped, apparently lost for the next words. Then he turned to face her. "I left here under a cloud, Grace. A very, very black cloud."

"Even so, can't you come and join the final hour of the party?" she urged, giving his sleeve a small tug of encouragement. "Have a drink for Christmas, forget your troubles for a little while. You can stick with us," she added, in case he was worried about more reactions like those of the couple who ran the pub in Roseby—briefly trying to imagine what he might have done to have caused them, then wishing she hadn't.

"I wish I could. I drove all the way over here because my sister told me to come—in fact she said it was an excellent idea—but now that I'm here I doubt it very much."

"I didn't know you had a sister," Grace said, pleased that he had shared this small confidence with her.

"I have four of them, Grace," Ben replied, "and three are in there right now, along with my mother, who hasn't spoken to me for fourteen years, and who still isn't ready to talk to me now."

Grace's mouth dropped open as her mind began clicking things into place.

"Meredith?" she breathed, unable to believe it.

"Yes, Grace," Ben said, "Meredith is my mother."

23

Grace was stunned, but as she sat beside Ben with no idea of what to say next, she caught sight of two people standing on the front steps to the hall, looking around while they talked agitatedly.

Ben had spotted them, too. "You'd better go."

"Will you be okay?"

He turned to smile at her, though his eyes were weary. I'm fine, Grace. You go now, I'll see you tomorrow."

She gave him a worried glance, climbed out of the car, and heard him reversing down the road. She waited a moment then began to walk up to the hall.

James and Annabel swooped on her as soon as they saw her. Annabel was beside herself, declaring that the party was definitely over and they were heading back.

"Don't you *EVER* do that to me again," she shouted at Grace. "Where the hell have you been?"

"I needed some time to myself," Grace told them, grateful that the music from inside was drowning out their remonstrations, and reluctant to tell them that she had been with Ben, knowing they were likely to read it all wrong.

They walked to the car in silence. Once inside, Annabel refused to speak to Grace for the rest of the journey. Grace looked to James for support, but he stared stonily ahead as he drove, and made no move to dispel the fraught atmosphere.

Grace glanced out the window, exhaustion creeping over her. The roads heading home were disturbingly hushed. The headlights' full beam did their best to penetrate the black night, but to little effect.

It was hard to believe it was Christmas Day. She had a suspicion that when they got up again in a few hours, it would feel more like going through the motions than a true celebration. She remembered Ben, standing outside the hall tonight, so close and yet so far removed from the rest of his family. What on earth had happened to make it that way?

She was tempted to share her discoveries—it might thaw the frostiness in the car—but stopped herself, feeling she would be betraying Ben's confidence. He would tell them about it himself if he wanted to. At least his revelation had distracted her from thoughts of Adam for a while.

"People were saying we're in for a heavy snowfall tomorrow," James said beside her, breaking her train of thought.

"Good job you stocked up today then," Grace responded, after which they said nothing further.

Grace was relieved when the Roseby village sign flashed by them. As they pulled up outside the cottage, she remembered Millie with a guilt-laden jolt. How could she have left her alone out here? What if something had gone wrong and Millie had needed her? She hurried inside and found Emma lazing sleepily on the sofa, the television burbling in the background. "Not a peep," she reassured Grace. "I hope you had a good time."

Grace said her thanks, and saw Emma out. Then she crept into Millie's room, peeked briefly at her daughter's peaceful, sleeping face, whispered, "Happy Christmas, little one," and took herself off to bed.

When Grace woke up, she was pleased to discover that it had been a rare night without dreams. Her head felt groggy, however, and a dull ache began as she remembered what Liza had told her about Adam. She went in to see Millie and found her standing, holding the bars of the crib, cuddling Mr. Pink while eying her full stocking in the corner with a mixture of wonder and apprehension.

Grace gave Millie a few presents to open. They had only gotten as far as unwrapping a board book and a jigsaw puzzle when the little girl began to lose interest, and Grace smiled as her daughter grabbed Mr. Pink, threw him ahead of her, and crawled towards the door. As they were going downstairs, Annabel appeared and headed towards the bathroom. "Merry Christmas," Grace said, but Annabel just grunted.

James was already up and drinking coffee at the kitchen table.

"I'm sorry if I scared you last night," Grace began as soon as she saw him.

"Never mind. As long as you're all right?"

"I am . . . though I don't know if Annabel will be talking to me today."

"Now don't be too hard on Annabel," James said. "Remember, Adam went missing around here. So when you go MIA, she worries—she's bound to."

Grace felt chastened. James looked like he wanted to add something more, but then Annabel appeared.

"Merry Christmas!" she greeted them, hugging them all before going across to the kettle. "When are we opening presents?"

"As soon as possible, I think," Grace replied, relieved that she appeared to have been forgiven. She jiggled Millie on her hip, then poked her tongue out to encourage her daughter to laugh.

"Come on then, little lady." Annabel plucked her niece from Grace's arms. "Let's go and see what we can find under the tree."

They spent the next couple of hours opening presents. Annabel's selections were always interesting. Crème de la Mer for Grace—"It's so overpriced, but I'm saving your skin from cracking up in these Arctic temperatures"—while James received Ted Baker boxer shorts, which he looked quite pleased with until he saw that the labels said EXTRA-LARGE. "I thought you'd take it as a compliment," Annabel laughed when he complained. Grace had bought Annabel some Smythson business accessories and a pair of pajamas, but had to apologize to James as he opened his gift. "In my defense, I didn't know you were coming."

In haste, she had managed to locate an empty photo frame and make a collage to go in it, by scanning old pictures onto the computer.

James beamed at her after he opened it. "A decade of Grace, James, and Annabel! Don't worry, it's perfect."

Despite her considerable pile of presents, Millie wasn't much interested in the unwrapping process. James had given her Mr. Men stories, and tried in vain to get her to sit with him while he read, but Millie's face grew increasingly wary and she kept crawling close to her mother. In the end he gave up, and began to help Annabel prepare the dinner, while Grace took the new toys out of their boxes. By the time Millie went down for her nap there was nothing much left to do. James switched on the television, and he and Annabel settled themselves in front of it. Grace tried to join them, but she couldn't concentrate, thinking about Liza's and Ben's revelations the previous night.

She sat there for a while feeling fidgety, then got up. "I might go for a quick walk."

"You and your walks," Annabel said absently, her eyes fixed on the television. "Just don't disappear for hours this time."

"Want me to come?" James asked, and looked half-relieved and half-disappointed when Grace replied, "No, it's fine—I won't be long. Just need a bit of fresh air. Millie shouldn't be up for at least another hour or so, but listen out for her, will you?"

She went into the hallway, pulled on her wellies, collected her jacket, gloves, and hat, and headed out. The sky was a strange color— almost yellow—and she sensed that the fresh snowfall they'd been warned about wasn't far away. She inhaled deeply, smelling the frosty grass and wet tarmac, feeling the cold air surging down her throat.

At the top of the hill, she turned off the road and made her way along a path of mud and flattened grass, skirting around the edge of dry stone walls. When she reached the familiar large flat stones, she sat there for a while, taking in the view. She looked across towards Lover's Leap, remembering Annabel describing it as the most haunted place on the moors. Then her mind returned again to the previous night—and Liza's urgent voice as she had confessed to Grace in the shadows of the lake.

She pictured Adam at a library computer, trying to trace his father, and knew she couldn't sit on this information. Grace was skeptical about rousing the police's interest with such a scant new lead, but they needed to know. Liza's name didn't have to come up unless they thought it was significant.

Grace jumped up from the stone slab as an idea came to her. What was stopping her from finding Adam's father herself? She could go to the library, try to retrace Adam's footsteps, and see what he might have uncovered. At least then she would have an idea of what he might have been going to tell her, the thing he'd referred to in his mysterious note.

She felt reinvigorated by this new sense of purpose, looking towards the sky and taking a few deep breaths. As she did so, the first specks of snow landed on her, sticking to her clothes and gloves. She kept her face upturned, flakes appearing out of the void above her in a soft white flurry. She spun around slowly, catching them on her tongue, feeling their frozen, gentle caress on her skin in the brief moment before they vanished.

A dog began barking nearby, and a voice said, "Having fun?"

Ben stood a short distance away, wearing a padded coat, beanie, and thick gloves. Bess was by his side, her tail wagging.

"Yes, I am," she said, smiling, feeling a glow of fresh color suffuse her cheeks.

"Merry Christmas, Grace." He came closer, until she could see small specks of snow clinging to the stubble on his chin.

"Merry Christmas," she replied, recalling him leaning over her in his car a few hours ago. It felt like a distant memory.

"What are you doing out here?" he asked.

"Oh, getting some fresh air and having a think. We all walked up here the other day, and Annabel was telling us your stories about Lover's Leap." She gestured beyond the railway line. "Is it really the most haunted spot around here, or were you having her on?"

"A bit of both, really." There was a glimmer of amusement in his eyes. "It is notorious—but the ghost stories are ancient. It's all cuckolded husbands and distressed maidens. I've spent more time there than most and I've never seen a ghost."

"Really?" she asked. "And what were you doing there?"

"Dealing with my teenage angst," he laughed. "It's an easy place to get to from the schoolhouse. There's a path that goes straight there, called the monks' trod. They're all over the moors—centuries ago the monks used them to navigate, and they were also known by smugglers bringing in contraband from the coast. The path eventually connects with this one. For a while, Claire and I would go and sit dangling our feet over the edge to smoke and complain about our family. We've always been close, although I'd stopped going there by the time Claire began taking Adam along. My next bolt-hole was one of the ruined workers' houses. By that time life was turning a bit more serious for me." He lost the smile, and as he gazed into the distance, Grace could tell that his thoughts were elsewhere. He looked back and paused, as though debating what to say. In the end, he said nothing, and as she met his eyes, she felt slightly off balance.

"I should be getting back," she said.

"I know a short cut. I'll show you." He began to walk away.

She hesitated, her mind still attuned to their conversation. She wondered what had turned him so somber, and felt a fleeting sense of disappointment that he hadn't confided in her.

Ben turned around. "Are you coming?"

"Yes," she replied hastily, snapping out of her trance and following him.

The snow's gentle fall was deceptive. Before long it flew heedlessly into her eyes, melted into cold drips that ran down her face, and soaked through her jeans. The journey seemed to be taking forever, when halfway along the path by the stone wall, they passed a gate.

Ben stopped. "Let's go through the field," he suggested, rubbing his hands together as though to warm them. "It's so much faster." He clambered over the gate. "Come on, Bess," he shouted, and the dog immediately bounded up onto the wall and down the other side.

Both of them turned to look at Grace. "Come on then," Ben urged.

"Isn't this trespassing?" she asked as she grasped the gate and started to climb, feeling awkward as she tried to swing her leg elegantly over the top—an impossible feat while wearing wellies.

"Only if they see you!" Ben replied. "And I don't think anyone else is daft enough to be out here on Christmas Day—too busy stuffing themselves with turkey and drinking themselves under the table."

His words conjured up the rich, spicy aroma of warm mulled wine, and this urged Grace onwards. She jumped down from the gate and found herself standing in a patch of sucking mud, deceptively slick. Ben grabbed her elbow, steadied her, and helped her to wade through the bog. Once clear, they all hurried across the field.

As they neared the next gate, Bess stopped and began barking, and Ben slowed beside her for a fraction of a second, turning to look behind them. Grace had kept her head down to keep the snow from getting in her eyes, but now she glanced up. Seeing Ben's alarm, she automatically twisted round to follow his stare.

Through the snow she could make out a large, shaggy-haired creature with solid, curved horns. It was ambling towards them. As they watched, it quickened its pace, some distance away yet, but getting closer much too fast for Grace's liking. Then it broke into a run.

Ben shouted, "Oh shit! Move, now!" He lifted up Bess while she was still barking, and practically threw her over the gate. Then he was by Grace's side, yelling, "You next, Grace, *hurry!*"

Her heartbeat charged into her ears like the thunderous thud of hooves. Ben's body was now close against hers, his breath warm on the back of her neck as she gripped the top beam. He pushed her, propelling her upwards, and she swung her leg frantically over the top. In her panic, she leaped rather than climbed down, landing in another patch of slippery mud. It took her legs out from beneath her so that her gloved hands and unprotected face went slap straight into it.

As Ben jumped down next to her, she struggled up onto her hands and knees, panting and gasping. Looking behind her, she saw a pair of large round eyes glaring at them through a gap in the gate, the bull snorting air heavily. Bess barked frantically, crouched with her front paws low and her hindquarters high in the air.

"Are you all right?" Ben squatted beside her.

"I'm fine. Just . . . filthy." She tried to wipe the hair from her eyes with her dirty gloves, knocking a big glob of muck from her nose as she did so.

She looked at Ben, expecting laughter, but instead saw concern. She didn't know where her giggle came from, but it began to bubble out of her until she couldn't stop. Ben looked surprised, then the creases around his eyes deepened as he joined in.

Grace surveyed her mud-splattered coat and jeans. "God, what a state," she exclaimed, wondering how it was that she was sitting in a field covered in dirt and snow, feeling the happiest she had been since she'd arrived.

"You should see your face," Ben chuckled. He offered her a hand, and she took it, pulling herself upright. Their bodies came briefly together, and Ben stepped swiftly away, bending down to reattach Bess's lead. "Come on, let's go. I need to make a phone call, then I'll come and join you for lunch."

Grace trudged after him, her mood deflating. Now she was keen to get indoors. Back at the cottage, Annabel's jaw dropped and James began laughing when they saw her.

"What the hell happened to you?" Annabel asked. "Been rolling around in a pig sty?"

"I got chased by a bull," Grace replied, then wished she hadn't, as they both looked at her incredulously, and then at each other, before they dissolved into more streams of mirth. She didn't know why she couldn't join in when she'd found it funny herself at the time. Now she muttered, "Yes, it's hilarious," and headed upstairs to get changed.

An hour later, the smell of roasting turkey wafted tantalizingly through the cottage. Grace was feeling much better after a bath and a change of clothes, and Millie had woken refreshed from her nap and was investigating more of her toys.

Annabel was up as soon as she heard the knock at the door. "I'll get it." She disappeared into the hallway, then Grace heard her exclaim, "Ben!" as though genuinely surprised to see him.

Ben caught Grace's eye as he came in, and smiled at her.

"Grace got chased by a bull this morning!" Annabel told him merrily.

"Really?" He raised his eyebrows at Grace, but said nothing more.

She was keen to change the subject. "Dinner's ready."

"I'll give you a hand, Grace," James offered.

As they concentrated on dishing up, Ben sat down on the floor, murmuring softly to Millie as he admired her presents. Annabel joined them and began to tell him about the ball.

A few minutes later, Grace and James put four plates of steaming food on the table. Grace strapped Millie into her high chair in front of her own small offering.

They took their places and started to eat. James speared a brussel sprout as he said, "So, Ben, it's been pretty handy for Grace that you've been able to help her get things moving here."

James's tone made Grace look at him sharply. Ben nodded. "Yes, lucky for her and for me—she's kept me from being at a loose end."

"Annabel tells me that you're house-sitting?" James persisted. "How long will you be here for?"

"Another few weeks," Ben replied as he poured gravy over his meal. "The owners are due back in early February."

Grace wondered if she would have finished the renovations by then. She imagined living in the village without Ben nearby, and was alarmed at how downhearted she felt. "Where will you go then?" she asked.

"Back to Australia. Pick up where I left off."

Annabel took the gravy boat from him. "And where was that?"

"I work for a small architecture firm in Sydney. I've had some time off for long service, among other things, but it finishes at the end of February." He sat back, studying them in turn. His eyes fell on James. "So what do you do?"

"I work for a Swiss bank." James straightened his shoulders as he spoke. "And spend most of my spare time on the ski slopes. I can't get enough of it. Don't suppose you have much chance to ski, living in Australia."

"Actually, there are some great spots in Victoria," Ben replied, his arm hooked casually around the back of his chair. "But I live close to Sydney and spend more of my time surfing. I'm lucky enough to have a place near the water. There's something pretty magical about catching waves. I really miss it, actually."

In the silence that followed, Annabel caught Grace's eye, raising an eyebrow almost imperceptibly, before she said, "Don't you have man-eating sharks in Australia?"

"We do," Ben grinned. "But so far I've been lucky." He looked at James and Annabel. "So how long are you two staying?"

"A few days," James said.

Grace could have sworn that Annabel tried to bat her eyelashes. "Until New Year's."

"Are you keeping an eye on the weather?" Ben asked. "Because it's forecasting snow at any time. You do know this village can easily get cut off in the snow?"

"Oh, I'm used to snow," James replied with a wave of his fork, before he turned to Grace. "Do you remember that year we stayed in the Cotswolds and it snowed the whole time? We made that snow-man and put Annabel's underwear on it."

"Yeah, I remember not talking to you both for the rest of the day," Annabel added. "That stuff cost a fortune."

"Ben has a good point, though," Grace interjected, trying to include him in the conversation. "I hope we've got everything we need."

"We bought plenty of food yesterday—we'll be fine," James said confidently. "Anyway, we could get out if we really needed to."

Ben took a sip of his beer. "I wouldn't be so sure about that, mate. Don't underestimate the weather around here—it can make things pretty hairy."

James looked irritated at being contradicted, and Grace tried to lighten the atmosphere. "All the better if they do get trapped in, Ben, because as you know there's a cellar full of crap below us that needs sorting through."

Ben laughed, while Annabel gave Grace a dirty look.

"You've not started that yet then?" Ben asked.

"No," Grace said, "it's so bloody cold."

James got up. "You'll have to show me what's down there. Perhaps you'll find something valuable—who knows, you might be sitting on a gold mine. Anyone else for seconds?"

As Grace watched him walk across to the kitchen counter, she thought briefly of the boxes waiting beneath them. Had she missed anything there? She was overtaken by an urgent need to check them again, but shook it off.

"I doubt there are any hidden gems in the cellar," she said

casually as James came back to the table, his plate replenished. "In the attic, maybe, or in here." She gestured around her, trying to quash the sense of disloyalty she felt towards Adam's family while they talked like this. "Adam thought the grandfather clock would be worth some-thing." As she spoke, she could hear it ticking steadily in the back-ground, punctuating the conversation. That was one thing she couldn't wait to be rid of. She remembered it stopping in the dead of night soon after she'd arrived. Had that been one of her strange dreams? No—she clearly recalled watching as it began working again.

"That clock is awesome," James said. "My aunt and uncle used to have a clock like that, and I loved it when they let me look inside. I wound it up for you earlier." He picked up on Grace's consternation, and glanced at the others, puzzled. "Was that the wrong thing to do?"

Ben excused himself soon after the meal, saying he didn't want to leave Bess on her own for too long. Grace and James washed up, then joined Annabel, who was applauding while Millie pulled a squawking plastic pelican around the room, its broad beak opening and shutting.

"Shall we play a game or something?" Grace asked, looking to Annabel, as it was something of a family tradition. "I've got cards—how about Hearts, or Spades, or Chase the Ace?"

"I'm too tired," Annabel moaned, and James didn't even reply.

Grace was beginning to accept that Christmas was officially over when the phone rang.

"Merry Christmas, love," her mother said when Grace picked up the phone. "Have you had a nice day?"

Grace couldn't help but acknowledge how homesick she felt upon hearing her mother's voice, but she tried to sound cheerful, not want-ing her mother to worry. They chatted inconsequentially for a while, telling each other about their days. Then her father came on the line, and after wishing her a Merry Christmas, asked, "So how are you getting on?"

"Good," Grace replied. "I had the kitchen wall knocked down last week."

"What on earth did you do that for?" He sounded horrified.

As she began to explain, she felt herself stumbling over the words. She knew him too well, and the silence on the other end of the line was a bad sign.

"I'm not sure you're fully aware of what you've taken on, Grace," he said when she'd finished. "These are big jobs—they'll all take time. Do you really want to be there for months?"

Grace felt her hackles rising. "I haven't just had the wall knocked down. You should see the amount of clearing out I've done. When that's finished I'll be able to get on with redecorating."

"Well, it's up to you." She hated the way he did this—his words offering her a choice, while his tone conveyed exactly what he thought. "But remember, after this holiday you'll be on your own. You can't expect Annabel to be driving up to see you every five minutes."

"I don't expect her to, Dad! For goodness sake! I thought you'd rung to wish us a happy Christmas, not to have a go at me."

"Calm down, love. I am wishing you Happy Christmas. I'm simply looking out for you—I don't want you to run into any trouble while you're there on your own."

"Well, it feels like you're getting at me," she said grumpily.

"I'm not. Now, have you got enough money to be getting on with?"

That question couldn't help but make Grace smile. Annabel and Grace had a joke that even if they became multimillionaires, their dad would still ask them if they had enough, as he had done when they were teenagers heading out for the evening.

"Yes, I have enough," she said, turning around to see her sister look up and grin. "Now, do you want to speak to Annabel?"

The rest of the evening passed in a weary haze of wine and television. When Grace climbed into bed, exhausted, she knew she would sleep the night.

Except she woke up three hours later, sweating, Annabel motionless beside her in the dark. The answer she'd been searching for earlier was right in front of her. She knew exactly what was troubling her about the cellar.

24

Grace crept downstairs, hoping she wouldn't wake James. There was no way this could wait till morning: despite her fears, she needed to look in the cellar right now.

Luckily James had left the TV on, so the flickering light filtered through the living-room door and flashed in staccato bursts on the passage walls. But as she got farther towards the back of the cottage, it became gloomier, the light dwindling to nothing. She ran her hands over the cellar door until she found the handle and pulled it open, hearing it creak. Then she made her careful way down the steps, engulfed in blackness, knowing that once she reached the bottom she could switch on the light.

She was jittery, jumping at every slight noise or rustle, feeling her way along the wall, nearly retreating in panic as something soft brushed against her hand, until she realized it was the belt from her robe. "Stop working yourself up," she scolded herself in a whisper.

When she reached the bottom, she felt along the wall, and flicked the light switch.

The change from total darkness to the stark white light of a bare bulb stung her eyes and left her mind reeling. Grace closed her eyes for a moment, making a conscious effort to slow her breathing, and then opened them again, squinting.

Everything was as she remembered, including the bitter cold. She headed straight for the box of Adam's personal effects—the one she knew he had brought with him from London. She began taking things out, pulling feverishly at the contents, piling them on a nearby shelf. This time she wouldn't be satisfied until she was sure she had checked everything.

Towards the bottom of the second box, she found what she was looking for. A small black plastic folder. And inside it was Adam's passport.

She pulled it out and opened the purple booklet, to double-check. There was his picture, the one that Grace had always laughingly told him looked like a police mug shot.

She stared at Adam's handsome face. A rush of tenderness weakened her legs, and she held on to a shelf to stop them from buckling. At last, this was evidence, surely, that he hadn't intended to run away? Or at least it made it less likely. But if that were so, then other possibilities, some unbearable, edged closer to being true.

Her mind swirling, she whirled around.

James was standing silently behind her.

She squealed with fright. "What the hell are you doing?" she shrieked.

"What the hell are *you* doing?" he shouted back. Barefoot and bleary-eyed, he was brandishing a large piece of wood. "For Christ's sake, Grace, you scared the life out of me. I woke up to a bloody door creaking, and then heard all this scraping and rustling. After what Annabel's been telling us, I was terrified I was about to confront the headless horseman rummaging about down here." He laughed, but when Grace didn't join in he immediately sobered up. "What's wrong?"

She shook the passport at him. "They asked me to find this last year, when they were suggesting that Adam had run away—and I couldn't. But I didn't know the bloody cellar existed then, did I? It suddenly dawned on me that I never checked the boxes he put here. Perhaps the police will take his absence more seriously now—though I somehow doubt it." She dropped her arm despondently.

"Grace," James began to rub his bare arms as he stood there in T-shirt and boxer shorts, "come upstairs and we'll talk about this. It's freezing down here."

He held out a hand. She went across and took it, and he began to lead her towards the stairs. "Hang on," she said, "we have to turn off the light."

He waited as she flicked the switch, then they edged slowly back up in the darkness. Once in the corridor, Grace dropped his hand and closed the door gently, trying to stop it from creaking.

James followed her down the hallway, but when she began to climb the stairs, heading back to bed, he said, "Grace, wait a minute."

She tried to look at him, though she could barely make out his face.

"Come and sit with me for a moment."

She went into the living room with him. He pulled her onto the sofa and unzipped his sleeping bag, covering them both with it.

"Lean on me for a while. Let yourself relax."

Grace did as he bid, and felt her eyes grow heavy. The next thing she knew she had woken up with James asleep next to her, his arm still around her. Quietly, she disentangled herself and got up. James stirred briefly as she kissed his forehead and whispered "Night," before tiptoeing from the room. Out in the hallway, the grandfather clock greeted her with its steady tick. The thought of it stopping sent her hurrying upstairs without looking to see what the time was and falling gratefully into bed next to Annabel.

Grace was woken again after what felt like just five minutes, to the sound of Millie crying. Grey light was beginning to poke through the curtains, but inside the cottage it was dim. She found Millie sitting up cuddling Mr. Pink, and Grace only needed one look at her wide-eyed tear-streaked face to know that Millie wouldn't be comforted back to sleep. She lifted her little girl out of the crib, trying to stave off her own tiredness by blinking hard and rubbing her eyes. They began to play together on the floor by the crib, but after a while Millie grew restless. Grace picked her up and tiptoed downstairs to get breakfast, trying not to wake James.

"What time is it?" James asked from the depths of the sofa.

"Too early," Grace muttered, then walked back out to check the grandfather clock, only registering the silence as she did so.

"The clock's stopped," she said anxiously. The hands were pointing to just past three.

"It must be stuck, I'll look at it later," James mumbled sleepily.

"Thanks." Grace went over to her mobile phone on the tabletop. "It's nearly eight o'clock," she said, surprised. Then she pulled back the curtain and looked out. "And I think you could say that we're snowed in."

She heard the sofa's springs creak as James pushed himself up, then he was behind her, peering through the window. "Bloody hell!"

The garden had disappeared. It looked as though someone had laid a sparkling white blanket from the level of the low garden wall right up to the cottage. The only things poking through were the tips of the taller hedges and the bare trellis arch midway along the path.

"I'll have to dig us out," James declared. "Have we got a spade somewhere?"

"I . . . I don't know," Grace said. "I didn't think about it—"

James made a noise of exasperation.

"Do we actually need to go outside?" Grace queried. "Unless you're going to shovel your way right over the top of the moors, I think it's safe to say we're stuck."

In reply, James threw himself onto a chair.

"What's the problem?" Grace asked, amused. "You're always talking about how much you love the snow."

"Yes, because in Switzerland I can ski on it," James grumbled. "It's completely different."

"You could take Millie sledding instead . . ."

"Well, we can't do anything much until we can get down the path." James began to pull on his jeans and a sweater. "I'll search around and see what I can find."

"Be my guest." Grace felt annoyed as she carried Millie across to the kitchen area and sat her in the high chair. James always had to make big issues out of little problems. Adam would have found it the perfect excuse to cuddle up in front of the television. She briefly wondered whether Ben would be shoveling snow right now.

Daylight had finally conquered the night by the time Annabel appeared downstairs. "What's that noise?" she asked, tuning in to a recurring scraping sound.

Grace went across to the window and pulled back the curtain. "James found a shovel, so he's clearing the path. I'm not sure why, but he obviously thinks it's important."

"Wow!" Annabel stared out of the window. "I don't think I've ever seen so much snow." She spun around, beaming. "Let's get our coats on and make snowmen all day, Millie." She ruffled her niece's hair, and was delighted when Millie looked up and grinned at her.

Grace laughed at them both. "Sounds great. But can you give me some help first?"

Annabel's eyes narrowed.

"Don't look at me like that. Last night I remembered I hadn't checked the boxes in the cellar for Adam's passport, and so I took a look, and sure enough—I found it."

"Really? Why on earth did he put it down there?"

"I don't know. I wish he'd told me about the damn cellar in the first place. I have no idea why he didn't."

"Maybe he thought you knew about it," Annabel suggested, shrugging.

"No, actually, he lied about it," Grace snapped, surprising herself with the ferocity of her reply. "And so I want it emptied while you two are here to help. It's too creepy to do it on my own."

"I don't believe you sometimes," Annabel muttered, flinging herself onto a chair. "Some Christmas holiday this is turning out to be. Well I'm sorry, but you can count me out—it's bloody freezing and I bet there are rats down there. Get James to bring up the boxes."

"It won't take long," Grace insisted. "And you can sit at the top and sort out the stuff. We'll get through it in no time if we all pitch in."

A few hours later, Grace felt like she was corralling unruly sheep. Annabel and James had agreed to help, but both would slip away endlessly—James to check on the football scores; Annabel for any reason that would avoid the task at hand. At least when Millie got up it meant that her enthusiastic auntie was happy to keep her entertained, leaving Grace free to go through things.

By midafternoon there were piles of full boxes and large bags destined for either the garbage or a charity shop. The cellar was now rimmed with bare, grimy shelves.

"Okay," Grace conceded, when she took stock of how much they had done. "Let's take a break."

"Finally, she lets us rest." James sat down heavily on the stairs and leaned against the wall.

"Let me tell you this before I forget," Annabel said. She patted the three boxes in front of her. "These look like they contain personal effects, letters and the like, so you'd better go through them. It's strange that they weren't in the attic with the rest."

"Perhaps Connie and Bill got too old to clamber about in the attic," Grace replied, opening one of them and rummaging inside, finding exercise books, notebooks, more photograph albums, newspaper clippings, and loose papers, all mishmashed together. She sighed. "There's so much of this stuff. I've got no idea why they held on to this." *God, it's never-ending*, she thought, and had a renewed rush of determination to harden her heart and plough through the swathe of papers. She needed to feel she was getting somewhere.

"If I take these upstairs, can you two entertain Millie for a while?" she asked them.

"Anything if it keeps me away from those damn boxes," Annabel replied, while James added, "Sure."

When Grace got into her room, she lifted the boxes one by one and tipped their contents onto the bedcovers, knowing that if she had to clear them away before she could go to sleep tonight it would make her work faster. She climbed up to sit amid the chaotic mountain of papers, and began rifling through them. Anything she wasn't interested in got tossed back into an empty crate, and she began to stack the rest in piles by her bedside, next to her neglected copy of *Rebecca*.

Her spirits sank as the collection of papers she wanted to look at more closely grew larger: bundles of letters, mainly; notepads that had been scribbled in; bank statements that she didn't feel she could throw away without checking; old greeting cards; photos, both in albums and loose; and a couple of school yearbooks that might well contain something about Adam. As she was going through them, it became clear that at least one of the boxes had contained Rachel's effects. It made her think of Connie and Bill facing the same task, whittling down their daughter's belongings to retain the official documents that proved her existence, and the photos and letters that could help them recapture Rachel, even if only for a moment, as her image or words briefly fleshed out the specter of her from the confines of memory. For all Grace knew, so many other things she had touched in the past few weeks had secrets of their own to tell, but they had died along with their keepers. All Grace could do was unwittingly dispose of the evidence.

She picked up a bundle of letters. They were written in the same handwriting, and she plucked one from the top and opened it. Without knowing the contents she couldn't determine their value, but she still felt as though she were snooping.

> *Dear Mum and Dad,*
>
> *I hope you are both all right. I know you will still be getting over the shock, but* <u>please</u>*, please keep writing and telling me your news. I am doing fine in York. I've found a flat, and there's plenty of space for the baby, who is kicking me all the time now—it's a strong little thing, that's for sure.*
>
> *When you see Meredith, please could you tell her that I'm sorry I didn't say good-bye. I've included a letter for you to pass on to her. I miss you all very much. I know it's*

hard, but I'm sure I am doing the right thing. Why don't you come and see us when the baby arrives?

> *All my love,*
> *Rachel*

Grace plucked the next one from the pile.

Dear Mum and Dad,

It's good to hear that they have fixed the road—it's hard enough driving up the bank without potholes to avoid! I'm glad to hear that the show went well, too, Mum, I'm sure you did a brilliant job of organizing it.

The whole city is talking about the Viking house found under the old Craven's factory. We went for a walk over there yesterday, but there's not much to see at the site. Plenty of people trying to have a look, though.

Thanks for the money, but please don't feel you have to keep sending it—I'm doing fine on social security, and I have earned a bit more doing some casual typing work— finally, all those hours practicing are paying off It's good work, because I can do it when Adam sleeps I'm lucky that at the moment he's a good sleeper in the day, though he keeps me up all night long sometimes! I can't wait for you to meet him—come and see us soon.

> *All my love,*
> *Rachel*

Grace stared out of the bedroom window at the wintry afternoon twilight. From the letters, it sounded as though Connie and Bill had been trying to support their daughter, however upset they must have been when she had run away pregnant. It was strange, seeing Rachel's handwriting; trying to imagine her in a tiny flat in York, caring for a new baby while working to make ends meet. Grace had conjured up Rachel so vividly that she felt a strong bond with the woman. However, these letters reminded Grace that she didn't really know anything about the flesh-and-blood person who had written them, the woman whose clothes Grace and Annabel had danced in.

Grace glanced at a few more pages to find that they contained similar themes. She would have to go through them one at a time, but it could probably wait. It seemed unlikely that Jonny's name was going to come up. Grace wasn't even sure how much Adam's grandparents had known of the boy who had gotten their daughter into trouble, but presumably since Jonny had emigrated there wasn't a lot left to say, and everyone would have had no choice but to move on.

She sat for a while, considering what to do next. If she didn't uncover any evidence of Jonny among these papers, she was going to have to look at other options. She could try to call the library tomorrow, but suspected it would be closed for the Christmas holiday.

Deep in thought, she went down the stairs and discovered Millie holding a biscuit in each hand, a half-empty packet on the table. "She won't eat her dinner now!" Grace said jokingly as she stroked Millie's hair.

"Oh, sorry, I didn't think of that." Annabel put the packet on one side. "Listen, I was wondering about going to see Meredith while we're snowed in. If I give her a call, maybe James can dig me up as far as the schoolhouse so I can interview her. What do you reckon?"

"Er, excuse me—I don't know about that," James interrupted. "Have you seen how high the snow is?"

"It'll be better in the morning," Annabel replied confidently.

"Fine by me," Grace said. "In fact, I might come with you." A new awareness reinvigorated her. There was another way to learn more about Jonny, after all. It was Meredith who had been able to tell her the most about him so far. Perhaps if Grace pressed her further she might remember more. Grace couldn't help but feel that locating Jonny was pivotal—that if she found him, she would find answers.

As her mind slowed, she became aware of the room again, and noticed that they were accompanied by a steady ticking.

"Did you fix the clock?" She looked at James.

He appeared confused. "No, I forgot all about it."

Grace turned to Annabel, who shook her head. She stiffened, then walked out into the hallway.

The pendulum was swinging steadily back and forth. Grace's head began to throb. "When did it start again?" she asked as she came back into the living room.

Annabel shrugged and James said, "I didn't notice, sorry."

Grace glanced at her watch, and frowned. "It's telling the right time."

"Perhaps it hadn't stopped after all," James suggested.

"You do remember it stopping, don't you?" Grace pressed him.

"Yeah, I think so." But he didn't look sure.

"Think, James—do you or don't you?"

She saw James exchange a look with Annabel, before he answered, "Don't worry, Grace, I remember."

25

Grace held the phone to her ear, irritated that she'd been placed on hold for over five minutes now. She was about to give up when a voice said, "I'm sorry, Constable Barton is on holiday until New Year's. Unless it's an emergency . . . ?"

"No," Grace said miserably. "It can probably wait."

She felt incredibly frustrated as she hung up. However, she had one more option. She searched around for the scrap of paper Niall had given her, and dialed the number.

"Hello?"

"Niall, it's Grace—Grace Lockwood."

"Grace! How are you?" He sounded surprised to hear from her.

"Fine. I'm sorry to ring you over the holidays, but I need your advice." Her foot began tapping out a nervous tic as she talked. "I just tried to ring Constable Barton but he's away till after New Year's, and I don't want to sit on my hands till then. A few things have happened over the last few days, concerning Adam's disappearance . . ."

"Go on." Niall sounded intrigued.

"Well, first of all, I went to the Christmas Eve ball at Freeborough Hall—and an old friend of Adam's came up to me and said she had seen him in the library at Ockton, the day before he disappeared. Apparently he told her he was looking for his dad. Adam's father was a man called Jonny Templeton—he abandoned Adam's mother when she got pregnant and moved overseas with his family. So I thought that might be significant . . ." She took a deep breath. "And then I found his passport. Down in the cellar. Adam had put some boxes there when we moved in, and one of them had his passport in it . . ."

"Didn't the police search there last year?" Niall asked.

"It was locked, and I thought it was only a cupboard back then I think one of the men that conducted the search asked me for the key, but I didn't know where to find it."

"Well, I'm amazed. They shouldn't have overlooked that."

Grace furrowed her brow—surely that was beside the point. "It doesn't matter now. I just want to know if this changes anything, with the investigation."

She was acutely aware of the silence on the other end of the line. "Doesn't this give us some new leads . . . ?" she pleaded. There was a tiny note of hysteria in her voice; she could hear it.

"I'm not sure. Look, you need to talk to Barton. And if the woman you spoke to can come down to the station, too, and tell them the same thing she told you, that'd be the best way of getting their attention."

Grace's optimism disappeared. "I'm not sure she will. She said she hadn't come forward earlier because she doesn't want to be involved . . ."

"Is that right? And did she say why?" The suspicion was clear in his voice.

"No."

SARA FOSTER

"Grace, perhaps you should think about your loyalty to this woman. She can talk to the police in confidence. No one else needs to know."

"In that case I'll speak to her again, see what she says."

"Right then." Niall sounded as though he were about to hang up.

"Isn't there anything else we can do?" Grace was aware of how desperate she sounded, and she hated it. Against her will, she was getting sucked back into the emotional turmoil of the last year.

She heard him sigh. "Remind me of Adam's father's name again?"

"Jonathan —Jonny—Templeton—I think he grew up on a farm around here."

"Well, I'll see what I can find out—might not be for a few days."

"Fine," Grace said dejectedly. "Thank you."

When she came off the phone she headed downstairs to rejoin the others. Millie was playing with her favorite stacking blocks, while James and Annabel were bickering about what to watch on television. Being cooped up wasn't suiting them very well.

"I just asked Niall's advice about the passport," she said. "He didn't sound that interested . . . which was pretty much what I expected." She sat down, trying hard to suppress her exasperation. "Adam didn't simply disappear, I'm sure of that. But I have no idea what happened. . . . How am I ever going to get to the bottom of it?" With fumbling fingers, she angrily wiped away the tears before they had a chance to fall.

"Now listen to me, Grace," Annabel said, coming across and putting an arm around her sister. "This place is no good for you. It's going to drive you insane. You can't spend your time obsessing about Adam—because, for whatever reason, he's gone, and there's no sign at all that he's about to come back. James and I will have to head off soon . . ."

188

Annabel hesitated and looked at James, who nodded.

Grace sat, waiting for the inevitable.

"We think you should come with us," James said. "We can't leave you up here all alone, Gracie. It's not right at all. It would feel like abandoning you, and this place is far too . . . well . . . remote," he finished.

"Mum and Dad are really worried about you," Annabel added.

Grace ran a hand through her hair. "Look, I know you're saying this because you love me, but I need to finish what I've started. It won't take long."

Annabel leaned back and blew out a long, frustrated breath. "Grace, this village is sucking the life out of you—you're so serious all the time."

Grace had had enough. She stood up. "I don't think it's this place, actually. I think I sobered up a bit when my husband disappeared on me and my child." She went across to Millie and picked her up to cuddle her, upset when Millie screamed and struggled until she was put back down.

"Grace, listen to us," James insisted. "You and Millie need looking after, and there's no chance of that while you live up here. Annabel's right, this isn't good for you. Where's the fun-loving girl we used to know, who could barely stand a day without going somewhere different or trying something new? Just look at yourself right now."

"I wouldn't be feeling like this if you two could start supporting me instead of antagonizing me," Grace retorted. "And I think you have forgotten that I have a baby now—much more has changed in my life than just my location. Besides, you live in Switzerland—I'll never see you, James, even if I do move back to London. What kind of support is that?"

"I'm thinking of moving back," he replied.

"Oh." She looked at him, unsure of what to say—they were getting completely sidetracked.

"Listen, I'm not isolated . . ." she said testily, trying to get the discussion back on course. "I've got Ben, and Meredith, and Claire, and Emma . . ."

Annabel threw her hands up in the air. "For God's sake, Grace. You hardly know any of them!"

They all glared at one another.

"I'm going for a walk," Grace told them defiantly.

Annabel shook her head then turned away. "Of course you are, Grace. That's your solution for everything nowadays."

Grace was already on her way out. "Just mind Millie for me," she called irritably over her shoulder. "I won't be long."

By the time she reached her front gate, she could feel the tears streaking down her face. Why did everyone she loved want to make things so much harder? James and Annabel's attitude was really getting to her. Life wasn't always about taking the easy option: sometimes there were things that needed to be done.

She stomped up the road, the hardened snow crunching under her feet, until she reached Feathery Jack's place. The chimney was puffing as usual, and in the front garden two small barn owls sat together on one perch. They barely moved, only the occasional twist of their heads signaling that they were alive. Sturdy leather straps were looped around their legs, and Grace felt sorry for them. She walked closer to the fence, glancing at their heart-shaped faces, their speckled breasts, the sharp hooks of their talons. The pure white among their dappled feathers stood out against the greying crust of snow.

"Come on over, then, lass."

The voice came from the doorway, and then a gaunt old man

appeared, beckoning her closer. His face was a scrunch of wrinkled skin beneath tufts of white hair. He wore a tweed jacket a few sizes too big for him, and his trousers were tied tight around his ankles with string. A pipe dangled from his mouth, jiggling up and down as he moved. He came across and opened the gate for her, and she followed him towards the owls. "Stroke her on her belly, like." He looked expectantly at Grace. She tentatively touched the owl's soft feathers. Its beak looked razor sharp, but the owl sat stoically and didn't move.

She stood back. "I'm Grace, I live at Hawthorn Cottage."

He gave no indication that he'd heard her. Instead he went back into the cottage for a moment, then came out holding something small, which he offered to one of the owls. It was snatched in an instant from his outstretched fingers. As the bird gripped the item in its talon and began to tear at it, Grace saw it was a dead mouse. She watched as skin was ripped away to reveal raw red flesh, feeling revolted.

"Er, thank you!" she said after a while, unable to bear it any longer. The old man didn't even acknowledge her, heading back towards his cottage again.

She let herself out through the gate, unsure whether to go home to try and make peace, or carry on walking. As she wavered, the door to the redbrick house opened, and Ben emerged with Bess on a lead. He raised a hand when he saw her, and then did the same to Jack, who was heading back across his garden. The old man called, "Now then," as he offered the second owl a dead mouse.

"I was going to come and see you later," Ben said as he drew near. "To find out when you want to start work again on your cottage?"

Grace smiled. "As soon as possible, but I think I need to wait until the others have left. It's far too crowded in there at the moment."

Her face or voice must have reflected her downcast thoughts, as Ben asked, "Everything all right?"

"No," she said. "Not really." She bit back the tears, feeling foolish, not wanting to cry in front of him.

"Would you like to take a walk with me and Bess? You don't have to talk if you don't want to. We'll just keep you company."

"That would be good. Though I can't leave Millie for too long."

"Don't worry—we weren't going far anyway. Perhaps we won't go through the fields this time, eh?"

As she laughed despite herself, she saw the lines around his eyes deepen as he grinned.

They were only gone for half an hour, but Grace felt so much better on her return to the cottage. They had walked in silence for a while, then Ben had begun to talk about the plans for the renovations, what they should do next. She had confessed her worries about the time it might take, and he had reassured her, saying that once they got started and she could see it all unfolding she'd feel a lot better.

When she got home, however, her mood came crashing down again. Millie was fractious and clung to her. Annabel took herself upstairs while James fixed them all lunch. Grace tried to talk to him but he gave her one-word answers, and she could feel the anger radiating from him even though his back was turned. She wondered if he was still upset at their earlier disagreement, but whatever it was, nothing could shake him out of it.

In the evening, after Millie had gone to bed, they got out a deck of cards and went through the motions, but no one had their heart in it. Grace tried to tell them about her encounter with Feathery Jack and his owls, but could see they weren't interested. She was debating whether she could excuse herself for bed at eight o'clock without inviting a barrage of sarcasm when, without warning, they were plunged into blackness.

"What the hell . . . ?" Annabel cried.

"I've seen the fuse box down in the cellar." Grace sighed, thinking that it was the perfect end to the day. "I'll get a flashlight and check it out."

"I'll come with you," she heard James say, and then there came the sound of his chair scraping along the floor as he stood up.

Grace collected the flashlight, and they made their way to the cellar. She went gingerly down the steps, feeling James close behind her. At the bottom, she directed the beam towards the wall, shining it along until she located the box. "Right," she said, "the switch should be in there . . ."

"Wait a minute, Grace," James said. She swung around, and he took the flashlight from her. She briefly made out his eyes in the dim light, the contrast between the white sclerae and dark irises. Then she felt his fingers brush her cheek, and his lips were pressing against hers.

Grace was stunned. James took this as a welcome sign, and dropped the flashlight, hands cupping her face now, kissing her harder. As he wrapped his arms around her, pressing her into him, her body began to crave this physical contact, and she collapsed against him, kissing him back. He was so solid, so reassuring. In the dark it might not be James. It could be anyone—and the tremble that ran through her had a thrill of desire in it. She was dissolving, becoming a million tangled threads of sensation, when the lights snapped back on.

And something else clicked into place in her head.

James opened his eyes, as Grace watched him with the horrible realization that their friendship had just turned in on itself. She saw the small flicker of his eyes trying to reach her, searching for somewhere he might comfortably settle within her gaze; and the dull veils of disappointment that descended as he found none. His whole body seemed to pull itself into a stiffer pose with one enormous effort of will, and he bent down to pick up the dropped flashlight. Grace knew they had just lost something between them that might never be found again.

"Come on." He headed for the stairs without looking back, and she followed him.

Upstairs, Annabel looked bemusedly at both their faces. "What happened?"

"The lights came on before we even touched the box," Grace said.

"Really?" Annabel glanced around. "Perhaps this cottage does have a ghost, after all—switching the lights on and off and stopping and starting the clock."

"Don't say that."

Annabel saw Grace's face and laughed. "Come on, I was joking. Don't get paranoid on me. Now, where were we?"

James picked up his cards, took a brief look at them, and threw them back on the table. "I'm done," he said. "Think I'll have an early night. It's time I went home—I've got a long drive tomorrow."

Annabel stared at him in astonishment, then at Grace for an explanation.

Grace pursed her lips, and glanced away.

They left James buried under a duvet on the sofa, and went up to bed. They both got ready in silence and then Grace put out the light. She lay there, knowing Annabel was awake.

"Something happened between you two just then," Annabel said.

Grace didn't reply.

"You're all over the place, Grace. You have to make up your mind what you want before we can help you."

Grace heard Annabel roll over, and gathered that was her sister's way of saying good night.

26

James was up and ready to leave by the time Grace headed downstairs with Millie the next morning. She put Millie on the floor, and then looked at him, weighing up how much she dared to say. "Don't leave like this," she pleaded.

James came across to her and stroked her cheek, his face so forlorn that it made her want to cry. "It's been lovely spending Christmas with you, Grace," he said. "But nothing's ever going to change, is it?"

He knelt on the ground next to Millie. "Bye, little lady."

Millie crawled rapidly over to Grace and clung to her mother's leg.

"I'm always here for you," he told her fiercely, getting to his feet. He picked up his bags and walked towards the door. "Say good-bye to Annabel for me."

And then he let himself out.

Grace stood by the door, using all her strength to resist the urge to follow him. She knew it would be for her own comfort, and would intimate to James that she wanted something more than his friendship. It wasn't fair to do that to him. So she listened to his car starting up and driving off, the engine noise getting fainter and fainter until it petered out. Then she sat down, feeling bereft, studying the frost that had formed intricate patterns on the window.

Annabel appeared moments later. "Has James gone already?" she asked in surprise. "I heard his car."

Grace nodded. "He said to say good-bye."

Annabel had softened this morning. She perched on the arm of Grace's chair. "What happened?"

"He tried to kiss me last night . . ."

"Really? I thought he was over all that . . ." She leaned back and blew out her breath.

They sat without speaking for a little while, then Annabel sprang up. "Jeez, how could I have been so stupid? I'm running through so many things in my head right now, and seeing them differently."

"Really?" Grace asked. "Like what?"

"Well, like yesterday, for one. He followed you outside, a few minutes after you left—and came back in looking really annoyed, saying he'd seen you walking off with Ben."

Grace felt obliged to explain. "I met him when I went out, and he offered to walk with me . . ."

Annabel said nothing in reply. Grace couldn't decipher her expression.

"Bel, are you interested in Ben . . . ?"

Annabel looked at her, amused. "Of course not," she said. "He's just the most handsome bloke around here to have some fun with. Anyway, he lives in Australia, Grace—I'm all for long-distance romance, but that's taking it a bit far."

They were interrupted by a loud crash. James marched into the living room, leaving the front door wide open, an icy blast of air rushing through the cottage. His face was an angry red.

"The road is coated in black ice—the bloody car keeps skidding on the damn hill. I can't even get out of this sodding place . . ."

"You'll never get past the schoolhouse," Annabel said. "It's really steep."

There was a rap on the door, and a moment later Ben poked his head into the living room. "I heard you having trouble out there, mate," he said, looking at James. "Can I give you a hand? If you're able to turn the car around I'll tow you up this way. It's not as steep—you can still get onto the motorway, it's just a bit of a longer way round."

James muttered a curse, and stormed out again. Ben looked across at the two women in confusion, and then followed James.

Annabel went over to the window, Grace behind her. Soon after the men disappeared, they heard the distant noises of engines, then saw Ben's Land Rover go past, closely followed by James's rented Passat, both men staring grimly ahead.

"Poor James," Annabel said, one eyebrow raised, and then collapsed in laughter. Grace joined in, but it felt more like a necessary release than true mirth.

When Annabel sobered, she patted Grace's arm. "Don't worry, Grace, he'll be fine—he loves you too much just to disappear out of your life."

Annabel hadn't seen his crushed expression last night, Grace thought, but she hoped her sister was right. Then she registered what Annabel had said.

He loves you too much just to disappear out of your life.

Had Adam not loved her enough? When all was said and done, was that it? Should she be trying to come to terms with it and move on, rather than dredging through the past like this?

It would mean letting go of her faith in him. Was she ready to do that? What if one day, against all the odds, he reappeared, and after he explained, she would understand?

But she didn't really believe it would happen. Such ideas might release her fears for a while, but in the long term she was binding herself to empty promises. Because if she really knew Adam as well as she thought, then the only reason he wouldn't come back was if he couldn't.

27

By the time they walked up to the schoolhouse to see Meredith, the snow had receded to the point where they could crunch through it in their Wellingtons; but now it glittered with crystals, forming patches of slick ice, and it took them twice as long to reach the gravel drive as it had done the last time. Grace was glad they had taken Millie in the stroller, as it was slightly less precarious than carrying her.

"Meredith definitely agreed to this?"

"Relax, Grace, she was fine about it," Annabel replied, trudging along next to her.

Before they'd even turned off the road, they could hear children squealing. As they watched, three boys raced into view, padded out in thick coats, hats, scarves, and gloves. They stopped their chase for a moment, gaping at Grace and Annabel.

"Is your grandma here?" Grace asked, at which the youngest boy came over, took her by the hand, and pulled her along towards the side of the house, leaving Annabel and Millie behind.

"No!" Grace said in protest, having to run to keep up, "I think she'd rather we knocked." But the child just giggled, and then burst through a door into a large kitchen. For a brief moment Grace hoped she might be able to sneak out again, but a couple she had never seen before had abruptly curtailed their conversation and turned to stare.

"Sorry," Grace said, as the boy who had brought her disappeared through another door. "I was looking for Meredith."

"Ah," said the woman, coming forward with her hand outstretched. "You must be Annabel. Mum said you were coming. I'm Veronica, her eldest, and this is my husband Steve."

Veronica was wearing jeans and a sweater, but Steve was in a suit and tie, as though he had just come from work. As he came across to shake Grace's hand, Meredith's dog Pippa barged through the inner door. The animal flew across the room, jumping up at Grace and sending her staggering backwards beneath its weight. Grace tried to catch the dog's paws to steady herself, but she was pushed out of the kitchen door into the garden, landing with a thump on the snow.

Annabel rounded the corner with Millie, as Steve rushed outside and grabbed the dog's collar. "Pippa, come here," he ordered, leading her back indoors.

"Are you all right?" Veronica asked apologetically, offering Grace a hand up. "I'm sorry. Bobby shouldn't have let her out."

"I'm fine," Grace said when she was on her feet, dusting herself off. "I'm Grace. This is Annabel." She looked towards Annabel to find that her sister was almost doubled up laughing, and gave her a pretend scowl. "And this is my daughter, Millie."

Millie was leaning forward in the stroller, her mouth hanging open as she looked between her mother and the door where the dog had disappeared.

"Come on in," Veronica said. "We'll give Mum a shout. Hasn't this weather been awful? Mind you, it keeps the kids busy—they've been out playing in it all day."

Once they were inside, Steve pointed to an open bottle of wine. "Can I get you both a drink?"

"One of those would be lovely," Annabel agreed.

"Water's fine for me, thanks," Grace said. "Did you all have a good Christmas?"

"Great, great," Veronica replied. "The snow's made it difficult to get back to Ockton, so we've been staying here. I don't think Mum was banking on us all being here for so long, but she's coping very well."

"She loves it," Steve said. "I've given her a shout, she'll be here in a second."

At that moment, Meredith appeared. As usual, the older woman had composed her expression to one of courteous welcome, and it was impossible to tell if there was genuine feeling behind it.

"Hello, Meredith," Annabel said, but Meredith was looking at Grace.

"I didn't know you were coming, Grace."

Grace was caught off guard—was she not welcome now? "I wanted a word with you."

The older woman's eyebrows rose a fraction. "Come through to the living room, then," she said.

Grace unbuckled Millie from her stroller, and followed Annabel through the house. They entered a cozy living room where a fire was blazing. Pippa sat by the hearth, and began to get up as they approached, until Meredith commanded, "Stay." The dog lay back down again and put her head on her paws.

Meredith made a formidable matriarch, Grace thought. Not someone to get on the wrong side of. She hadn't seen any photos of Ben around the place, and wondered how his mother felt about his return to the village.

Meredith invited them to sit on a sofa, and perched on a chair, facing them. Grace had brought a few small board books to keep Millie entertained, and now she sat her daughter on her lap and handed her the pile.

"Right," Meredith said, "I'm happy to answer questions, Annabel, but I don't want my photograph taken."

"All right then," Annabel agreed, fishing a notepad and pen from her bag. "I'll find something else." She looked beyond Meredith for a moment. "That's a really unusual fireplace."

Grace looked at the tall post which was standing beside the fireplace, strange markings carved into the top.

"That's a witching post," Meredith said, without turning around. She looked at the sisters, registering their apprehensive glances. "My grandfather knocked down some crumbling old cottages that had been here for centuries when he built this house. The witching post was found in one and he set it into the fireplace—he was too superstitious not to."

"And what is a witching post?" Annabel asked, staring spellbound at the hearth.

"There are various legends—often to do with them offering protection from witches," Meredith told them. "Although I've also heard they marked safe places to hold Catholic Mass, back in the 1600s when you could be killed for it. But you're here to ask me about Timmy . . ."

"Yes." Annabel shifted in her seat. "So, you say you have the ghost of a young child living with you?"

"We *do* have Timmy's ghost living with us," Meredith replied sternly.

"Have you ever seen him?"

"No. But as I told you before, two of my girls have—and I'm

sure they'll tell you about it if you ask them. I've only heard the banging of doors, and a child's laughter, which are the more obvious indications of his presence . . . but there are subtle things, too—usually items being moved around in certain rooms. And he also has a fondness for playing with the time on our mantelpiece clock."

Grace started upon hearing this, and caught Meredith's eye briefly, before Annabel diverted their attention, asking, "When was the first time you became aware of his presence?"

"There have been stories in my family for years," Meredith told them, "but I never experienced him as a young child. He became more active in the seventies . . . my father always said it was because . . ." Meredith stopped.

"Because . . . ?" Annabel encouraged.

". . . Because I had young children in the house," Meredith finished, looking briefly at her hands as she spoke, then back at Annabel. "Perhaps my brood reminded him of when the place was a school, and he hoped to join in with their games."

Grace looked down at Millie, who was still busy with her books. She was glad Millie wouldn't understand the topic of conversation.

"And when was the last time anyone saw him?" Annabel asked.

"It was when Jenny was a child. She was playing in her room and saw a young boy standing in the doorway, watching her. But she wasn't frightened."

"No one's seen him since?"

"No, Annabel, I'm afraid not."

"So can you describe what it's like, living with a ghost?"

Meredith gave a weary sigh. "It's like living without a ghost, except for a few unexpected bumps and bangs now and again, and having to hunt for your pens or papers because the little scamp has moved them."

"It doesn't scare you?"

Meredith gave a tight smile. "No, it doesn't. It's probably the least of my worries, in fact. Sorry."

Annabel sighed. "Well, if there's anything else you think of that might be interesting—now or later—could you let me know?"

"Yes, of course."

"And would you mind if I call again if I have any more questions?"

"That's fine." Meredith got to her feet. "Now, I'd better check how the cooking is going. Would you like a word with Veronica, while she's here?"

"Yes, please," Annabel perked up, but before Meredith could leave, Grace set Millie on the floor and stood up. "Actually, Meredith, I have something to ask you as well—on a different subject."

Meredith stopped in her tracks and turned slowly back around.

"I'm trying to trace Jonny Templeton," Grace explained. "Can you tell me where he lived before he moved to Australia?"

"Of course," Meredith said, and Grace thought she heard a trace of disdain in her voice. "Gilldale—a little village near Ockton. His family had a farm there called Riverview. His sister didn't go to Australia with the family, she got married to an Ockton man and moved into town. I think she still lives there. She might be able to help you."

"Great—do you know her name?"

"Josephine," Meredith replied. "I'll let you know if I think of anything else, shall I?"

Grace nodded. "Thank you for your help."

"I'll ask Veronica to come in now," Meredith said over her shoulder as she left the room.

While they waited, it was clear to Grace that her sister had been riled by Meredith's offhand manner. Annabel looked like she were about to start talking, but Grace muttered, "Not now." A few moments later, a face poked hesitantly around the door.

"Mum said you wanted to see me?"

"Yes." Annabel indicated the sofa opposite her with a wave of her pad. "I'd love to ask you a few questions—about Timmy."

Veronica regarded them worriedly.

"The ghost?" Annabel prompted.

Veronica closed the door gently behind her and sat down. "Look, Annabel, this is a bit embarrassing—what's Mum told you?"

"That you and Jenny saw Timmy as children."

Veronica seemed sheepish. "Okay, please don't tell Mum this . . . but . . . we made it up. We wanted attention . . . If we'd known Mum would tell these stories until the end of time, we might have thought twice. I'm not saying he doesn't exist, but I don't think either of us wants to start talking about him with a journalist. Can you drop it? I'm really sorry."

Annabel sat back and closed her eyes for a moment. "Don't worry, I'll work something else out."

Grace could see that her sister was inwardly seething. She sat there embarrassed, as Veronica asked, "Would you like to stay for another drink?"

Before Annabel could say anything, Grace answered, "No, it's fine, we need to get back for lunch. Thanks anyway."

Veronica showed them out. They set off in silence, but as soon as they were away from the house Annabel blurted, "Well, that's my story down the toilet."

"Come on, Bel, there are loads of ghost stories around here. You'll just have to think of a new angle."

"That's not the point," Annabel grumbled, and they lapsed back into silence.

A few minutes later, Grace saw Jenny and Claire crossing the bridge and heading up the hill towards them. She wondered if they had been to see their brother, and was about to give them a wave, when Claire looked up and saw them, then threaded her arm through Jenny's. There was something out of place about the gesture, Grace thought. Something that made her keep her arm by her side as they got closer. When they passed one another, Claire gave a cheerful hello, but both women kept up their stride.

"That was a bit odd," Grace said as soon as they were out of earshot.

"What?" Annabel asked distractedly. "Oh . . . It was fine, Grace, stop being so suspicious of everything. Come on, let's hurry up and get back. I need to see what I can do to rescue this piece. I wish I hadn't told the features editor about it now. I'm going to look like a total idiot."

They carried on, occasionally having to clutch at one another to steady themselves when they hit a patch of slick ice. When they reached the bridge at the dip of the road, Grace took the opportunity to glance back up the hill. Jenny was looking around, too. A second later Claire followed her sister's gaze, said something, and Jenny turned away.

28

"I'm going to take a drive," Annabel announced the next day. A snowplow had been through, and the roads were clear, the remaining snow piled in dirty grey-brown heaps on the sides. "Do you remember me telling you about the pub Ben took me to, the one with the ghost chair? I'm going to have a word with the landlord and see where I go from there."

"Ben might have more ideas, too," Grace said. "Or what about Feathery Jack? He looks like a man who'd have plenty of stories to tell. You could even feed his birds a mouse or two while you're with him."

Annabel gave her sister a sarcastic grin. "No thank you. Perhaps I'll flick through Connie's book, though, see if I can come up with anything that way."

When Annabel had left, Grace decided to go and see Ben to discuss restarting work on the cottage. She carried Millie up the lane, her arms aching, hoping it wouldn't be long before her daughter began to walk.

"Grace!" Ben appeared pleased to see her as he opened the door, which brightened her mood. He invited her in, though she noticed he shut the door to the living room before she walked past, and ushered her into the kitchen. *Was that deliberate, she wondered, or am I becoming completely paranoid about everyone here?*

"As you know, James has gone now," she told him, "so we could do a bit more work downstairs. I'd like to get on with it."

"Sure," he agreed. "Why don't I take a look at some of the smaller jobs while Annabel is still with you? Have you decided what kind of cabinets you'll get for the kitchen, or sorted out the flooring?"

"I haven't even thought about it," Grace admitted. "But I'll make a start today. I'll take Millie into town."

"It's a good time to shop with the sales on," Ben agreed. "I'll come around tomorrow morning and we'll go from there."

When he showed her out, Grace glanced again at the closed living room door. She was sure they were becoming friends—and yet she was convinced he was withholding things, despite all he had told her.

She tried to push away her doubts as she walked back down the lane. Adam's disappearance had made her too distrustful—she had to stop approaching everyone as though something mysterious or sinister might be going on beneath the surface. She couldn't live the rest of her life with a prevailing sense of suspicion.

Grace was determined to make it into town—she knew she'd feel better when she was progressing again with work on the cottage. She packed a lunch for Millie, then headed for the car. She hadn't used it since before Christmas, and was thankful that the engine started right up. She switched the heating on full blast while she was strapping Millie in, then traipsed around the outside of the vehicle, clearing the windows of the remaining snow and ice.

Once they set off, Millie began to fuss before they'd even gotten up the hill, and Grace fervently hoped she wouldn't keep it up for the whole journey. The car only warmed up properly as they reached the top of the moors. Grace was beginning to settle into the drive, when her eye caught some marks on the windshield.

She looked closer. There were greasy letters smeared on the glass, only just visible.

As she tried to make out what they said, she lost concentration and had to swerve to avoid running off the road. She slowed to a crawl and then pulled over, still scanning the windshield.

Whatever it was, it had been written on the outside. She got out and went around to the front of the car, standing back so she could see.

Running the length and width of her windshield were five large letters. Very faint, but there nonetheless. Spelling out one word.

LEAVE.

Fear and bewilderment made her insensible for a moment, and she cast around wildly as though someone might be standing nearby. All she saw was flat, desolate moorland. She collected a rag from the car and scrubbed furiously at the letters until she couldn't see them any longer. Back inside, she switched on the windshield wipers, briefly mesmerized by the tick tock of their rhythmic sway.

She had a flash of longing for another life. She wanted to feel carefree and safe. She wanted to sit in a café for a long, lazy afternoon, drinking hot chocolate and reading her book without interruption. She wanted to take a holiday and lie in sweltering golden sunshine or swim in a refreshing sea. She wanted her mind to stop whirring. She wanted to feel like herself again, and not this frightened stranger.

Millie's restless cries reached into her daydreams and drew her back to the present. In the cold white light her hands looked grey-blue, curved rigid around the steering wheel. She hunted in her bag and handed Millie a biscuit, then sat for a moment in indecision. She wasn't sure she wanted to drive while she felt so frightened, but as she looked behind her, towards the village, she knew she didn't want to go there either.

She put the car into gear and set off again, trying to figure out who might have done such a petty, cruel thing. Her mind went first of all to James. Had he been so vindictive as to write that on her windshield as he left? Why would he have gone to the trouble? Unless he'd been trying to scare her into leaving? It was a pretty outrageous thing to do, but then she'd never seen him so angry.

Or was it Annabel, playing a joke—or perhaps both of them in it together, thinking that if they couldn't reason her away from the village, they could spook her out.

Then she pictured Meredith and her cool, indifferent manner. Her children were all staying for Christmas: Liza with her secrets; Jenny with her standoffishness. Claire and Veronica appeared pretty normal, but Grace hardly knew them. She couldn't imagine any of them walking deliberately down from the schoolhouse to scrawl a word on her car, but then she'd seen Jenny and Claire coming from that direction just yesterday.

What about Ben? After all, she was convinced he wasn't being entirely honest with her. It was Ben who walked past her car each time he came to work. She had trusted him enough to let him into the cottage, and their lives. But what if her instincts about him were wrong?

And there was Emma's son, who looked ghoulish and might think it a good joke, scaring the new neighbor. Or Feathery Jack, who lived in a world of screeching owls and dead mice. He'd seemed cordial enough, but perhaps he didn't want a newcomer in the village.

You've just named the whole of Roseby, she told herself. *Who have you left out? Meredith's dog? Timmy the ghost?* She laughed, but it felt uncomfortably close to hysteria. Perhaps Annabel and James were right—perhaps this place was getting to her more than she realized.

29

Grace got back to the cottage a few hours later, as dusk began to fall. She opened the door with Millie half-asleep in her arms, and was about to call hello, but stopped as she heard Annabel talking. She didn't mean to eavesdrop, but she couldn't help but hear what Annabel was saying.

"Don't worry, I'll make the deadline . . . I got some good stuff today, so I'll write it up quickly." There was a pause, then, "Really? Oh, that's so exciting, I can't believe I'll miss it. I don't think we're doing anything for New Year's—Grace has barely mentioned it. I'm stuck here in this crappy cottage, freezing my arse off. My sister seems obsessed with the place, and it's beginning to freak me out—"

Grace pushed open the living room door with a bang and saw Annabel's shock turn to dismay. "Zoe, I'll have to call you back," she said, and hung up. She came across. "Look, Grace, I'm sorry—I didn't mean . . ."

"No one is forcing you to stay," Grace told her grimly. "Why don't you go if you hate it that much?"

"What is your problem, Grace? I'm not leaving you . . ."

"Annabel, I'm thirty-two, I don't need a sodding babysitter, thank you. Just go. If that's how you really feel then I'm probably better off without you."

Annabel's temper snapped. "Oh, is that so? Fine. If I'm not needed then I'll get my things," she said, and barged past Grace, running up the stairs.

Grace set Millie in her high chair and went to the cupboard, ignoring her unsteady fingers as she collected a jar of food. She was watching Millie eat when she heard her sister clomping down the stairs, her case bumping behind her.

Annabel's flustered face appeared in the doorway. "You're right, Grace. We need a break from each other. Otherwise you're going to drive *me* crazy as well as yourself."

As Annabel headed for the front door, Grace's anger disappeared, leaving fear in its stead. "I'm sorry, Annabel," she said. "It's just—you didn't write the word *leave* on my car, did you? As a joke?"

"What are you talking about?" Annabel stopped and faced her. Grace saw her sister's alarmed expression, and faltered.

What was the point in explaining? Annabel would only tell her that it was another reason to get away from this place.

"It's nothing," she said.

Annabel shook her head, flung open the door, and began dragging her case down the path.

Grace tried to tell herself that this was a good thing—it was time to stand on her own two feet, and with everyone gone she could get on. But when she heard Annabel start her engine, she ran out of the cottage towards the garden gate. The little red car had already zoomed off down the road, and Grace used all her willpower to keep herself from running after it and screaming for it to stop. Instead she stood motionless, holding her breath until the noise of the engine had completely faded away.

They were alone.

She looked up at the cottage. It stared back at her obliquely, its windows blank eyes. She steeled herself, straightening her posture, and headed inside. She was staying here for one fundamental reason—Adam. She wouldn't lose sight of that. Once the cottage was empty, she would reassess. If her efforts had revealed nothing, then she would accept the inevitable hollow good-bye. In fact, nowadays she often found herself hoping for its benign release, rather than anything else. For it was the gathering phantoms of other possibilities that kept on waking her at night to an icy darkness, sweating and shaking, repeatedly grasping for the light.

30

Grace lay awake for much of the night, wishing Annabel had come back, while telling herself over and over that she was doing the right thing by staying. She flinched at every strange noise she didn't recognize, however slight. Thankfully, the clock ticked steadily, but there was definitely some scratching going on in the wardrobe. It sounded like a mouse, but there was no way she would be investigating. Finally, she dozed until the day broke and Millie woke up.

She was tremendously tired that morning. She felt like the air was treacly, slowing her down—everything taking twice as long as it usually did.

She was still in her pajamas when Ben knocked on the door. She answered it, resigned to him seeing her like this, and straight-away his face conveyed his concern.

"Grace . . . what's happened?"

"Nothing . . . It's just that everyone's gone and it all seems a bit daunting."

"You look exhausted." He came in and set his toolbox down near where Millie was playing. Millie crawled over and tried to open it.

Ben kneeled down next to her. "Hmmm . . . not sure you're

216

ready to help me out yet . . . But what have you been doing here, Millie?" He indicated the blocks spread out over the floor. "Shall we give your mum a hand and put these away?"

Grace sat down on the sofa and watched the two of them together. When Millie began to take blocks back out of the bag, Ben built her a tower, and she gleefully knocked it down. Grace leaned back, and her head began to drift.

The next thing she knew, she was waking up. Bewildered, a surge of panic rushed over her as she opened her eyes. In front of her, Millie was strapped into her high chair, with Ben feeding her a sandwich.

Ben registered her movement and looked across, seeing her alarm. "It's okay, Grace, you fell asleep," he said. "You've been out for the count. I decided I'd leave you to it, though to be honest I don't think an elephant stampede through the living room would have woken you."

Relief flooded over her. She felt momentarily weepy, but pulled herself together as she sat up. Millie held up her sandwich to show Grace.

"Thank you so much," she said to Ben. "It's a rare treat to have a morning nap."

"I can imagine," Ben replied. "And you're welcome. Any time."

"Don't say that unless you mean it," Grace laughed. "I might take you up on it."

"I do mean it, Grace." He held her gaze.

Grace felt compelled to break the protracted silence that followed. "I had a falling-out with Annabel," she confided, finding herself glad to talk to someone. "And she left while she was angry with me. We don't usually fight, not seriously . . ."

"Don't worry," Ben reassured her. "My sisters argue all the time—always have. There's invariably some sort of upset going on in my family. Of course, I've been on the outside for a long time now, but from what I can gather it still goes on. Everyone is so stubborn— they insist on blaming each other for their problems, so one drama gets replaced by another."

"I gather you haven't seen your mum yet?" Grace asked gently.

Ben grimaced. "Unless she meets me halfway, nothing will ever change."

"Have you tried to talk to her, or does she just know that you're here?"

"Claire's been acting as a go-between so far," he admitted.

"Perhaps you should cut Claire out and try speaking to her yourself," Grace suggested as she got up from the sofa.

"You don't know my mother."

"Actually, I do, a little bit—and she's pretty formidable. But what choice does she have if you confront her—she has to listen, surely. And there must be a part of her that is longing to see you."

"Perhaps . . ." Ben didn't look convinced, but he sat there in silence for a while, thinking. "Maybe I'm still not sure whether I want to see her . . ."

Grace waited for him to continue, but he added nothing further. She collected some yoghurt from the fridge, and offered Millie a few spoonfuls, before she said, "Ben . . . can I ask you a favor?"

"Of course."

"I feel a bit of a wimp saying this, but catching mice is not my forte. Can you set a trap for me upstairs, and then check it tomorrow? One of those humane ones . . ."

Ben smiled at her. "I think I can manage that—although do you have the trap already?"

She shook her head.

"Then I don't know where you'll find one around here. Not

many care about seeing the mice live . . . but I'll tell you what, I'll try to make something if you like." He contemplated the idea for a moment. "I'll need a plastic box or bowl, at least five centimeters high, then something like a nail file or a cocktail stick . . ."

An hour later, the homemade trap was ready to go. Grace had run about finding materials, then looked on in admiration as Ben had constructed it. He lifted it carefully and they headed upstairs to her bedroom. Grace set Millie on the bed.

"I think it's somewhere in here," she said, opening the door of the built-in wardrobe.

Ben put down the trap and knelt beside it. "I'll just have a peek and see if I can spot where the little nuisance has been," he told her. He began checking the floor, and Grace watched him while she and Millie sat on the bed. He lifted up a piece of carpet. Then he paused.

"Er . . . you might want to come and look at this . . ."

"If it's a dead mouse then I'd really rather not," she told him, staying put.

"Well, there's no mouse, but he's left his mark," Ben said, and he lifted up a bundle of chewed bank notes.

"Where the hell did that come from?" Grace asked, beginning to understand what it was that she was looking at.

"There's a loose floorboard under here, with a space beneath it."

"Oh my god, that's got to be the money Adam took out of the bank, the day before he disappeared. He told me he was going to get some cash to keep at the cottage, but he never told me where he was planning on putting it. And I couldn't find it . . . It was one of the reasons the police thought he'd run away . . ."

Ben sat back with his arms wrapped around his knees, studying her carefully.

"But you don't think he did run away now, do you, Grace?"

31

After Ben had gone, Grace didn't even bother contacting the police, knowing Ken Barton was away. Instead she called Niall again.

"It's Grace Lockwood," she said in a rush as he answered. "I've found the thousand pounds that Adam took out of the bank. It was hidden under a floorboard—I came across it this afternoon while I was looking for a mouse. He must have put it there for safekeeping, and he just didn't get a chance to tell me." She hesitated, then went on. "It seems highly unlikely that Adam would suddenly decide to leave without any money on him . . . there's got to be more to it. So how do I get the police interested?"

She waited for his answer, her heart thumping hard.

"Look, you really need to have a word with someone at the station. I'm not back there until Monday, but if you haven't gotten anywhere by then, come down while I'm on duty, and I'll make sure you get some attention."

Grace knew he was trying to help, but the lack of urgency in Niall's tone was dispiriting. For the next few days it looked like all she could do was sit on her hands.

Niall sensed her disappointment. "I know the waiting's hard, but although you've made some discoveries, I'm not sure there's much that'll give us any new leads." He thought for a moment. "Look, I might be in Ockton later today. I'll see if I can do a bit of digging about Jonny Templeton."

"Thank you. His sister's name is Josephine, if that helps—I don't know her married name, but I think she still lives in Ockton."

"All right then," Niall said. "I'll be in touch if I find anything."

Grace hung up and went over to Millie, picking her up. "So what shall we do now?" she asked her daughter. In reply, Millie screeched and pushed hard against her, struggling until Grace put her down. Grace sat and watched as Millie crawled over to a pile of books, picked them up one by one and riffled briefly through the pages before flinging them aside. Her daughter seemed increasingly unsettled of late. Grace wished Millie could tell her what she had seen on the day Adam had disappeared. *Her little mind might hold all the answers*, Grace thought, if only she could access them.

She leaned deeper into the chair cushions, thinking. Adam couldn't have met with an accident, or Millie would have been found with him. So either he'd run away and chosen to leave his baby behind, or he had been an unsuspecting victim of some sort. Everyone seemed to think that the first option was more likely, but what if something sinister had happened? In that case, Millie had been left on the doorstep by someone else. Which meant they had known where Grace and Adam lived. And they were probably aware that Grace was back here now.

Her thoughts flashed back to the word *leave*, its spectral appearance on her car windshield. Her throat constricted and her lungs began to heave, struggling to draw in oxygen. She looked at her car keys on the table, then towards Millie. Why wasn't she going? She could make the decision right now, and it would all be over.

It will never be over while you have so many questions, she reminded herself. She just had to keep listening to the calm, rational part of herself and ignore the shrieking voice in her head issuing a stream of dire warnings. After all, she had been living here for a month, and nothing much had actually happened. Only that word written on her car windshield, which might have been a twisted prank. The rest of it could be put down to chance, or paranoia.

Meanwhile, she was getting closer to uncovering some answers, she knew it. She could at least stay until Monday, and go to the station. In the meantime she would pack up the rest of the cottage; organize it so she was ready to leave whenever she wanted to.

She felt better after running things through in her mind. When Millie went for her lunchtime nap, Grace made herself a sandwich and brought the rest of the papers down from her bedroom to read at the small dining table. There were more letters in Rachel's handwriting, and she leafed through them. They looked to be newsy—no mention of Jonny, though some lovely references to Adam as a baby which made her nostalgic for Millie's early days back in London. She bundled all of them together. She would take them with her as keepsakes for Millie.

As she picked up the final envelope, she found a stack of notes underneath, in handwriting she hadn't seen before. They were written on identical sheets of white notepad paper, folded in half.

She picked up the first one.

If you go, I will die.

Grace was stunned. Quickly, she found the next one.

I can't bear the thought of being apart from you. Please don't go. We can work this out, whatever our folks say.
I love you.
Jonny

Grace put it down and picked up another.

I love you.

Then another.

Don't leave me.

And the last one.

Don't make me hate you forever.

Grace frowned. In the accounts she had heard so far, it was always Jonny who had abandoned Rachel—but these notes told a totally different story. One with an unsettling undertone.

She wished now that she hadn't jumbled up the contents in the boxes from the cellar by tipping them onto her bed together. If she'd gone through them one at a time, she would have known exactly which box these had come from, and what else had been in there. She was curious as to whether Adam knew about these notes. Surely if he'd read them he would reconsider what he knew of his father—and want to find him in order to learn the full story.

She fervently hoped Niall could uncover more information about Jonny. She was convinced that he was somehow important.

She couldn't settle to looking through the more mundane

papers after this. Instead, she went upstairs and grabbed the dog-eared copy of *Rebecca*, then lay down on the bed and tried to immerse herself in it. Soon she was engrossed, and she was just reaching the end of a chapter when Millie woke and began to call out to her. Maxim de Winter had faced his wife with the truth, and as Grace got up and hurried to her daughter, his final question still rang in her ears: *"Will you look into my eyes, and tell me that you love me now?"*

32

Grace had expected to spend the whole of New Year's Eve with only Millie for company, but in the afternoon Emma came around with a request. "My sister's having a charity sale at church tomorrow, and she's tearing her hair out trying to get enough donations. All the money goes to the homeless. You don't have anything she can sell, do you?"

"Are you kidding?" Grace replied, stepping back so Emma could see the boxes stacked up in the hallway behind her. It was a valuable opportunity to hasten the clearance, and Grace's spirits rallied as they filled Emma's car with as much as it could hold.

Emma looked longingly at what was left behind. "It's such a shame to leave it, but we're staying over in Ockton tonight for New Year's, and I'm helping her set up the sale first thing. I should have thought about this earlier." Her shoulders slumped regretfully.

"Well, I could bring these to Ockton for you, if you like," Grace offered.

"Oh, don't you worry," Emma said hastily. "There's no need to go to any bother."

But Grace was thinking of Jonny. She had a burgeoning desire to see the farm at Gilldale for herself, and Ockton was only a few miles farther. "I'd be happy to," she insisted. "Just give me directions."

Emma's face brightened. "Well, that's ever so kind of you! My sister will be thrilled. If you've got a paper and pen handy, I'll draw you a map."

As they finished and Grace closed the door, she surveyed the half-empty hallway. This had been a stroke of luck for her as well as for Emma's sister. Tomorrow this area would be clear again. It was amazing how the knowledge made her mind feel so much lighter.

As she walked into the living room and looked around, she felt a fresh impetus to clear out as much as she could today. Most of the contents of the china cabinet could go to tomorrow's sale, not to mention the extra table linen. She grabbed a few empty boxes from the hall and began to pull things out of drawers and pack them up. It was satisfying work, and she was stacking yet another full box in the hallway when she heard someone crunching down the garden path.

She opened the door to see Claire standing there. "Ben told me that your guests have gone, so I decided to pop round and see how you are."

Grace was touched by Claire's thoughtfulness. "Come in. Would you like a hot drink?"

"A tea would be great, thanks."

They went through to the living room. Claire took a seat and began talking to Millie while Grace boiled the kettle.

When their mugs were on the table, Claire asked, "So, what are you doing for New Year's tonight?"

"Not a lot," Grace admitted. She had been half hoping that Ben would come and find her to suggest they spend it together. Since he hadn't, there weren't many other options.

"Would you like to come up to the schoolhouse? All my sisters will be there, we usually have a bit of a get-together. It isn't right to see it in alone . . ."

Grace wasn't keen to spend an evening outnumbered by Meredith and her family. However, she realized that it might give her the opportunity to speak to Liza again, and persuade her to talk to the police.

Before she could reply, Claire leaned forward.

"Actually, I have to confess, I'm hoping that Ben might come, too, if he knows you'll be there . . ."

Grace coughed as a large gulp of hot tea hit her throat unexpectedly fast. "What makes you say that?"

"Well, he seems to think a lot of you. And I'm willing to try anything, to be honest. I am so sick of him skulking up there in that house, and Mum sitting in her castle . . . and never the twain shall meet. It's ridiculous, they're as bad as each other. If I'd known how this was going to pan out I wouldn't have suggested he come back . . ."

Grace put down her mug. "I don't know much about it. He's only said that he had a big falling out with your parents and they've been estranged for years."

"Well, I bet he didn't mention how much grief he caused Mum and Dad when he was younger—he was quite the rebel for a while. . . . Perhaps he was sick of being stuck out here with a load of teenage girls—it can't have been easy. He crashed Dad's car into the pub one night after he'd had too much to drink . . . lost control and it skidded right down the hill."

"So is that why he's still barred?" Grace asked. "I saw him getting thrown out."

Claire smiled. "Len and Joyce think '*yance a bad egg, allas a bad egg*'—as do most people round here. They probably don't realize how much time has passed. Once Ben got his reputation it was always going to be difficult for him to shake it off. Moving away was probably his only option—but then he set our house on fire . . ."

"What!"

"Oh, he didn't mean to. He fell asleep in our old living room and left a candle burning. Woke up to find the room ablaze. Mum and Dad were out at the time, but all us girls were home. Ben came flying up the stairs to warn us, but we couldn't get down past the fire, so we ended up climbing out of Veronica's window and over the schoolhouse roof. It took the fire engine nearly an hour to get here, and half the house had burned down by the time they got it under control. We were lucky not to lose everything, but Mum and Dad never really forgave him. They pretty much kicked him out—or should I say they made his life hell from then on, until he'd had enough."

Grace pictured the elegant room at the back of the house. "So the huge dining room with the picture window is part of the refurbishment?"

"Yes."

"And how did you keep in touch with Ben, after he left?"

"He would write to us. Mum and Dad never mentioned him, but we would tell them bits and pieces about what he was doing. The rift appeared to come from both sides, though I thought Mum might back down now Dad has gone. At least it has jolted Ben into making an effort, even if it is too late with Dad. But I don't know why he's come all this way and now seems stuck at the last hurdle, even if Mum should be meeting him halfway. Perhaps he's just too proud to beg . . ."

"Well, I hope they can sort it out."

Claire finished her tea and stood up. "So will you come tonight?"

Grace hedged. "It's a really kind offer, but it's difficult with Millie . . ."

"She can sleep in the living room, if you like—it's right next door to the dining room, and we have a baby monitor we can put in there as well. That's what we did when Veronica's boys were babies."

Grace couldn't think of another reason not to go, and so found herself reluctantly acquiescing. "Okay, I'll come. Thanks."

"Great." Claire began to pull on her gloves. "Come around eight."

They walked to the door. "Good luck with Ben," Grace said as she showed Claire out.

"Thanks." Claire paused. "He's fond of you—you and Millie. You're doing him good. When he talks about you, he smiles—and it makes a change. It's almost like we have the old Ben back."

And she walked down the path towards the garden gate without waiting for a reply.

33

Grace stood in front of the schoolhouse, her hands gripping Millie's stroller, summoning up the courage to go in. Tonight, thoughts of Adam set off squalls of pain behind her shoulder blades, and produced a hot ache in her stomach. Two years ago they had been standing in Times Square together, after Adam whisked her away to New York as a surprise. They had only been married a few months, and were thinking about trying for a baby sometime in the next year—unaware that Millie would be conceived ahead of schedule a month later. As they had held one another close, wrapped within a crowd of thousands all rejoicing, life was crammed with excitement and opportunity.

Last year she had been in her parents' villa. Her mum had given her two sleeping pills and she had gone to bed at ten.

She peered up at the forbidding house, the only Christmas decoration a prickly wreath of holly on the door. However, despite her hesitation, she had to admit to herself that spending the evening with Meredith's family was more appealing than sitting in her musty old cottage on her own, watching TV. And maybe Ben would be there, too.

Claire greeted her at the door.

"Did you speak to Ben?" Grace asked as she maneuvered Millie's stroller inside.

"Yes. He didn't agree to show up, but he heard me out and said he'd think about it," Claire confided in a whisper. "I reminded him that there's never going to be a perfect time for this. I've told Mum he might be coming—she grimaced and has avoided me since, so I've no idea what she makes of it. But that's Mum for you. All my sisters have seen him already, so there won't be any big reunions. It's just him and Mum finally being in the same room together. Keep your fingers crossed for us all, won't you?"

As she led Grace inside, two small boys ran past, the first one trailing a balloon while the smaller one tried gleefully to catch it.

"Careful!" Veronica said, appearing in a doorway and glaring at her children. "Sorry, guys, they've had too much lemonade today. We're in for a heap of trouble tonight, I think."

"Millie's asleep," Grace said, indicating the stroller, its hood down.

"Pop her in here then." Veronica opened the door to the living room. "The heating's on, so it's nice and warm, and I've set the monitor up for you."

Grace peeped inside. The room was softly lit by a small lamp next to the sofa, and she remembered Annabel sitting there, trying to interview Meredith. She looked at the tall witching post next to the fireplace and thought sadly of her sister—how she wished Annabel were here tonight, cracking jokes and being sarcastic.

Grace wheeled Millie's stroller over to one corner, checked her daughter was still asleep, then came out and gently closed the door. The dining room door was ajar, light blazing through the gap, and she followed Claire to join the party.

It was the first time she had seen all of Meredith's daughters together. Veronica was next to Liza on one of the sofas, talking animatedly while pressing her hand against Liza's protruding belly. Jenny sat opposite, her eyes on her sisters. The husbands were standing by the picture window, its curtains drawn. Dan wore a thick leather jacket, in contrast to Steve's polo shirt and smart trousers. They looked unlikely friends, and as Grace watched, Dan said something with a chuckle that made Steve look uneasy. In the corner, three young boys were attempting to play Twister. Last of all, Grace spotted Feathery Jack, seated at the table on his own with a sherry glass in his hand.

Claire had gone to find her mother, and Grace looked around wondering who she should talk to. She was already beginning to regret coming, feeling like the specter in the room that nobody had noticed.

"Grace?"

She turned to see Meredith, her face stiff with that familiar veneer of politeness.

"Hello, Meredith, thank you for inviting me." She handed over a bottle of wine.

"You're welcome." Meredith took the gift and forced her smile a little wider. "There's food on the side table, please, help yourself."

Grace went obediently across to the buffet. As she picked up a plate, she surreptitiously looked back to see Meredith surveying the room. Slowly, her children stopped talking.

"Well, come and eat," Meredith said to them, and they began to get up.

"Ah'll turn sixty-nine this year," a voice piped up behind Grace. She turned to find Feathery Jack hunched in a chair. His eyes were wide, as though he couldn't quite believe his own words.

Grace wasn't sure what she should say in reply. He looked far older.

Her parents were already in their sixties, but retirement was rejuvenating them—they could easily be mistaken for Jack's children.

"Next year, Jack, you'll be sixty-nine next year. The New Year hasn't come yet," Claire added as she reappeared next to Grace. She didn't get a response, nor did she seem to expect one.

"Ah's last of the old school," Jack added gruffly. "Rest gone to meet their maker."

Grace didn't know what to say to that. Instead, she began to gather food on her plate, then sat down at the large dining table. The others slowly joined her, and Steve took a seat opposite. "So, how are you finding living on the moors, Grace?"

"I like it," Grace replied. "But I've got a lot to do. I wish I had more time to explore the area."

Dan cut in. "No word from that husband of yours, then?"

All other conversation stopped.

"Dan, leave her be . . ." Claire sounded irritated.

"I was only asking . . ."

"Dan was in the police force for a while," Liza explained. "He had friends working on the investigation . . ."

Grace could feel her face burning with embarrassment as she met Liza's eyes. The plea in them was clear, and Grace remembered her words as they had talked by the lake. *I'm begging you not to get me involved.*

Dan glared at his wife. "That's right, Liza. And it's the strangest case of a missing person that I've ever heard of . . ."

"That's as maybe, but I'm sure Grace doesn't want to talk to us about it," Meredith said stonily.

Dan scowled and lowered his gaze.

It seemed Meredith was able to silence her son-in-law easily, even though he was ready to pick a fight with his wife. Grace glanced gratefully at Meredith, but she was concentrating on her meal.

As Grace picked up her knife and fork again, she hoped the conversation was over, but the next voice was female, and obviously directed at her.

"Don't you feel scared, living out here alone with your baby? It's pretty isolated. You must be lonely?"

Grace looked up to see Jenny observing her curiously.

"Sometimes . . ." she admitted. "But we're adjusting . . ."

"I don't think I could live back here, now," Veronica remarked. "No offense," she said as Meredith raised her head, "I've just gotten too used to having a supermarket on hand 24/7. I don't know how you did it, Mum—I'm always running in there for something or other."

"You just need a better routine," Meredith said. "You have it too easy nowadays—it makes you lazy."

"No it doesn't," Veronica cried. "Disorganized, maybe. Lazy, no."

Meredith smiled thinly and began to help herself to more potato salad.

"How old is your daughter, Grace?" Jenny asked.

"Millie is fifteen months." Grace couldn't help smiling as Millie's petite little face came into her mind. "She's developing a strong will of her own already—though she hasn't started walking yet." She looked across at Liza. "How long till your baby arrives?"

"Five weeks," Liza replied. "I can't believe it."

"It changes your life, that's for sure." Grace tried to catch Veronica's eye for backup, and Veronica smiled but didn't seem willing to comment. Grace fell silent again, feeling as though she had hit on an awkward subject.

She was relieved that everyone's attention moved next to Claire, who was roundly berated for planning yet another trip abroad, with no sense of, in Dan's words, "long-term responsibility." Grace had always been a little envious of big families, but as she listened she realized that they could be quite claustrophobic, too—particularly if everyone decided to gang up on you and tell you how to live your life. Perhaps that's what had happened to Ben. She looked at the mantelpiece clock. It was after nine and there was no sign of him. It didn't seem as though he were coming—which meant that she had a long night ahead of her with the rest of his family.

She had just finished eating when the conversation swung her way again. "So, Grace, how are you getting on with the cottage?" It was Steve, Veronica's husband, who had spoken.

"Slowly," Grace admitted. "But hopefully things will speed up a bit, now that all the festivities are out of the way."

"Meredith told me about her suggestion," he continued, and Grace recalled Meredith saying that he was a lawyer. She looked over to see that Meredith had her head tilted to one side as she listened, like a bird suddenly aware of an interesting morsel.

"When people go missing the spouse can get tied into their property for years, even if it is in joint names," Steve continued.

Grace tried to keep her face fixed as she said, "Yes, I'm aware of that . . ." Her voice was hostile, and she avoided everyone's gaze.

"Meredith's idea might be advantageous for both of you," Steve persisted. "And I'd be happy to find out what can be done legally. If you rent it to someone you know, you might avoid a few problems—particularly if Adam comes back and isn't happy with the arrangement."

"That's unlikely to happen now," Dan added as he ate, waving his fork in the air. "Sorry, Grace, but you don't often find a missing person after all this time."

Grace was seething. How dare they casually discuss her

decisions, her life, and her husband over dinner like this. She was on the verge of losing her temper, when the conversation moved on as though nothing had happened. Veronica started to reprimand one of their children for running around with their food. Jenny got up and began collecting plates.

Grace met Claire's eyes and saw her sympathy. Meredith was scrutinizing her, too, but as soon as Grace noticed, the older woman got to her feet and busied herself helping Jenny with the dishes.

People began to leave the table, and Liza hurried from the room. "I'm going to check on Millie," Grace announced to no one in particular, and followed. At least if she could press Liza to talk to the police, this night wouldn't be a total waste of time.

However, by the time she reached the hallway, Liza was nowhere to be seen. Frustrated, Grace headed instead to the living room and peeked under the stroller hood, reassured by the sight of Millie's peaceful face. She sat down, and was considering whether to rejoin the party or sneak back to the cottage, when she realized she could hear talking. It was coming from behind her, beyond a window that looked out over the front of the house. She wanted to move, but the curtains were open, and if she got up she would probably be seen in the lamplight. So she sat there uncomfortably, unable to avoid hearing what was being said.

"Liza, listen to me," came a male voice. "You can't stay with him. He's an idiot."

"What choice have I got? I'm not asking for anything from you, so leave me alone—I can't do this anymore."

"We're not doing *anything*, I'm just talking to you . . ."

"You know exactly what I mean. It should never have happened in the first place. If anyone finds out . . . If Veronica—"

"They won't . . ."

"They would suspect right this second if they opened the door. I have to get back."

"Liza, wait . . ."

But then there was the sound of the front door opening and shutting, and footsteps hurrying along the corridor.

Grace sat there, stunned. It was unbelievable. This family became increasingly complicated the more she knew of them. Surely Veronica would have some idea of what was going on right under her nose. She couldn't live with someone and not know . . .

Then she realized where her thoughts would lead, and cut them dead.

There had been no sound since she heard the front door, and her anger had faded to resignation. There was little point in sitting here. She would go back to the party and at least try to see in the New Year.

She had another peep at Millie, who was still soundly asleep, then headed back out. She was in the corridor, about to reenter the dining room, when the front door opened.

Steve regarded her in astonishment, but as he saw the look on her face, his eyes turned guilt-ridden. Grace could only hope that she did a passable job of feigning disinterest before she turned away.

A few people asked after Millie when she returned. They had all moved across to the comfier seating, and as the wine flowed, most of the family gradually forgot Grace was there. At one point her phone beeped in her pocket and, collecting it, she saw she had a text from James.

Looks like our friendship is finished.

She would have been disturbed by it if she didn't know him so well. He would have had too much to drink for the New Year's countdown. *Don't be daft*, she quickly replied. But after that she heard nothing more.

When the clock read a quarter to eleven, Claire leaned over and said sadly, "I can't believe Ben isn't going to come."

Claire had seemed so hopeful that this evening might be a step forward for them all, and Grace felt sorry for her. "I'm sure he has his reasons."

"Yes, he's as stubborn as Mum," Claire muttered.

As the year met its final hour, the conversation began to turn maudlin. Veronica had eventually got her boys off to bed and appeared to be determined to make up for the drinking time she'd missed. She was lying on the couch with her head propped against Steve's thigh when she said, "I can't believe this is the first New Year's without Dad."

"I know," Claire agreed. "He did love a good knees-up."

"He loved the *idea* of a party," Liza said with a smile, "but let's face it, often by this time he'd be exactly like Jack . . ."

They all looked across. Feathery Jack was slumped in an armchair, his head lolling forward over his chest as his body rose and fell rhythmically.

"Not on New Year's," Meredith said. "That was different."

Grace turned with the others towards Meredith, who had hovered between the kitchen and the dining room all night. She had kept on the outskirts of the conversation, and yet the girls hadn't noticed. They treated this place as though it belonged to them, and their mother like she was part of the furniture. But Grace had the feeling that Meredith was the glue that held them all invisibly together.

Grace felt a rush of sympathy as the older woman stooped to collect some empty glasses. She got up and went across, determined to make an effort.

"Can I help you with anything?"

Meredith abruptly straightened. It was as though she had been lost in her own world and Grace was interrupting her. Lamplight bounced off her eyes and made them appear moist, but perhaps it was just a trick of light—after she moved, all Grace could see on Meredith's face was the emotionless expression she was used to.

"I'm fine, Grace," she said, "but thank you for asking."

"Mum . . . Grace . . ." came Veronica's voice from across the room. "Steve's going to do first-footing. No reason why we can't keep up Dad's tradition. Dad always made a big deal about it," she explained to Grace. "We had to go outside before twelve, and then follow him back in after midnight." She glanced at her watch. "In fact, we'd better get on with it." She got to her feet and whipped a whisky bottle from the table in the corner, then picked a lump of coal out of the fireplace. "Mum, what else do we need?"

"I'll get the rest," Meredith said, and left the room. Veronica surveyed them all sitting there. "Come on, everyone."

"What's all this about?" Grace asked Liza as they began to haul themselves up.

"First-footing is meant to bring luck to the house. A tall dark man has to enter first after midnight, and bring gifts—whisky for good cheer, coal for warmth, bread for food, salt for flavor, and a coin for prosperity. Mum and Dad did it every year."

As they made their way towards the door, Claire asked, "What about Jack?"

"Leave him," Veronica said. "He won't even notice."

They filed down the corridor towards the front door and Grace followed them. Outside, Veronica gave Steve the whisky bottle and the coal, and Meredith gave him a loaf of bread and a pot of salt. She looked at the others. "We still need a coin."

Dan held out a coin, his stance, hand on hip, clearly indicating his contempt for the proceedings. Steve juggled the other items in his arms to receive it. Then they gathered around, and Claire looked at her watch and counted down the seconds.

"Three . . . two . . . one . . . Happy New Year, everyone!"

Grace had expected lots of hugging and kissing, as would have happened in her family, but instead, after a few choruses of "Happy New Year," Dan piped up, "All right then, back inside—hurry up, Steve, it's bloody freezing."

Steve walked towards the front door, twisted the handle and pushed, but nothing happened.

"It's locked," he said. He put the items in his arms on the ground, and tried it again, first with one hand and then with both, rattling it.

"Let me see." Meredith sounded annoyed. She shook the handle, but it didn't budge.

Grace began to shiver. Please get the bloody door open, she prayed. Then she heard a long, piercing scream.

At first she thought it was one of Jack's screeching owls, but as it came again, she registered the familiar pitch of it.

"That's Millie," she shouted, charging towards the door. "Get the bloody door open *NOW!*"

34

Grace barged in front of Meredith, grasped the door handle and shook it hard, but it wouldn't budge. She looked at it in a panic, mind and heart galloping together.

A hand grasped her arm and she instinctively shook it off. "Grace," Claire shouted, "this way, come on."

They charged along the side of the house to the back, flinging open the door. Grace raced through the dimly lit kitchen, into the corridor towards the living room. When she reached the room, she paused in horror.

In the muted light, a shadowy figure stooped over Millie's stroller. As he straightened, Grace saw that it was Feathery Jack, with Millie in his arms. Millie's small face was panic-stricken. Grace rushed across and snatched her daughter.

"What the hell is going on?" she demanded, fright becoming fury in an instant.

Jack appeared confused as he looked from Grace to Claire. "Ah heard the bairn skrikin'," he said.

Millie began to cry hysterically and Grace tried to shush her.

She whirled around, her only aim to get away from this house, but her escape route was blocked by a crowd of worried faces.

"What happened?" Veronica asked.

"She must have had a nightmare or something," Claire said.

Grace could feel all their eyes fixed on her, burning into her, bringing her close to screaming herself.

"Poor little mite," Liza murmured. "Will she be all right, Grace?"

"She'll be fine," Grace replied through clenched teeth, "but I think I'll take her home."

She walked across to try to put Millie back in the stroller, but Millie clung tight and sobbed harder. Grace attempted to soothe her, rocking her gently back and forth.

"Bit of a bad omen, that, isn't it, us all sprinting round the back," Dan commented. "I think you were the last-footer, Steve, not the first," he chuckled.

"Rubbish," Meredith said. "This'll be Timmy, up to a bit of mischief, no doubt."

Grace's blood ran cold at the idea of a ghost child in here alone with her daughter on the stroke of midnight, while she stood locked outside with this strange family. A spike of fear shot through her. "I need to take Millie home," she said. "Now." Her voice came out low and strange. "Let me out."

No one moved, everyone just kept staring, but then Claire's kind face appeared in front of her. She held Grace's arms as she said gently, "I'll walk you home."

"Can you take the stroller?" Grace asked, and then headed towards the door, holding a shrieking Millie tightly to her. Everyone parted to let her through, but no one said a word. She avoided their eyes, making her way quickly outside and onto the road. The cold hit her like a blow as the darkness enveloped her, and she hurried down the hill. The light was on in the pub, and she used that as a guide. They were almost at the cottage when she heard footsteps behind them.

"Is Millie all right?" Claire asked breathlessly as she caught up.

Grace had Millie cradled against her, but the little girl had gone quiet now. Grace nodded and didn't speak further until they were at the cottage gate. "Thank you for bringing the stroller. You can leave it by the porch—I'll put Millie to bed and then I'll come back for it."

She didn't wait for a response, and hurried upstairs to settle Millie in her cot. The little girl rolled to face the wall without a sound. Grace watched her sleeping for a while, wanting to make sure she was all right, but Millie didn't move again. By the time Grace headed back downstairs, she was both relieved and exhausted.

She went to collect the stroller, to discover that Claire was still hovering in the garden.

"I wanted to check you were both okay."

"Really, we're fine," Grace replied wearily.

"Are you sure?"

Grace took in Claire's earnest face. This woman was a Blakeney—and she wanted little more to do with them after tonight. But Claire had always seemed different, and Grace felt a sudden need for company, so she found herself saying, "You're welcome to stay for a drink if you like. Then I have to get to bed."

Claire followed her into the living room.

"Tea or something stronger?"

"Tea is fine."

Grace made the drinks, then they sat down. Claire fiddled with the handle of her mug for a while before she looked up. "I feel I should apologize for my family . . ."

Grace shook her head. "Perhaps I'm overreacting—my head's a bit all over the place."

"Well, at least take no notice of the Timmy comments. He was a bit of a joke among us when we were little, but Mum really believes in him—she gets extremely irate if we push her too far on it."

"Well, maybe she's right. Maybe he does exist, and he scared the hell out of Millie tonight."

Claire seemed astonished. "Do you really believe that?"

Grace ran a hand over her face. "I didn't. If you'd told me a few months ago that I'd be talking seriously to somebody about seeing ghosts, I would have laughed. But since I've been here, I've been dreaming of black dogs, hearing spooky stories everywhere, and standing in front of a clock that appears to choose when it stops and starts . . . I don't know anymore . . ."

"But Grace, there are perfectly reasonable explanations for those things. . . . The clock might have a fault. And perhaps the dreams about black dogs are happening because you've made them significant, so your subconscious keeps throwing them back up again. All the ghost stuff is just hearsay. Until you see some incontrovertible evidence for yourself, don't believe it."

Grace smiled at her. "You're probably right." She hesitated. "You're different from the rest of your family, Claire. More . . ." She wasn't sure how to finish.

"I'm hoping you're going to be the first person ever to say normal," Claire chuckled, indicating her piercings as she did so. "These usually make me stand out for a start. But I am very different from them. I think Ben and I have more trouble hiding our feelings than the others. And there's so much going on in our family that I'd rather not know about. You'll have to excuse Jenny, for a start. She's all bitter and twisted at the moment because Liza is pregnant. Jenny would love a family, but she had to have an emergency hysterectomy a few years ago. She's trying to live with it, but she doesn't do a great job at times. . . . She's had a tough time of it lately, anyway—she was always Dad's baby and it hit her particularly hard when he died. No doubt she's envious of you having Millie—I remember her having a bit of a crush on Adam when he lived here. She always used to tag along when I went out for a sneaky cigarette with him. It annoyed the crap out of me, I quite liked him myself."

Grace smiled, still having trouble picturing Adam as a chain-smoking teenager.

"My role in the family is primarily as the dumping ground for everyone else's stress and problems," Claire continued, "most of which, if not all, are self-inflicted. You can see why I like to go on long trips away . . ." Claire smiled as she said it, but her underlying frustration was clear. "And what about you, Grace?" she asked. "What are your plans now?"

"I have no idea," Grace replied. "I've only been on my own here for a couple of days, and it feels like everything is getting on top of me again. I'm not sure if I'll be able to see this out. I'm normally pretty strong—but I underestimated how challenging this would be . . ."

"Well, you've been through a lot," Claire said. "Give yourself a break. Besides, struggling doesn't make you weak, Grace. Considering what you're dealing with, it would probably be more of a concern if you weren't struggling . . ."

Grace put her head in her hands. "Well, I'm fed up with it. I don't know how much longer I can live here without going crazy, but there's still so much to do . . ." But she didn't want to talk about that, and searched for a change of subject. "I'm sorry Ben didn't come tonight."

Claire shrugged. "He has his reasons. I should stop interfering, he's a big boy."

"So, if you and Adam were good friends when you were younger," Grace asked, "how come Ben didn't know him very well?"

"Oh, Ben was doing his own thing by the time we were eighteen, certainly not hanging around with me. It's that strange twin thing—we've got a strong bond, but we can irritate the hell out of each other as well."

Grace stared at her in astonishment. "You're twins?"

"Yes—I thought you knew."

Grace shook her head. "It makes sense though—Ben seems so much closer to you than the others, and you share certain similarities."

"Yes—as Mum used to say, we're both willful and pigheaded," Claire laughed. She finished her drink. "It also makes me piggy in the middle in the case of everyone versus Ben. But then my brother doesn't help that really—he's so hard to predict, or prize information from. Well, thanks for letting me stay for a chat. I'd best get back to the house now and see what's happening. Will you be okay?"

"I'll be fine, thanks." Grace followed her to the front door.

"Happy New Year," she called out belatedly, a few seconds after Claire had closed the gate behind her.

"Happy New Year," came Claire's disembodied voice in reply, her body already engulfed by the night.

When Grace shut the front door, she went back into the living room and poured herself a glass of wine. She took it out to the hallway and stood in front of the grandfather clock, feeling impetuous. "Happy New Year, and fuck you," she said to the clock, raising her glass to it.

The clock ticked on.

It was after two a.m. She knew she was going to regret staying up in a few hours, but the night had thrown up so many things to think about. Pieces were beginning to come together in her mind. From what she had overheard earlier, there could be little doubt that

Liza and Steve were having an affair. Perhaps Liza wasn't meant to be in Ockton on the day she had bumped into Adam? It would certainly explain her reluctance to get involved. Especially if Dan was friends with people on the investigation.

She remembered what Claire had said about Adam. She smiled to herself, wondering if Adam knew what Meredith's girls had thought of him.

Rachel's papers lay in front of her and she idly studied them. On the top was one of those strange notes from Jonny. As she reread it, all her questions drifted together to become one bold suggestion, and she froze.

Jesus, she thought. If she were right, this would change everything.

She searched quickly for the only one that was signed. She had read it as Jonny. But that *o* could easily be an *e*. In fact it was an *e*, the more she looked at it.

If you go, I will die.

I love you

Don't leave me.

Don't make me hate you forever.

I can't bear the thought of being apart from you. Please don't go. We can work this out, whatever our folks say. I love you.

Jenny

35

Grace sat staring at the notes in front of her, then reached out and topped up her wineglass without even thinking about it.

These letters were obviously written by a girl who was hopelessly in love. The one that she had signed bothered Grace the most. "... *whatever our folks say* ..." implied that Adam had reciprocated, didn't it? She remembered Claire saying that Jenny had just turned thirty—so there were only a couple of years between her and Adam. She would have been sweet sixteen when Adam had moved into the village.

If the two of them had had a secret romance, and their families had conspired to separate them, Meredith might not be pleased to see Adam back. But that was fourteen years ago. Surely this couldn't have any bearing on Adam's disappearance, could it?

Moreover, surely Adam wouldn't have brought Grace and Millie to live here if he had any notion that there was a big problem lurking in these backwaters. No, whatever the notes indicated, it had to be firmly in the past as far as Adam was concerned. After all, Grace had never heard him talk about the Blakeneys before. He obviously hadn't

248

kept in touch with any of the girls after he moved away. They couldn't have been that important to him in the long run.

Unless . . . What if Adam had been searching for Jenny in the library, and Jonny was a cover story he'd given to Liza? Perhaps he had really wanted to find Jenny again? But then why not ask Liza where Jenny was? Maybe Liza had left that part out? Perhaps they were all in it together, determined to throw Grace off the scent?

Off the scent of what, though? Grace felt increasingly confused. She was going around in circles, with no idea whether she was getting any closer to the truth. Frustrated, she took another slug of wine.

Where did this new information leave her search for Adam's father? She'd never thought about it before, but she only really had Liza's word that Jonny was relevant anyway. She tried to think back. She could still picture Liza's face on the steps of Freeborough Hall. She had seemed so earnest. Why would she lie?

She would lie if Jenny asked her to. She would lie if Adam's disappearance involved her sister. Perhaps they all would. Had Grace experienced any genuine friendliness or hospitality from them since she'd been here, or was it all an elaborate subterfuge to get her to leave? Perhaps Ben was involved too—passing information along from inside Hawthorn Cottage, keeping them posted on what she was up to.

As her theories grew more and more elaborate, Grace felt as though she was losing her grip on reality. She looked at her half-full glass and went across and poured it down the sink. Then she took herself upstairs to bed.

As her foot touched the top step, the clock began to chime three. And then it stopped.

She couldn't even summon the energy to be frightened. In fact, she felt fury coursing through her instead—at everything and everyone who had led her to this point.

She flung open her bedroom door, and halted. Finally, fear got sharp teeth into her, and instantly clamped down.

On her pillow was *Ghosts of the Moors*. Connie's book. Grace knew, without a doubt, that she had packed it ready to leave, but now it lay spread open, face down, as though she had paused in reading it.

She picked it up. It was open at a page she recognized.

The black barghest.

A fearsome hound with razor-sharp teeth and claws. Seen shortly before the death of a local. She flung it across the room. Then she took her duvet, wrapped it around herself, and went to lie down on the floor next to Millie's crib; trembling, her mind tumbling over and over, not daring to close her eyes even though she wanted to, her ears straining for any hint of movement close by.

36

As light began to spread over the moors, Grace crept around the cottage, hurriedly packing suitcases, putting items in the last of the boxes they would take with them, and stacking the ones for the charity sale together.

Last night she had been scared senseless, but this morning she realized what a fool she had been. The Adam she loved would not want her here, falling apart while trying to find him. The Adam she knew would have urged her to put Millie first. There were more important things in life than having all the answers. Today, they were leaving.

Much of the organizing was done, but the kitchen was still full of odds and ends. She walked past the now ticking grandfather clock and headed into the living room. There, she paused, looking at the hole where the kitchen wall had been. The ceiling was a mess, too, and the floor needed finishing. She would ask Ben to sort it out after she'd gone. The rest of the renovations could be done by somebody else. She didn't care anymore.

She pictured herself storming up to the schoolhouse, getting everyone out of bed and demanding answers. Someone had put that book on her pillow last night, she was sure of it. Claire had been the last person in the cottage with her, but she couldn't remember Claire having the opportunity to go upstairs without Grace noticing. Besides, if Meredith had a copy of the key to the cottage, any of them could have done it.

Unless the cottage had its own ghost? Stopping the clock and moving things around, just like Timmy. Perhaps Timmy had come back with them last night; perhaps Millie really had seen him?

Grace shook herself out of that daydream. She would begin to fall apart if she believed that. She couldn't afford to consider it.

Before Millie woke up, she called Annabel.

"Grace," came her sister's tired voice. "Why are you calling so early? I've only just got to sleep! How was New Year's?"

"Rubbish," Grace said. "How was yours?"

"It was fine," Annabel replied. "But it would have been better with you. I feel horrible for leaving you. I'm sorry. Mum and Dad are really cross with me. How are you getting on?"

"You don't have to apologize," Grace said, hearing her voice crack slightly. "You've done so much for me in the last twelve months. But, listen, I'm thinking about taking a breather. We might come down to London—can we stay with you?"

"Oh Grace," there was no mistaking the delight in Annabel's voice, "that's great. Of course you can. You're doing the right thing. I know you want to sort out the cottage, but you don't have to put yourself through hell to do it. You've done enough—the rest can be taken care of without you having to live there."

As she listened to her sister's comforting words, a few tears broke loose and ran down Grace's face. When she hung up, she walked upstairs and looked out the window across the moors. There are so many reasons why I can't wait to get out of here, she reminded herself as she surveyed the bleak view. *Yet I still feel this galling pull to stay.* She knew why. She was abandoning much more than the place, and it was still so hard to let go.

But her mind was made up. When Millie woke up, Grace dressed her warmly. "We're leaving today," she whispered to her daughter.

Millie played at her feet for most of the morning while Grace rushed about packing up the kitchen. She was emptying the cutlery drawer when there was a loud rap on the door. She dropped the spoons she was holding, and they fell to the floor with a clatter, causing Millie to flinch.

Grace walked across to the window and pulled back the curtain to see Ben jiggling impatiently on the doorstep, his hands pushed into his pockets. Bess sat patiently next to him. As she looked at the dog, Grace remembered the open book on her bedside: a black dog that foretold death. *Don't be so silly,* she told herself, finding that in daylight it was a little easier to repel her fears.

She walked to the front door and pulled it open. He smiled easily at her. "Happy New Year, Grace."

"Happy New Year," she echoed, feeling unaccountably pleased to see him.

"I came to see what you'd like to do next on the cottage."

"Come in."

He knelt close to Bess. "I won't be long. Stay here."

Bess lay down on the doorstep in resigned reply.

As Grace brewed the kettle, Ben crouched down on the living room floor and spoke to Millie. Grace watched as Millie pulled herself up against Ben and stared into his face, putting a tiny finger out to poke at his nose, making him laugh.

"Here you go," Grace said a few minutes later, offering him a mug of steaming tea.

He got to his feet, took it from her, then they both sat down opposite one another.

Grace looked at his hopeful face. "I'm sorry, Ben, but I've decided to go away for a while—so everything will have to be put on hold." She tried to pretend she didn't care that they would be saying good-bye, but she couldn't hold his gaze. This gentle, unexpected bond she'd formed with Ben was one she would miss.

Ben looked surprised. "Where will you go?"

"We're going to stay with Annabel, figure things out from there. I'm hoping to leave today."

Ben cradled his mug in his hands. "Well, I'm sure you're doing the right thing. But for what it's worth, I will miss you both."

Their eyes met. Ben looked away first, back down at his tea, as he said, "Now, can I do anything to help you, before you go? You're going to need to get cracking, Grace, the snow is due again this afternoon—you don't want to be driving in that in daylight, never mind at night."

There was nothing tying them together anymore, but Grace didn't want to say good-bye yet. So she hunted around for how he might help.

"I'm pretty organized, I think. I just need to get the stuff in the hallway over to Ockton—I promised Emma that her sister could have them today for a rummage sale."

"Right then, I'll load them up for you." He finished his drink, went through to the hallway and began taking boxes out to the car. After ten minutes, he was back at the door. "I don't think I can get any more in."

Grace walked out into the hallway. There was one box left.

Millie had crawled behind her, and now she clung on to her mother's leg, wanting to be picked up. Grace stooped to get her, and Millie rubbed her eyes and leaned her head on Grace's shoulder.

"You'll have to sleep in the car today, Millie," Grace said. "We've got to go to town." As Millie began to grumble, Grace realized that they hadn't eaten anything since breakfast, and it was now almost lunchtime.

Ben was watching them. "I'll tell you what," he said. "Why don't I mind Millie for you? Then you can put that box on her car seat, pop Millie into bed and spare her the trip to Ockton? And if you like, while Millie's asleep I'll sort that out for you a bit more." He gestured to the mess where the kitchen wall had been.

As always, Ben's presence was calming, and quashed all her earlier fears. She could trust him—when she looked at his gentle face, she was in no doubt about that. Millie obviously adored him, and it would really help her out. If Millie stayed with Ben she could have her lunch and then a proper nap, which would make her much better tempered for the journey later. Meanwhile, Grace could get through everything as fast as possible. She could drive to Gilldale before heading to Ockton and dropping off the boxes. She'd be back to pack up the car again and get well clear before the snow began. She didn't want to spend another night in the cottage.

"I'd really appreciate that," she agreed. "I'll be as fast as I can. There's a bowl of pasta for her in the fridge—can you give her that and then put her down for her sleep?"

Ben nodded. "Sure."

Yet still, Grace hesitated.

"Well, what are you waiting for?" Ben asked. "Go on."

As she looked at his open face she had an urgent desire to tell him everything. Her suspicions about his family. The word *leave* written on her car. Her vague concerns about Millie. How frightened she was that she would never shake off her torment over Adam's disappearance. And beneath it all lay her growing doubts about herself, and her state of mind. She opened her mouth to speak, but then he held his hands out to take Millie, and the moment passed.

She lifted her little girl up, looking into her eyes. "Mummy's stepping out for a while," she told her. *And then we'll leave—go and figure out the next part of our life together. As long as we have each other, Millie, I know it will work out . . .*

Millie reached a hand out and touched her mother's cheek, as though she was giving Grace a small, reassuring caress. Grace kissed her daughter's forehead, feeling unaccountably emotional, then held her out to Ben, relieved that Millie went to him willingly.

They followed Grace into the hallway as she collected her coat. "I'll be as fast as I can," she said, opening the door and wavering on seeing the dismal grey sky.

"Don't worry, take your time," Ben said from the porch, bending down to give Bess a pat. "I've got no particular plans today."

Grace smiled, "Thank you, Ben."

He straightened, and she saw a flash of deep emotion in his eyes, gone in the moment it took her to blink.

She walked down the path and through the gate, then climbed into her car and set off on the drive along the top of the moors. As she headed away from the village, she reassured herself that in a few hours she could make this journey for the final time.

37

As Grace took the turn for Gilldale, a few early snowflakes began to fall. Tall trees huddled either side of the road, their branches leaning over the car and dripping water onto the windshield. Gilldale was a larger village than Roseby, but there was still nothing much to it except a row of houses set on a bend. As Grace pulled the car up at a T-junction, she had no idea where to find Riverview Farm, Jonny's childhood home, and she didn't have much spare time. She looked in both directions, and then decided to turn towards Ockton.

Less than a mile later, she struck lucky. There was the sign, "Riverview," hanging from a steel gate, and a muddy track headed off through a field. Without a second thought, she took the turn, and the wheels began churning through the mud.

A small whitewashed house came into view a short time later. Grace stopped the car by the front door and climbed out. Her head began to pound. It seemed unlikely that anything good or useful would come of this, yet she had been determined to come. It was as though her quest for information had become a compulsion, driving her on regardless of reason. Her increasing resolve to abandon her search had also strengthened an innate pull to pursue these final, tenuous leads. She hated how desperate she felt.

However, she wasn't given much time for second thoughts, as before she had even knocked the door swung open. A teenage girl stood there eyeing her uncertainly.

"Sorry to trouble you," Grace said. "I'm looking for the Templeton family."

The girl shook her head. "We're the Wetherfields. Templetons ain't been here for years."

"Do you know where any of the family live now?"

"No." The girl looked genuinely sorry. "Mam and Dad might, but they've gone out."

Grace looked around frantically. This was where Jonny had lived. It should reveal something to her, surely.

The girl began to look worried. "Are you all right?" she asked.

"I'm not sure," Grace admitted, running her fingers through her hair. "But I'm going now. Thanks for your help."

The girl's eyes were wide and wary as she closed the door.

Grace drove the car back down the muddy track, having a disturbing flash of herself as the girl must have seen her: on edge, with bags under her eyes and unkempt hair, asking questions about people who hadn't lived there for years. A crazy woman. There was no longer any doubt that she needed to get away.

She felt deflated as she rejoined the tarmac road. It took a long time to reach Ockton along the winding lanes, but gradually the road widened and houses began to appear in unbroken rows. She followed Emma's directions to the church hall, and was greeted by Emma and her sister Sally, who couldn't stop thanking Grace for her generous contribution.

"I've decided not to stay. Millie and I are going to London today," Grace told them.

Emma flung her arms around Grace. "I understand, although I'm sad to see you go. I was looking forward to getting to know you better."

Grace was touched by Emma's words, but they didn't change the fact that she couldn't wait to leave. She checked her watch as she returned to the car, horrified to realize that it was nearly two o'clock. She got in, started the engine, and began to head out of town. As she drove along the main road, a few more specks of snow landed on her windshield. She glanced up at the sky. It loomed close and grey.

She stopped at a service station and hurried inside in search of food to tide her over, finding only a sandwich that looked unappetizing. As she came out again, a bitterly cold wind began to drive gusts of snow along the ground. She put her head down and pulled her mobile phone from her pocket to call Ben, tell him how she was getting on.

He didn't pick up his mobile, or the cottage phone. Unease prickled her skin as she got back behind the wheel.

Then her mobile rang in her hand. She looked at it in relief, expecting it to be Ben, but she didn't recognize the number, so answered with a hesitant "Hello?"

"Grace? It's Niall. I've just been to your cottage, and the fella there said you'd gone to Ockton."

Grace was immediately wary. "Have you found something?"

"Perhaps," Niall replied. "Where are you?"

"I'm in Ockton, I was just heading back."

"Wait there. I'm driving over now. Meet me at the police station in ten minutes."

He hung up before she could even ask what was going on. She felt herself trembling; his tone suggested he had uncovered something significant.

She had seen the police station on the main road through town, near the church. She swung the car around, reminding herself that she shouldn't be long. But at least Niall had seen Ben, so he and Millie must be okay, even if Ben wasn't answering his phone.

As she drove, the snow fell steadily, her tires slushing through a thin layer that had formed on the road. She discarded her sandwich, no longer hungry. The weather was making her nervous.

She pulled up in front of the police station. Niall wasn't there. She took out her phone, but there were no messages. She decided to try Ben again to tell him she would be delayed.

This time he answered straightaway. "Are you all right, Grace? A policeman was here looking for you. Said he had some information he needed to pass on." He sounded concerned.

"Yes, I'm about to meet him—I don't know what he wants yet," Grace replied. "How's Millie?"

"She's still asleep. I hope you don't mind, but I've brought Bess inside as it's snowing quite a bit now. Don't be too long if you want to get out of here today."

"Don't worry," she assured him. "I'll be back as soon as I can." As she spoke, she looked in her rearview mirror and saw a car pulling up behind her. Niall climbed out. "He's here. I'll see you shortly." She hung up.

Niall walked over to her door. "Now then, Grace," he said as she opened it. "Thanks for meeting me. I wanted to have a word with you in person."

"What's going on?"

"Let's get out of the snow for a minute while we have a chat," he said. Then to her surprise he headed for the church rather than the police station.

Grace followed him, watching the snow beginning to coat his

hair. As Niall held the gate open for her, she said to him, "Please, just tell me."

Niall walked past her, beckoning her up the church path. When they got underneath the porch, he finally stopped and said, "Grace, I'm afraid I found Jonny here."

Grace briefly imagined a man waiting inside the church, ready to talk to her—perhaps with news of Adam. Then, as she looked back at Niall, taking in his sober expression, it clicked.

"He's dead." Her voice was dull.

"Yes," Niall said, watching her carefully. "I thought it might be best for you to see for yourself."

He moved out into the snow again and headed around the side of the church, treading on the patches of grass that grew in between the gravestones. Grace followed him, still trying to absorb the news.

Adam's father was dead?

Why hadn't she even considered that possibility?

Niall stopped at a low headstone. Grace focused on what was written there.

JONATHAN CHRISTOPHER TEMPLETON

BORN 2 MAY 1956

DIED 11 OCTOBER 2004

BELOVED SON OF GEORGE AND DOROTHY, AND

BROTHER TO JOSEPHINE

REST IN PEACE

Grace felt her whole body sag. She had been so sure that finding Jonny would lead to answers. She pictured Adam—unwittingly searching for a father who had passed away years before. She looked at Niall. "Do you know what happened?"

"I've had a talk with his sister. He was in an accident in Australia. A car crash. Apparently his parents have been dead for years, and the sister stayed behind in Ockton to get married when the rest of them went overseas. He had no other family, so her husband flew over and collected his ashes, brought him back to be buried here."

"Did you tell her about Adam?"

"No, I asked a few questions, and mentioned that her brother's name had come up in an investigation and I wanted to rule him out. She was ever so curious, as you'd imagine, but I haven't said any more for now. If you want to meet her then I'm sure something can be worked out. But that's up to you—and her, of course." He fumbled in his pocket and pulled out a piece of paper. "Looks like he'd done well for himself," he said, handing it to her.

It was a photocopy of an Australian newspaper article, under the headline LOCAL PROFESSOR IN FATAL CRASH, featuring a head shot of a balding middle-aged man, gazing to the right of the camera lens and smiling. Grace studied the picture, trying to take in the fact that this was Adam's father, searching for something in his features that would link them; but Adam had looked much more like his mother.

"You can keep hold of that," Niall said.

"Thanks," Grace replied, folding the sheet and putting it into her pocket before the snow ruined it. She looked at the gravestone again.

"Are you all right?"

"I'm wondering whether Adam knew about this."

"If he found out, that day in the library, do you think it could have affected his state of mind?" Niall asked gently.

Grace shook her head. "I would have seen it that evening, I'm sure of it . . ." Unless he found out the day he disappeared, while she was out shopping. If he had discovered anything in the library, he could have made some follow-up inquiries that afternoon. Was that what his note was about? Had his emotions overtaken him once he'd written it?

Why didn't you tell me what you were doing, Adam?

She bit her lip to stem her distress.

Niall patted her shoulder. "I'm sorry, Grace. Come down to the station tomorrow, eh, and tell them what you've found over Christmas. Take it from there."

"I don't think I can," she admitted. "I've had a bit of a change of heart about living in the cottage. I'm planning to leave later today."

"Well, give Barton a call instead, then."

Niall obviously wasn't convinced that she'd found anything worth investigating, or he wouldn't be so accepting of her going. He was just being kind, she realized, helping her tie up loose ends for her own peace of mind. There was no point being here—hanging on to an empty hope. Everyone else was focused on other things. Life had moved on.

They traipsed back over the grass. Niall walked beside her, and didn't say another word until they were next to Grace's car.

He held open her door for her as she climbed in. As he did so, he looked up at the snow-laden sky. "Best get going, if you're planning to," he said, the warning clear within his words. "It can be pretty dangerous driving on the moors with snow around—and it'll be getting dark within the hour."

38

It was barely three o'clock by the time Grace got back onto the main road, but Niall was right—already the daylight was beginning to fade. As she headed out of town she was slowed down by the drifting snow. She drove as quickly as she dared, trying not to be reckless.

She was only a couple of miles from the moor road turnoff when she met a queue. She sat there impatiently, eyes fixed on the blur of red lights from the car in front of her, trapped in stuffy air as the heating hit full blast. Now and again they edged forward, but it must have taken a good twenty minutes before she reached the cause of the delay. Two cars had crashed at a junction and the accident took up one side of the road. She glanced at it as she passed, but the people involved were no longer there, only the empty shells of their badly damaged vehicles. It looked like it had been nasty, and Grace rapidly reassessed her plans. Was she doing the right thing rushing Millie away? She looked nervously at her watch. Yes, she told herself—all she had to do was pack the car and turn around when she got back. She'd persuade Ben to tow her out of the village if she had to.

She left the traffic behind as she signaled right and turned onto the empty road that cut through the moors, dismayed by the heavy grey sky. Five miles to Roseby, the sign said. As she tried to speed up, the snow became millions of tiny white specks shooting towards her windshield from the gloom. It was mesmerizing, and Grace had to focus hard to keep her eyes on the tarmac.

The minutes ticked by, and the way in front of her swiftly became a blank white nothingness. Soon she could no longer see where the roadside ended and the moors began—the only things to help her were the tall slim markers spaced every fifty meters or so, their reflective red tips lighting the way.

She was moving slower and slower, and her low spirits sank even further. She couldn't risk bringing Millie out in this. Herself, yes, but not her daughter. They were going to have to spend another night in the cottage. She wasn't sure she could get through it without going mad. She could sleep with the light on, but she didn't know if she was more terrified of the shadows that crept along the walls or the obliterating dark.

Fear bred upon fear, as the storm of white outside grew stronger. The car was forced to a crawl. Grace had lost all points of reference, even the markers. She was frantic now, blinded by whiteness, desperate to reach the cottage, all thoughts of getting out again forgotten. It felt like she'd been on the moors forever—surely she should have been back by now? Perhaps she had unwittingly taken a wrong turn.

She was on the point of hysteria when a tall stone marker came into view. She stared at it, sure she had never seen it on this route before, but it looked familiar. Then she recognized it with a shock: it was the picture on the front of Connie's book of ghosts, a stone marker with a simple cross, like a gravestone.

It loomed closer, the headlights' illumination giving it a spectral sheen. She would be familiar with it, surely, if she were on the right road. Where the hell was she?

Transfixed, she neglected to steer, and the tires came off the tarmac, immediately floundering as they struggled for traction on the sodden moorland. She whipped the steering wheel hard around, but the car skidded and vibrated, and she had to brake sharply.

She peered through the windshield, her fingers still clutching the wheel. Daylight had faded to nothing; night was in ascendance. She had no idea where the road was anymore. She leaned against the steering wheel for a moment to stop herself from hyperventilating. When she looked up, snow pelted the car in frozen fury. Blackness surrounded her. She couldn't even see the stone marker now.

She tentatively pressed her accelerator. The engine roared, the tires spun, but she didn't move.

She kept the engine running and fumbled in her pocket for her phone, willing it to have reception out here. She almost wept when the little screen lit up and showed a good signal. She had two missed calls from Ben. She hadn't even heard it ring, but now she pressed redial rapidly, her hands shaking.

"Grace?" He answered immediately, sounding agitated. "I've been really worried, where are you?"

"Ben, is Millie all right?"

"Yes, of course, she's fine—she's playing. Now, where the hell are you?"

"I'm stuck on the moor top." She tried and failed to keep the panic out of her voice. "I've driven off the road, but I must be close to the village—I've been travelling long enough. I've just passed a stone marker with a cross on it. What should I do? Shall I try to walk back?"

"No," he said sharply. "Don't leave the car, Grace. I told you, the snow can cause all sorts of trouble. Listen . . . I'll come and get you. Wait there."

He hung up, leaving her so relieved that she dropped her head and finally let the dam of her emotions loose. She sobbed loudly into her hands, releasing all her pain, her frustration, her anger, and her sorrow, gulping in air until she felt spent. When she looked up again, she was resigned and ready for the long night ahead.

Now that the car had stopped moving, the snow wasn't as fierce, but it still fell relentlessly, and it was hard to make out much else. If there really were ghosts on the moors, it would be the perfect time for them to take a walk. Her eyes flickered from side to side, searching for unexpected movement. Her ears strained to hear anything out of the ordinary. She looked in her rearview mirror, but the stone marker had been annihilated by darkness. It had been tall enough for a man to hide behind. What if there was somebody there, just out of sight?

She put her head in her hands. What was she doing? Why was she insisting on terrorizing herself?

Too afraid to look out again, she kept her eyes down, trying to hold herself together. She ran through everything that had happened since she had arrived—right through from her first memories with Adam . . . the night he had disappeared . . . coming back, and the lonely weeks since, as she had tried to figure everything out. All of which had led her to this point—lost within the fall of night, snow suffocating the world.

She felt for the newspaper article in her pocket, and switched on the overhead light. She stared at the photo of Jonny, wondering how much he knew of Adam, and if this amiable-looking man had ever tried to make contact with his son.

Something told her that she was close to uncovering the truth. Everything she had discovered had proved that her suspicions were well-founded. So if Jonny didn't hold the answer, who did?

Finally, she saw the glow of headlights on the horizon, gradually becoming brighter. She kept concentrating on the newspaper article, and her memories and discoveries of the past few weeks spun and whirled. As Ben's Land Rover drew nearer, an idea flitted across her mind, so rapidly that it was almost gone before she caught it and reeled it in. It danced in front of her so vividly that for a moment she was spellbound. At first it seemed absurd, but as she twisted this strange notion over in her head, it began to make perfect, awful sense.

By the time Ben got close enough to see her, she had jumped out of her car and was racing across to him. She flung open the passenger door, breathless and agitated.

Ben stared at her. "Grace, are you okay? I'm sorry but you're going to have to spend another night here—there's no point in attempting to get your car out until morning. It's too treacherous to drive in the dark anyway."

Bess was there, trying to scramble across Ben to greet her, but Grace wasn't paying attention to either of them. Instead she was looking frantically through all the windows. "Where's Millie?" Panic filled her throat.

"Claire's got her, at the schoolhouse—I didn't dare drive up the hill in this weather without her strapped into a car seat. We'll pick her up on the way back."

"Oh god, Ben," Grace screamed at him. "What have you done? We need to go and get her *NOW*."

39

"Grace, I don't understand." Ben was frowning, while the snow sprayed up against either side of the Land Rover as it ploughed down the hill. Bess leaned between the seats, her nose pressed onto Ben's shoulder. "Why are you so upset? What's going on?"

Grace gripped the front dashboard, steadying herself while willing him to go faster. "Do you remember Adam having a fling with Jenny while he lived here? Back when you were teenagers?"

Ben shook his head. "No, I don't—he was always with Claire, if anyone."

Grace could see the lights of the schoolhouse getting closer. She concentrated on them, collecting all her energy together so she could use it to spring out of the Land Rover and run as fast as she could to get Millie.

"Grace, talk to me," Ben insisted, alarm plain on his face. "I don't understand—why are you so worried about Millie? She'll be fine, I promise—I know my family can be difficult, but I wouldn't have left her there if she was in danger."

"I know you wouldn't," Grace said hastily as the car pulled onto the gravel drive. "I have to get Millie back first, and then I'll explain."

She opened the door before he'd even stopped, leapt out, and ran towards the house.

As she neared the front door, she saw there weren't many lights on. She nearly barged right in, but at the last minute something told her to play it a little cooler, at least until she had Millie in her arms.

Ben came up behind her as she knocked. "Grace, what the hell—"

The door opened and Claire stood there. She looked worried. "Grace—are you all right? Ben told us you got stuck."

"Yes, thanks, I've come for Millie." Grace was trying to act normally but she could tell it wasn't working. Her voice was strange—high-pitched and too rushed.

"Right," Claire said. "She's in the dining room, with Jenny."

Headlights illuminated them all as another car roared onto the gravel. Grace looked to see Meredith climbing out of her four-wheel drive, and for once her face was a true picture of uncertainty. "Grace—I saw your car up there. Has something happened?" she asked.

"I'm here for Millie," Grace said. She turned back to Claire. "I'll just go and get her." She headed inside without waiting for Claire's answer, aware of worried voices close behind her. Footsteps followed, but all she wanted was to find Millie.

The corridor was dim, only a halo of light shining through the crack of the closed dining room door. She flung open the door, rushing into the brightness of the room, praying that her fears were unfounded, and that she was only being foolish.

The room was empty.

Claire came in behind her, her curiosity edging towards concern as she took in the empty space. "They were just here . . . I'll go and find them."

As Claire went back into the corridor, Ben and Meredith appeared. Ben looked confused, but Meredith regarded the room evenly.

"Where are they?" Ben asked Grace.

She went across and gripped his arm. "We have to find Jenny," she said, her panic increasing with every word. "I think she's taken Millie."

Claire rejoined them. "They're not in the kitchen . . ." She registered what Grace was saying. "Why on earth would she take Millie?"

"We need to find them quickly," Grace shouted. "I can explain later. Where the hell have they gone?"

"They can't have gone far." Claire looked frightened now. "She hasn't got a car."

"Ben," Meredith's voice was controlled and low, "I think you should take the monks' trod to the Leap, now, check she hasn't gone there."

"Why would she go to the Leap?" Claire asked, sounding totally confused. "It's pitch-black and snowing outside."

But Ben took one look at his mother's face and sprinted into the hallway, with Grace right behind him. He raced through the front door, heading for his car. Grace rushed around to the passenger side, but he said, "No, Grace, I'm just getting a flashlight. I have to go on foot." As he spoke, Bess bounded out of the car and began springing at his heels.

"I'm coming with you," she insisted.

Ben slammed the door shut and came around to her, pulling her to face him. "Listen to me. I know the trod well. I'll be faster on my own."

"You don't have to wait for me," she panted. "I'll keep up."

"Let's go then." He was already dashing towards the path.

It was impossible to sprint through snow, but Grace was running as hard as she could, thankful that the outlines of the uneven flat stones were still just about visible. Ben jogged beside her, shining the torch to light their way. Bess was yapping, disappearing into the night and occasionally reappearing around them again, enjoying the unexpected exercise.

"How much farther?" she gasped.

"We're nearly there," Ben urged. "Come on." And he quickened his pace, haring off into the darkness with Bess at his heels, the dog's barking becoming increasingly frenzied. Then Grace heard something ahead—a whimper that rapidly grew into a full-blown wail. "Millie," she screamed as she fought past a thick bush of sharp, deadened twigs that scratched and tore at her hands and face.

She slammed into something solid that almost knocked her off her feet. She staggered backwards, recovering her balance, and saw that Ben was ahead of her, standing stock-still, his back to her.

She walked closer. "Ben?" She put a hand on his arm. He didn't move. Then the noise came again, and she looked past him.

In the silvery moonlight, she could make out a figure sitting in front of them, legs dangling over the edge of the drop ahead. In her arms, something was moving, and Grace knew straightaway that it was Millie.

Without a second thought, she began to creep forward. Ben tried to pull her back, but she shook him off and kept going towards the ledge. She saw Bess had gone over to Jenny and was nudging her, but Jenny seemed mesmerized, staring out into the night, swaying gently back and forth.

Grace tiptoed slowly, keeping her eyes on Jenny all the time, terrified that she might cause her to startle. She was operating purely on instinct, knowing she couldn't stand back and do nothing.

She deliberately aimed for a point a few meters away. As she reached the edge, she tried not to look down, but her feet dislodged a pile of snow and it fell away into the hidden maw below. All Grace's senses screamed at her to get back, but she couldn't. Not yet.

Jenny's face was just visible, and she looked calm and dreamy— which was more terrifying to Grace than tears. Millie was crying and wriggling, and Jenny was patting her back absently, as though to pacify her.

"Jenny?" Grace said softly into the night.

Jenny gave no response, just stared out towards nothingness. Millie didn't appear to hear Grace either, and kept squirming to be free.

Grace edged towards them. "Jenny?" she said when she was only a couple of meters away. "Millie is cold and frightened. She needs to go inside. May I take her?"

"He moved on without a second thought..." Jenny said abruptly. Her tone was eerily composed. Grace began to shuffle closer, not stopping until she could almost reach out and touch them.

"I'm really sorry, Jenny," she said. "I think we should talk about it. But first we need to get Millie inside where it's warm."

Jenny looked up at Grace as though she had only just realized that someone was there. She frowned. "He married you."

"Yes." Grace's voice shook. She had a flash of Adam's joyous face on their wedding day, and felt a tear slide down her cheek. "And then he vanished, Jenny. I lost him, too—so did Millie. I understand exactly how you feel. And now I need your help. We have to get Millie out of the snow."

Grace moved within range of them and held her arms out. *Give her to me*, she implored silently.

Millie suddenly seemed to realize that her mother was there.

She screamed and pushed away from Jenny violently, trying to get to Grace. For a moment Jenny lost her hold on the child, caught unawares by Millie's unexpected movement, and Grace's terrified heart skipped a beat as she saw Millie rock backwards. She lunged forward to grab her daughter, feeling herself lose her own balance as she did so. She plucked Millie from Jenny's hands and willed herself upright, but it was too late, her momentum was forwards, they were going together. To right herself she needed to let go of Millie, so there was no hope, and they were tipping towards the edge. While panic ripped through her body, her mind began to accept the inevitable. *This is it, then.*

Strong hands grabbed her and pulled. She staggered backwards, regaining her balance. She looked to see that Ben was behind her, his face deathly white. "Thank you," she said, but he was staring beyond her.

Jenny had twisted to watch them, her expression unfathomable, but then she turned away and peered over the edge, as though thinking. Ben rushed across and gripped her under the arms, dragging her away from the drop. "Don't you dare," he shouted.

Silence enveloped them. Then Jenny began to cry.

Grace stroked Millie's face, and found it was icy. Millie's wails were weakening now, to intermittent exhausted sobs. Something screeched overhead, but Grace didn't care what ghouls might emerge from the shadows tonight to chase her. Nothing was more frightening than how close she had come to losing Millie.

"Grace," Jenny gasped, "I'm so sorry. I didn't mean to scare you. I only wanted to hold her for a little while . . ."

There was an ominous edge to Grace's next words. "What happened to Adam last year?"

Jenny froze, as though she'd been struck. "I have no idea—I

didn't even realize he'd been living here until after he'd disappeared. Why would you ask me that?"

"Because someone in your family knows the truth."

Now Jenny's expression was one of utter confusion.

"Why do you say that, Grace?" Ben cut in.

Grace had a very brief moment of hesitation. But the more she thought about it, the more she was convinced she was right. To hell with secrets and silence, she decided.

"Because I think Adam was your half-brother."

40

Ben and Jenny stared at Grace.

"What the hell are you talking about?" Ben said eventually.

Grace felt with her free hand and pulled the newspaper article from her pocket, brandishing it at them. "I was looking at this in the car while I was waiting for you, and I said to myself that Adam doesn't resemble this man at all—he looks more like your dad. It was only a casual thought, but something made me reexamine it. And the more I considered it, the more I felt it had the potential to explain a lot of things . . ."

Jenny was watching Grace intently, her eyes wide and wary, as though Grace were insane.

Ben got up, and held out his hand to his sister. "Look, let's go back to the house, get warm, then we can talk."

They stumbled along in silence, Ben supporting Jenny and using his free hand to shine the flashlight ahead. Grace followed, hugging Millie close as she concentrated on the path. Millie was quiet now, her face nestled into her mother's neck.

Finally, they saw the lights in the distance. As they got closer to the schoolhouse, Claire was waiting on the doorstep. She ran a hand over her face in relief as soon as she spotted them.

Grace didn't want to go inside. Instead, she headed towards Ben's car. Her fingers were closing on the handle when a voice hissed from the darkness behind her, "Why couldn't you just *leave*?"

The distant light from the schoolhouse cast a low glow on Meredith's face, and her eyes were furious, the hollows beneath them sunken furrows.

Grace was too livid to know where to start. "How *dare* you," she replied, as Millie began snuffling against her shoulder.

Jenny caught up and grasped her mother's arm, spinning her around, flinging words in her face. "Is it true? Was Adam our *brother*?"

When Meredith didn't say anything, Jenny began to shake her. Ben pulled her away.

"You made me think he didn't care rather than tell me the truth," Jenny shouted, tears streaming down her face. "How could you?"

"Jenny, you were a young girl, we didn't think—"

"I *LOVED* him, Mum," Jenny cut in. "It's been fourteen years, and nobody has ever made me feel like that since. And now I'm barren as well as alone . . ."

Grace flinched.

"Jenny, this was your father's doing, not mine!" Meredith's voice turned pleading.

"Don't you dare, Mum—you . . . you . . ."

"Everybody, *stop*," Claire demanded, her face distressed. "Come inside, Jenny."

Jenny let Claire lead her away. When they had gone, Meredith threw her icy stare upon Grace again. "I have held this family together for longer than you've been alive . . . and you have just blown it apart. Are you satisfied now?"

Grace stood defiant before those glacial eyes. "I'm calling the police," she said stonily. "And you can tell them exactly where my husband is . . . because I would bet both my life and Millie's that you know what happened."

They glared at one another.

Ben came and pressed a hand against Grace's back. "Grace, let's go."

She let him guide her to the car. He helped her in with Millie, then closed their door and walked around to the driver's side, saying, "Come on, Bess," and letting the dog jump through into the back.

"I'll go really slowly," he said as he got in. "Just hold her tight in case we skid."

They exchanged a tense look before he began to reverse. As the headlights swept around, Grace saw Meredith one last time, standing on her driveway, her posture as rigid as always, watching them leave.

They made their way in silence. The snow had lightened but continued to float down; the village was hushed and still. When Ben pulled up at the cottage, Grace tried to persuade her legs to move, but she kept on sitting there.

"Grace . . . ?" Ben said gently. "Would you like to stay with me tonight?"

"Yes, please." Relief flooded through her. "Thank you. I just need to get some things from inside for Millie. Can you come with us?"

"Of course." Ben switched off the car engine and came around to open the door for her. Millie's eyes were glazed and sleepy now, and Grace passed her to Ben while she climbed out, then he handed her straight back. "Stay, Bess," he said, as the dog tried to jump out.

Inside the cottage, Grace snapped on the light as Ben asked, "What do you need?"

"Can you get her pajamas from the top drawer upstairs, and some nappies? I'll go and get her some food for morning."

In the living room, she glanced at the packed cases and boxes. Only one more night, she told herself. She took some jars of food from the top of a box, using one hand to push them into a small bag while she held on to Millie. As she stood up, she thought she saw a flash of light in the darkness outside. She went over to the window and heard Bess's distant bark.

She peered harder through the glass, trying to force her vision to penetrate the black void.

"Ben," she called. "We're ready."

She turned and jumped to find him standing right behind her.

"I've got everything here," he said, holding up the pile in his hands. Then he registered the expression on her face as she looked wide-eyed over his shoulder.

"Grace . . . ?"

He swung around.

Meredith stood behind them

41

"Mum, what are you doing here?" Ben demanded.

"We need to talk," she replied, glaring at Grace.

Grace held Millie tighter. "I have nothing to say to you. Now get out."

"Grace, I would like to speak to you alone."

Grace gave a loud bark of derisive laughter. "Are you serious? Ben, I want you to stay right here."

Ben didn't reply, but went across and sat down on the sofa, looking rebelliously at his mother.

Meredith took a small step closer to Grace. "I know you're frightened of me," she said softly. "And it is ridiculous. I have been on your side, you know. I haven't done anything wrong. In fact, I'm the reason your daughter is safe—"

Grace froze. Ben got up again from the chair and came to stand next to her. "Mum, get on with whatever it is you want to say." There was a warning note in his voice.

Meredith held his gaze. "I don't even understand it all myself . . . but I will tell you what I know."

She waited for a moment, eyes turned fixedly towards the window as though steeling her nerves, and then she began.

"The first I knew that Adam existed was when he came here after Rachel died. I had my suspicions about his true paternity as soon as I realized how old he was. However, Bill and Connie thought that Jonny was his father—the timely move to Australia had made him a convenient scapegoat. I've always been unsure of why Rachel kept up the pretense when she knew she was dying. I'm surprised she let them bring Adam back here."

"I don't think he was meant to live with his grandparents," Grace said. "Rachel asked her boyfriend to take care of Adam financially—but when Adam found out the man had a second family, he wouldn't take his money. He chose to come and stay with Bill and Connie instead."

Meredith grimaced. "Well, in that case I understand now." She glanced at them, and Grace finally saw flashes of anxiety in her eyes. "I had confronted Rachel about her affair with Ted before she left— but the last I'd heard from her was a letter containing a brief apology, and an assurance that she was gone for good, which was passed on to me by her father. I'm not sure whether Ted knew of Adam either until he arrived . . ." The corner of Meredith's lip had begun to twitch, and she brushed at it absentmindedly. "However, I only had to tell Ted that his youngest daughter was in love with Adam to be sure my fears were well-founded.

"When Ted felt threatened, his first response was always attack. I know he warned Adam to stay away from Jenny. I wasn't privy to the conversation, so I don't know what was said. However, Adam left for university soon afterwards, and he never contacted the girls again. We were both hugely relieved."

"So tell me what happened last year?" Grace insisted.

Meredith closed her eyes, but her eyelids quivered as though wild activity were going on beneath the surface. Her hand came up as if she might hide behind it, but instead she rubbed repeatedly at her face.

"We didn't foresee what would happen to Jenny after Adam left. Her heart was broken. She had always been Ted's baby, and I think it destroyed him to see her like that and know it was his fault. She became a wraith, little more than skin and bone; she didn't care about anything, and nothing we did could rouse her spirits. We were very worried for a long time, we truly thought she might never recover. And even though, in the end, slowly, she came back to life . . . she was never the same carefree girl we'd known before. And she's had such rotten luck with men since. I think perhaps she made Adam into a god, and no one else could measure up. And then a couple of years ago she had an operation—went in thinking they were removing a growth, but things got more complicated, and as a result she had to have a hysterectomy."

Grace had no intention of cultivating compassion for the Blakeneys. "I don't need to hear all this, Meredith. Just tell me about last year."

Meredith met Grace's frosty stare. "Again, I had no idea you had even moved here until Ted rushed through our kitchen door. He was out of his mind. He told me that he had met Adam walking on the Leap. Ted just kept repeating, 'He's gone over, he's gone over . . .'"

Grace felt her mind and body sway together, as her world hardened into this new shape; one she was incapable of altering. The wound was real. The space beside her was permanent. He was gone.

She had pursued the truth relentlessly, and she had her answer. But there was no relief. Instead, its price was unendurable. She gasped for air, struggling with all her strength to control herself and listen, because Meredith was still talking.

"It took a while to get him coherent enough to talk to me. He never admitted any part in Adam falling, just said they'd had words and Adam had fallen over the edge. And he'd left her there," Meredith said, indicating Millie, who was now asleep in Grace's arms. "At the Leap—in her stroller, all by herself. When he told me, I ran to find her, and there she was, crying her eyes out. I wheeled the stroller back, unsure of what to do, and in the meantime she wore herself out and fell asleep. So I kept on going, up here." She gestured outside. "I opened the gate, half-expecting you to come out and find us, and I had no idea what I was going to say. I was still in shock myself. When you didn't come outside, it occurred to me that I could leave her and you could discover her that way, without me needing to be involved. She was wrapped up nice and warm, and I could come back later and check that you had taken her inside. So I walked away. And we didn't have to wait long till we knew she'd been found, as we saw the police cars go by.

"Meanwhile, I started running through everything in my head. Ted wasn't admitting to anything but an accident, and all I could think of was what it would do to our girls—to Jenny in particular—if he was accused of anything more sinister. I had an idea, and I talked it through with him. Gradually, as he saw that there might be a way out, he began to come round . . ."

Horror flooded through Grace. Less than two hours ago, she'd stood in roughly the same spot that Adam had fallen. She had been so close to going over the edge herself, into the abyss. She stumbled over to a chair and sank down in it, cuddling Millie close, trying not to think about her baby all alone on the wild, empty moor top, next to the Leap.

"What happened next, Mum?" Ben persisted.

Meredith looked towards the window. "While the police were out searching, we didn't dare return to the Leap. We were expecting them to discover Adam down there and rule it as a suicide. We thought if we moved him it would look more suspicious."

Grace frowned. "Why didn't they find him?"

Meredith couldn't meet their eyes. "Well, they didn't go to the bottom of the Leap. It's difficult to get back up, so they relied on the helicopter . . . but they should have seen him. . . . However, later we discovered that Adam must have moved, after he'd fallen . . . . When Ted went back, he was under a ledge—hard to see from the air."

"You mean you left him down there and he wasn't even dead?" Ben cried, horrified.

Meredith looked at him. "I didn't leave him anywhere," she snapped, her tone sliding closer to panic. "I didn't even look over when I went and got the baby—I couldn't bear to—and I didn't hear anything while I was there. It was your father who did the rest. He tagged on to the search party that went to the top of the Leap, tramping his boots through the mud so that when they found Adam it wouldn't look odd that he'd been there. Then after the search was called off, Ted went back to find out what had happened. Two things had changed when he came home that day. First, he was clearly heartbroken—so perhaps Adam really did fall by accident, as Ted never once said he pushed him—"

"Stop . . . stop . . ." Grace jumped up, Millie startling in her arms. She fought the urge to run from the room, wanting to hear everything that Meredith had to say, however terrible. After so long, she needed the truth. A sob rose up and threatened to engulf her. "How can you talk about *his* heart breaking . . . ?" Her voice cracked on the words.

"What else had changed, Mum?" Ben asked. "You said there were two things."

"His face was haunted for the rest of his days." Meredith spoke in a soft, shivering whisper. "Whatever he saw down there, it never left him. Even after the stroke had robbed him of his faculties, right to the end, he still had that same terrible look in his eyes."

Ben came over and put his arm around Grace. "So where is Adam now?"

"Ted buried him where he found him. We stayed up all night deciding what to do for the best. He was talking about going to the police, but I persuaded him not to. What would be the point of more lives falling apart? I kept reminding him of what it would do to the girls. So at dawn the next morning he took everything he needed and drove the car towards Skeldale, parked up on the roadside and walked over the moors to the Leap. You can get to the bottom of it that way, but it's a long hike. He didn't come home till after dark. And the next morning we carried on as normal. Neither of us ever spoke about it again."

"Adam's still at the bottom of the Leap?" Ben sounded incredulous.

"Yes."

Grace was overtaken by a sudden vile rush of nausea. She remembered Annabel talking about the Leap. Sitting nearby on Christmas Day, looking towards the spot. Standing on the precipice tonight. And all that time, Adam was down there, in the ground.

A great wound deep inside her began to claw at itself, tearing her open and digging deeper and deeper, hollowing her, until she was empty from the inside out. Up to this moment she had sometimes allowed herself to imagine him coming through the front door, throwing his arms around her, making it all right. But now he was lost forever. She could picture his easy smile, could well remember the deep vibration his voice made if she pressed her ear to his chest, and the concave space where her hand nestled between the muscles there. She still knew the solidity of him, his warmth, his breath, the place where his cheek merged from softness to sandpaper as his stubble grew. Now, as horror flooded her, she imagined that same body beneath layers of earth, the leeched lifelessness of it, the decay. Numbing shock began to edge its way along her limbs. Whatever she had been searching for it was never this—all hope permanently extinguished, leaving behind a blind despair. Abandonment had once felt so objectionable, yet at least it had cast flickering images of Adam into the future. Now she would do anything to bring back such possibilities.

She closed her eyes and gripped Millie tighter. Hold on, she told herself. Just hold on to Millie. Yet she felt her body begin to sway until Ben's strong hands reached out and caught her, guiding her back to a chair.

"Tell me the rest," Grace said, her eyes still closed.

"I've told you all I know."

"No." Grace opened her eyes and glowered at Meredith. "I want to know about the book I found open on my bed. The damn clock stopping and starting. The word written on my car . . . You obviously still have a key to this place."

Meredith paused, which told Grace all she needed to know. "That clock has been known to stop at three a.m. on occasion. Connie and Bill talked about it for years—Bill always found it a great joke, it was his heirloom. Connie hated it. . . . As for the rest, they were only minor things. I didn't know what else to do. From the moment you got here I was terrified that this would all come out eventually, unless I could get you to leave . . . and you seemed unnerved by the ghost stories."

Grace was going over everything else that had happened. She realized how close she had been to abandoning the cottage without putting all this together. Would she have been better off that way? It didn't matter now.

"Grace," Meredith said, interrupting her thoughts. "I know I've played a part, but I don't know what else I could have done. I was desperate to protect my family. All I've ever wanted was to try to shield my children from having to bear the consequences of such horrific mistakes."

At this, Ben made a strange sound and threw his hands in the air.

"You too, Ben," Meredith said defiantly. "Perhaps now you know what Ted did, you might understand . . ." Then she turned to Grace. "All I ask is that you don't call the police until the morning. I would like the time to speak to my daughters tonight; to explain. I would appreciate it if you could grant me that much. Because I brought your child back, Grace. I didn't know anything about Adam's birth or his death until things were set in stone—there was nothing I could have done to change either. And I told Ben straightaway where he could find Jenny and Millie tonight. I didn't deliberately set out to cause you any harm. So I'm asking you to allow me a little bit of time."

As Grace sat in stunned silence, Ben said, "This is unbelievable."

"I know you're angry with me, Ben," Meredith said. "But life is not always simple—surely you know that by now."

Ben looked stone-faced at this, but said nothing.

"I brought Millie back to you," Meredith repeated. "And I didn't take Adam away. Now I just want the chance to console my own daughters before their worlds collapse." She paused. "Just a few hours. Please."

Grace glared at her. She thought of Millie lying snug in her stroller by the front door. If it weren't for Meredith, her baby would have been left alone by a sheer drop. This woman had played havoc with her life, but, to Grace's horror, when Meredith had mentioned protecting her children, for a small moment Grace could almost understand why.

"I'll give you until dawn. And then I'm calling the police," she said. She tried to look into the depths of Meredith's fixed stare, to see if there was more to uncover, but her eyes were black marbles. Grace had been sure she'd spotted cracks forming, but they had closed over now, and she was banished from whatever else lay beneath.

Meredith turned swiftly and headed towards the hallway. In the doorway, she paused, listening. "Your clock appears to have stopped, Grace."

And then she was gone.

42

Ben let them into his house, with Bess running ahead of them.

"You can both sleep in my room if you like. Will she be okay in the double bed?" He nodded at Millie, who was semislumbering on Grace's shoulder, occasionally shifting her head from side to side.

"Thank you," Grace replied, weariness overtaking her. It was only early evening, but it felt like the dead of night—it had been dark for hours, and so much had happened.

Ben showed her up to his room and flicked on a bedside light. He paused at the door, "Can I get you anything?"

Grace just wanted to sleep. "We'll be fine. Thank you."

He left them alone. Grace put Millie on the double bed, rearranged pillows so she wouldn't fall out, and lay down next to her fully clothed. And then, although it was painful beyond measure, she let herself remember Adam. Tears streamed down her face and soaked the pillow.

After a while she was exhausted, but sleep wouldn't come. She did nothing but toss and turn, until finally, defeated, she headed downstairs for some water.

It was after midnight, and she was surprised to hear music

coming from the living room. The door was wide open, light shining beyond it, and she peered inside.

Ben was lounging on the sofa, staring into the distance with a glass of golden liquid in his hand. At his feet, Bess gave a gentle woof but then put her head back onto her paws. Ben glanced up. "Can't sleep?"

Grace barely heard him, for she was taking in the contents of the room. In addition to the furniture, there were half a dozen large canvasses stacked against one wall, and an easel stood by the front window. A photograph was clipped to the top of it, and on a canvas beneath, the face had been replicated in charcoal outline.

Without a word, she moved closer. It was a little girl, not much older than Millie, with blonde ringlets and blue eyes that shone with merriment.

"Who is this?"

"My daughter." Ben sat forward, his incisive eyes searching Grace's for her reaction.

"Oh!" Grace couldn't hide her astonishment.

"She's two, and she lives in Australia with her mum." Ben's voice was tender, his eyes fixed on the easel. "Catherine and I were married for five years—happily, I thought—but when Sophie was six months old, she left me for someone else." He caught Grace's eye before his gaze fell towards the floor. "I still find it very difficult to talk about. I was completely taken by surprise, and it blew my world apart—made me question everything I thought I knew. I hadn't even known that Cath was unhappy . . ."

Grace went across and sat next to him. "I'm so sorry."

"I'm not very good at sympathy," he said, swirling his drink and watching it spin. "When my walls start to crumble, I'm so damn frightened of what's behind them that I fix them straight back up again. Basically, I'm a mess . . ."

Grace's laugh was ironic. "Well, I understand *that* feeling." She gestured around them. "But you certainly have a hidden talent." She pointed to the canvases, most portraying the moors at varying times of day.

"I needed something to keep me busy—before your cottage came along, of course. I find painting very therapeutic." He watched her studying the pictures. "Since I've been back I've noticed just how different the tones of daylight can be—in Australia it's all yellows, here it's much more about blues and greys."

At the mention of his other life, Grace was reminded of all the questions she still wanted to ask. "So why are you here? Did you think it would help you to come to terms with your divorce if you sorted out your relationship with your mother?"

"Not really," Ben said. "There's far too much unspoken between me and Mum. We're both pretty fixed in our beliefs. To change to the extent that we could even have a rational discussion would require a degree of strength that I'm not sure either of us possesses."

"Is it because of the fire?" Grace asked.

He looked surprised. 'How do you know about that?'

"Claire told me."

"Ah." He hesitated. "Well, I'm pretty sure Mum knows I lied about starting the fire—but it was convenient for all of us if I were the guilty one. I wanted an excuse to get out of there; and they needed to believe that their little girl wasn't capable of it . . ."

"Oh my god. Jenny started it?"

"Yes—although I don't think she meant to burn down half the house. I'm not sure what she was doing. The first I knew was when she shook me awake. She was beside herself in the chaos that followed, but I persuaded her that I should take the blame." He noticed Grace's expression. "Don't feel too sorry for me, Grace. I wasn't particularly easy to be around back then. I'm sure everyone breathed a sigh of relief when I went, my sisters included."

"But I don't get it—if you've always known that you and Meredith were unlikely to work things out, then why did you decide to live here again?"

"I came back for my dad."

Grace looked at him in confusion.

"Jack is my dad, Grace, not Ted."

In the ensuing silence, Grace willed herself to open her mouth and say something, but she couldn't find the words.

"Are you beginning to see just how tightly the Blakeneys have wound their very tangled web?" Ben's voice grew darker as he added, "After tonight I think that Claire and I are probably the result of my mother's revenge affair."

Grace was confused. "You're saying your mother had an affair . . . with Jack?" She almost laughed, until she saw Ben's face.

"Yes."

"How do you know that?"

"Because I went into our house one day when I wasn't meant to be there, and heard my parents screaming at each other—Mum and Ted, that is . . . In fact, now that things are clicking into place, it might have been around the time that Adam was staying with his grandparents— that could have been the reason for their fight. But the bit I overheard was Ted saying that he was bringing up his brother's bastards, so what more did she want?" He took a large swig of his drink. "I went off the rails a bit after that. I planned to tell Claire, but Dad was always really good to my sisters, and I didn't want to break her heart—so I never have."

"She doesn't even know now?"

"No." Ben sighed. "It's complicated. Jack won't acknowledge that we're his. The one time I tried to broach the subject he got really angry and upset—so I've never brought it up again. Men around here don't discuss their deepest feelings—they're pretty much incapable of it. But I think he moved to the village to be nearer to Claire and me . . ."

"But how did he get along with Ted?" Grace asked. "Surely they would hate one another after that?"

"I've come to the conclusion that the most important thing for my family is appearances. As long as everyone else sees what my family wants them to, and they can avoid anything that makes them too uncomfortable, it doesn't matter what has really gone on, or who is getting hurt along the way. Jack was always invited for Christmas, and the rest of the time we just bumped into him now and again. He keeps himself to himself anyway, he loves his birds most of all. . . . He was never any threat. I can't imagine what Mum saw in him—they've never done much more than be civil to one another while I've been around. As I said, perhaps it was just an opportunity to get even."

"So how have you been getting along with Jack since you got back?"

"Oh, I go and see him every day, check he's all right, say hi to the birds, then we carry on with our lives." Ben put down his glass. "But I'm glad I've been here for a while to be able to do that. It's meant I've also had time and space for reflection—there's nothing worse than feeling lonely in a crowd of people. At least now when I head back to Sydney I might be able to pick myself up and begin enjoying life again."

Grace knew immediately what he meant, but was still choosing the right words with which to respond when he added, "It's been great having you here, Grace. . . . It's like you know me without me having to explain. If only . . ." he stalled, appearing to swallow his words.

Their eyes met. Ben took a deep breath. "Grace . . . there is a little gallery in Sydney that has kindly taken a few of my paintings, and it serves the best coffee and cake in the city. I would love to take you there . . . when you are ready."

There was much she wanted to say to him, but she was so tired. Yet, as they looked at one another, he nodded as though he had heard her thought.

"Thank you," she whispered, on the verge of tears. "I think I'd love that." And she looked down at his fingers resting on hers.

Grace drifted in and out of unsettling dreams, until Millie began crying. As she opened her eyes, she was puzzled by her surroundings until the events of the previous day came rushing back to her. She felt sick. She wanted to get on with calling the police, then get away from here.

But first she needed to be practical. She got Millie up and dressed, and took her downstairs for something to eat. Morning light began to infuse the night, creeping warily into the kitchen and casting insipid colors on every surface. Bess lay on her side, her gait tired but her eyes wide, watching the room changing. Millie crawled across and began patting Bess's fur a little too enthusiastically, then giggled when the dog licked her face. Grace picked her up, grabbed some plastic tubs from a drawer, and set her down to play with them, hoping it might keep her amused for a few more minutes. She fingered her phone nervously. She wanted Ben to be here when she called the police, but she didn't want to wait too much longer.

Moments later she heard a faint ringing upstairs. There was a protracted silence, but then Ben's footsteps thundered along the landing. Grace had already jumped up from her seat in alarm, heading for the door, when she met him coming in the other direction. He was wearing only a T-shirt and boxer shorts. His face was drawn, his eyes fearful.

"Claire just called me," he said breathlessly. "I'm so sorry, Grace, but Mum's disappeared. Her car isn't there, and Pippa's gone, too."

Grace stared at him, disbelieving, as he added, "Claire's distraught, I'm going to have to get up there."

He raced away, back up the stairs. Moments later he ran down again, pulling a sweater over his head and then doing up the belt buckle on his jeans. He sat on the floor by the front door and began lacing up his boots.

Grace had already snatched up her mobile and dialed 999. A few moments later a voice said calmly, "Emergency—which service do you require?"

"Police," she said. She was shaking with fury. How could she have been so naïve as to think that Meredith would stick to her word?

43

Ben stayed with Grace while she spoke to the emergency operator. She was surprised at how composed she sounded as she answered his questions. Inside, she was seething.

"I'm going to have to go and find out what's happening," he told her when she'd finished.

"I know."

"I'll come back as quickly as I can."

He headed out, but as soon as the front door banged shut, Grace knew she couldn't wait there alone doing nothing. She pushed her mobile into her pocket, picked up Millie and grabbed their coats. Then she wrenched open the door and charged down the path. "Ben, wait . . ."

Bess ran out with them, bounding eagerly towards the Land Rover, her tail wagging. Ben was already inside, his hand poised to pull the door closed, but he stopped when he saw them.

Grace unlatched the gate and rushed around to the passenger side, opening the back door first so that Bess could jump in. "We're coming with you. The police will take an age to get here from town. I'm not sitting on my hands in there. I've done enough of that."

He shook his head. "This is not a good idea, Grace."

She ignored him, handing Millie over and climbing in. "Yes, it is. I want to hear firsthand exactly what went on last night. I can't believe I let this happen. I should have phoned the police straightaway."

Ben said nothing more as he gave Millie back to her, but his grim expression made his reservations clear. As they set off, Grace saw that the snow had come to stay this time. It lay in deep shrouds over hedges and paths, formed delicate lacework over smaller nooks and branches, and magnified all it touched. Not much was left uncovered, only a few dark patches lying like shadows delineating a world of white. Overnight, the village had been transformed.

The Land Rover struggled the short distance up the hill, its tires grinding hard to keep traction. Grace's mind turned to her own car, abandoned on the top of the moors. Until the snow subsided she doubted she could even get back to it, never mind drive it further. And if she had problems getting out of the village, how easily would the police get here? Four-wheel drives like Ben's and Meredith's were the only vehicles that stood a chance of moving in this weather.

Unlike last night, today Millie was wide awake and not keen to keep still. Grace was struggling to hold on to her by the time the Land Rover reached the gravel drive. The schoolhouse roof had been smothered by snow, and a row of icicles had formed underneath the ledges of the upper windows, their spikes glinting in the morning light.

The front door opened before they were out of the car. Claire waited on the step for them, her face haggard and pale.

Ben hurried around to help Grace with Millie. Bess scrabbled between the seats, trying to come, too, but Ben snapped a stern "Wait" and shut the door on her. Bess began to scratch at the windows, barking and whining, as they headed away.

"What the hell happened?" Ben asked as they got near the door.

Claire pulled her dressing gown tighter around her. "Last night, Mum and Jenny had the row to end all rows. Or, rather, Jenny poured her scorn out on Mum, while Mum sat and listened. I tried to intervene, but Jenny was too furious. She basically told Mum what a terrible person she was, and that as soon as she could get away from here Mum would never set eyes on her again." She paused, peering past them. "Are you going to let Bess out?"

They all looked at the Land Rover. Bess was still up at the windows, barking indignantly at being left behind. Millie pointed at the dog, her little face concerned.

"I'm worried she'll run off when she's like this," Ben said. "I should have left her back at the house . . . So tell us, what happened in the end?"

"The conversation went round in circles, until Jenny was hysterically ranting and crying, and I managed to drag her off up to bed. I checked on her a moment ago—she's still asleep."

"And what about Mum?"

"Mum was just . . . weird. She sat there and took everything Jenny hurled at her and didn't say a word. She flinched a few times, but she pretty much gave Jenny a free rein. I know Jenny has a lot to be furious about, but I wish Mum had fought back a bit. After I'd sorted Jenny out, I sat with Mum and tried to hold her hand, but she shook me off, got up and said she was going to bed. I stayed downstairs for a while, knocked back a glass of brandy or two, and by that time it was all quiet. But this morning when I looked in on them, Mum wasn't there—and her bed hasn't been slept in."

Claire's voice was now barely audible over the sound of Bess's barking. "I'll have to let her out," Ben grumbled, dashing back to the car and opening the door.

In a flash, Bess leapt down and hared around the bushes towards the moorland beyond, still barking. "Bess," Ben yelled angrily, "come back here." He threw his hands in the air in frustration. "I bloody knew it. I'll have to go and fetch her."

As Ben jogged away, Grace and Claire were left alone. They listened to Bess's barking in uncomfortable silence. Even Millie's attention seemed held by the noise, as she sat quietly in her mother's arms. Eventually, Grace murmured, "I'm sorry, Claire."

Claire gave no reply. She was still listening. Grace watched as her features changed, a frown forming. "That's not just Bess barking," Claire said. "I think it's Pippa, too. It sounds like they're near the Leap."

At once, her tired eyes filled with terror. She dashed over to the garage and heaved up the door.

Meredith's four-wheel drive sat snugly inside.

Claire turned to Grace in horror. "She always leaves it on the drive. Except sometimes—in snow . . . I just assumed . . ." And then she began to run towards the noise.

Grace and Millie were left alone on the driveway. Everything around them was frozen, but in the distance the dogs' demented barking was a dreaded omen. There was another noise now, too, very faint—perhaps she was imagining it, but it sounded like a siren.

Ben's car door hung open. Grace walked across and sat on the back seat, settling Millie next to her and pulling out her phone. She spoke quickly and urgently when her mother answered, and once she knew that her family were on their way, she held her daughter close, waiting for whatever would come next.

44

After Grace had fastened Millie into her car seat, she turned back towards the cottage, her eyes passing over the brand-new "For Sale" sign beside the gate. Now that spring had arrived, the place looked much more inviting. The grey stone glowed in the weak sunshine, and the garden was beginning to burst into flower.

"You ready?" she asked her daughter, not really expecting an answer, but still delighted when Millie grinned and replied with a stream of babble.

She got into the car, her gaze lingering on the cottage one last time. Then she set off down the lane, past the pub at the bottom, on towards the hill. As she went, wisps of memories floated alongside her: Adam carrying Millie; Annabel complaining about the weather; James in his tux; Ben whistling to Bess. . . . She was surprised at how fondly she recalled some of them. But there were many others she was glad to be leaving behind, and a few she knew would always be with her. Most vividly, the terrible day that Adam's body had been brought up from the bottom of the Leap, alongside Meredith's. Grace had kept her composure remarkably well, until she had watched the ambulance heading silently down the lane. Then the tears had begun to stream down her face. That phase had lasted a long time—way beyond the point that her parents and Annabel had arrived, and they had all moved to stay in Ockton while an autopsy was conducted. The verdict had been inconclusive. They would never know for certain what had happened that day—whether Adam had fallen or been pushed.

She had been touched at how full the church had been for Adam's funeral—all sorts of people coming up from London, including James, who sat towards the back, on the opposite side to Ben. After that, Grace and Millie had gone to stay with Annabel for a time, before returning briefly to oversee the final details on the cottage and put it up for sale. Yesterday, soon after she had arrived in Ockton, Grace had spotted Liza hurrying along the street with a stroller. Before she could decide what to do next, Liza had looked across and caught her eye. Grace had smiled, and was about to go over to congratulate her, but Liza's stare was empty. She had put her head down and hurried away. Grace wasn't entirely surprised. According to Ben, the family had fractured in the last few months. Claire had gone away. Liza and Veronica weren't speaking.

While Grace had been lost in her memories, the car had begun its final steep climb out of the village. They were nearing the schoolhouse, which stood dark and empty, its "For Sale" sign battered and weathered. Each time Grace went past she didn't dare look at the windows in case she saw a small boy's lonely face—or, worse, the viperous eyes of a woman who felt herself wronged. She put her foot down and they sped by, before she braked suddenly at the next bend, swearing as a sheep hurried out of harm's way, two small lambs scampering behind.

Instinctively, she leaned round to check on Millie, who was turning the pages of a board book, unaware of anything amiss. Seeing her daughter was safe and content, Grace settled back into her seat and let out a long, slow breath. Her eyes fell again on her handbag, which lay on the passenger seat. She resisted the irrational urge to check it again—she knew the plane tickets were there—and felt a growing surge of excitement. She was longing to see a tall, dark-haired man who lived on the other side of the world, whose presence she'd missed for close to two months, despite e-mails and phone calls.

She smiled at the memory of her father's high-pitched voice when she'd told him what her plans were. "For goodness' sake, Grace, I don't see the need to rush off overseas. Come and stay with your mother and me for a little while."

"Dad, I've got the tickets booked! I won't be gone for long—and I need a holiday," she added, knowing that her reason for going was much more than that.

"Millie will be a horror on the flight."

"Dad, stop!"

"I know you, Gracie, I know exactly why you're going. And I don't like him."

"Why not?"

"Because he lives twelve thousand miles away, for Christ's sake."

"Hang on a minute, you moved to France—Australia is just a longer plane journey."

"Hmm." He didn't sound impressed. "Well, when you get back, come and stay with me and your mother."

"Dad, I'm not staying with you again while Mum insists on keeping that clock," Grace said, only half-joking. "It stops when it chooses, you know, usually on witching hour. Why she wants it is beyond me."

"It's an heirloom for Millie, apparently. Your mum didn't think it was right to part with it—we can mind it for her until she's old enough to decide what to do with it."

Grace acquiesced. "Well, it's nice of you. But if it gives you any trouble . . ."

"Don't worry, I'm sure someone on the Internet can tell me how to conduct an exorcism."

Grace laughed at the recollection, watching the houses beginning to appear along the road in sporadic bursts. They were coming into Ockton now, and she could see the church spire ahead. She drove a short distance farther, then parked, heading around the car to collect Millie. There were four elegantly wrapped flowers on the backseat—roses, each with a sprig of rosemary tied to the stem. She handed them to Millie, who clutched them bemusedly as they set off down the churchyard path. Grace carried Millie as she picked her way across the grass until they reached three headstones. The grass was damp but Grace knelt anyway, setting Millie down and gently prizing two of the flowers from Millie's grip. She laid them at the foot of one stone. For Connie and Bill. Then they moved to the next one and placed another flower in front of it. For Rachel. Turning to the final grave, Grace put her fingers over Millie's and together they set the last red rose on top of it. Millie toddled away, then turned and walked back unsteadily towards the upright stone. She stopped briefly next to the flower, squatting to pick it up and examine it, before setting it down again, and turned to celebrate her cleverness by beaming at her mother. Grace smiled, wishing she could share the moment. She put her hand on the cool stone in front of her, closing her eyes for a second, conjuring up Adam's beloved face.

A gentle breeze blew from behind her, caressing the back of her neck. She felt the light press of a hand on her shoulder and spun around, opening her eyes, expecting to see someone there. But all she saw was a weak yellow sun, beyond the small clouds that freckled the palest of blue skies.

ACKNOWLEDGMENTS

This book would not exist had I not been introduced to the wonderful North Yorkshire moors by my husband Matt and his family. Thank you to all of you for your steady support over the long writing process, in particular to Jo and Steve for letting me quiz you and for all the research you have done on my behalf. And thank you James and Dan for your creativity and cinematic know-how. I must also add that I have met many locals over the years I have visited the area, and all of them have been far friendlier than some of the people portrayed in this book—so I hope they will forgive me my artistic license! Thanks also to Big Jon and Caroline Foster, Neil Raynsford, and Fiona Thorp for answering police-procedural questions, and to Rosemary Johns for the legal input.

During the launch preparations for *Beneath the Shadows* I have been able to call on some very talented friends. My thanks go to Punita Mandalia for bringing Grace's cottage to life, and to Kirsty Aldridge for the beautiful photos. Yet more shout-outs to Julie Graham, Claire Moritz and Louise Clarke for being generous with their time and friendship while I was writing.

Having great agents makes the business of writing a whole lot easier. Thanks to Tara Wynne, Fiona Inglis, Catherine Drayton, and everyone at Curtis Brown and Inkwell Management for championing my work, and for all that you do. Additional thanks to Jenny Witherell for your practical support.

A huge thank you to everyone at Thomas Dunne Books, in particular to Anne Bensson: I am so grateful for your belief in this book, and for your ongoing insight and encouragement.

To Jen Shelton: you are a gift to our family, and we know how lucky we are to have found you.

To Marian and Raymond Agombar: your unwavering support is inspiring. Thank you for everything you have done for all of us over the past few years. You know how much you have helped to bring this book to life.

And finally, to my husband Matt and my daughter Hannah. When it comes to you two, thank you doesn't even begin to cover it.